A CHRISTMAS CORDIAL

A CHRISTMAS CORDIAL

And Other Stories

Laura Kalpakian

CHIVERS

British Library Cataloguing in Publication Data available

This Large Print edition published by AudioGO Ltd, Bath, 2013.
Published by arrangement with the Author

U.K. Hardcover   ISBN   978 1 4713 5975 0
U.K. Softcover   ISBN   978 1 4713 5976 7

Printed and bound in Great Britain by TJ International Limited

For Maudie and Dahbee
and
Bear and Brendan

Table of Contents

A CHRISTMAS CORDIAL

Among the family there prevailed the sentiment that Louisa Wyatt ought somehow to have 'done something' with her life, though quite what remained unspecified, since she had not done the obvious thing and got married. At least those closest to her used to express such thoughts, but gradually everyone who had known Louisa as a lively girl, an ebullient Oxford student, as a capable intelligent young woman had died off, or emigrated, and those who remained viewed her without that benign veil of youth or promise, in short, as a potty old woman of rigid habits and vague ways, she of the battered Burberry, the mothy scarf and galoshes, the hat pulled down tight over wiry, white hair, she who enjoyed alarmingly good health for her three-quarters of a century, who persisted in working part-time when she might have retired ten years before, who lived all alone in an enormous house in Holland Park bequeathed to her by her parents where she fussed with ancient cookbooks and tended (in her own potty fashion) a large herb garden that had got away from her; the thyme ran wild, the sage and celandine quarreled, the basil died every summer for want of sunlight and the mint reigned supreme.

Certainly her cousin Enid (second

1

or third cousin, Louisa had lost track) thought it unfair that Louisa should have an enormous, unattached four-story house with rooms galore when Enid, her dyspeptic husband and her numerous brood were jammed, crammed, boxed and burrowed into considerably lesser quarters in Shepherd's Bush. Mr. Basil Shillingcote, the solicitor who represented Louisa's affairs (for a firm that had represented the affairs of her father and grandfather before him), thought it foolhardy that the old woman should persist in the huge house when the land, the neighborhood, the very address were worth a small fortune *(better than no fortune at all,* he always added with a wink that had become so predictable it resembled a tic). Moreover, as administrator of Louisa's affairs, Mr. Shillingcote knew that her will had not (as yet) designated an heir to the house and he entertained himself with the notion that she would gratefully confer the house on him; all these possibilities he contemplated as one might an opera performed by a huge cast of pounds and pence. Louisa's co-worker at the Explorers' Club, Diana Dufour, thought that a woman living alone in such grand quarters was, quite simply, politically incorrect.

Diana Dufour had come to work at the Explorers' Club in 1970 when it had the rather grander name of The Society for Overseas Exploration, which was what it was called when Louisa went to work there as an indexer in 1955. That title too was a comedown from the Society for Imperial Exploration, which was what it was called for its first 130 years. Whatever its designation, the Club was rather incongruously housed between legations and far more affluent associations in Belgrave Square, the quarters willed to the Club in 1878 by Sir William Barry, the famous Imperial explorer. It sat in that graceful London square, testifying with its neighbors to a more leisurely age, less uncertain times, to a set of assumptions long since tested and discarded. Unlike its neighbors, the Club was proud but penniless, and lest its interior shabbiness be immediately apparent, the brass plate, the marble stairs were shined and swept daily by Mrs. Jobson, the Club's charwoman and bedmaker. Inside, however, and away from the prying eyes of those who might judge it harshly, the Club was dusty, dim, faded and tarnished; the heads and antlers, the glass eyes, the fangs and horns and tusks of animals shot in the course of Imperial Explorations (including the enormous upright polar bear in the foyer, his expression forever frozen into outrage) in fact were only cleaned and dusted once a year, in December, always close to Christmas.

'It's a dreadful waste of money,' Diana asserted of the animal cleaning as she stood negligently in the doorway of Louisa's small office with its glassed-in bookshelves and wooden filing cabinets and potted plants on the sill. Diana could stand negligently, but she could never be said to have lounged under any circumstances; she was a woman of large proportions and her political views were in keeping with her physical stature. 'Besides, the place smells of old wet hair for days after they've cleaned.'

'That's why we have it done close to Christmas,' Louisa replied as she continued jotting notes of the Index of Journals she maintained for the Club. 'We only have to endure the smell for a day or two and then we're off for the holidays.'

Their conversation was punctuated by the sound of a crashing bucket, a male voice cursing and a female voice urging him to clean it up before it stained the parquet floor. Louisa closed up the journal from which she had copied the last entry in the table of contents and regarded the impassive clock, remarking casually on the hour, hoping that Diana would go back to her own cubicle.

Diana remained impervious, commenting loudly on the ineptitude of the animal cleaners and adding in no uncertain terms that such clumsiness only underscored what the country had come to. As Louisa expected, Diana elaborated on this theme (her favorite) for about ten minutes, and then posed to Louisa the question she had asked each December

4

22 since 1973: would Louisa care to join her (and whatever leftish political group she was currently allied with) for Christmas Day? This year the Women's Anti-Nuke Coalition would hold a Christmas protest and—

'Thank you very much, Diana,' (Louisa had always given the same reply since 1973), 'but I'm sure my cousin Enid will invite me and as I've no other family but her, I shall probably spend the day with them.'

'You ought to think in terms of the Family of Man,' Diana counseled, preface to one of her speeches in which the Family of Man was depicted living happy, full, politically correct lives on the straight and narrow-gauge tracks laid out by Diana and her right-thinking leftish cohorts.

Louisa might have been afflicted with the entire speech, but Mr. Shotworth appeared, advising the ladies that they might leave a little early today if they wished. Mr. Shotworth was their superior, the Club's longtime administrator. Such was the shrunken grandeur of the Explorers' Club in these days of the shrunken globe that these three, and the pensioned porter, Mr. (once Sergeant) Taft (who lost money on the horses) and the charwoman, Mrs. Jobson (who lost money at the pub), were the only employees of an institution that had once boasted, indeed required, four or five times that many people, whose halls had once rung with the hearty

5

voices of adventuresome men. Mr. Shotworth was a conscientious man of indeterminate middle age whose good humor only failed him when he reflected at any length on the poverty and obscurity of the Explorers' Club, on its dwindling list of trustees, on its meager prospects for the future. However, he tried to remain always professional and even-tempered at the Club, confining his bouts of unhappiness to his home where he inflicted them on Mrs. Shotworth, who told him many times she didn't deserve it and it wasn't her fault.

Mr. Shotworth was pulling on his gloves. 'Christmas always creeps up on me,' he told Louisa and Diana. 'These last few years I'm scarcely aware of the season until they come in to clean the—' His last word was lost in the clang and scuffle of a falling ladder and a male voice advising the animals to perform unnatural acts. Mr. Shotworth winced simultaneously at the crash and the vulgarity. 'Well, Miss Wyatt,' he continued bravely, 'my wife and 1 are certainly looking forward to your Christmas Cordial again this year.'

'It's not mine, Mr. Shotworth,' Louisa reminded him, 'It's Lady Aylesbury's.'

'Yes, but she is long dead—'

'More than two hundred fifty years, I should think.'

'—and so the Cordial might very properly be said to be yours now. No one else makes it, do they?' To this Louisa assented. 'My

6

wife says you should bottle up your Christmas Cordial and sell it at Boots and make a fortune.'

'I've no need of a fortune,' Louisa replied.

'Perhaps not, but the world could use such a cordial—eh, Miss Dufour? The Family of Man?'

'The remedy for the ills of our time are political, economic and social,' Diana reminded him. 'They are not to be found in a bottle, although,' she added, an uncharacteristic gentleness softening her voice, 'if such a thing could be done, it could be done only with Louisa's Christmas Cordial, if it could be administered to punks and plutocrats alike, then perhaps . . .' Her tone became almost dreamy before Diana recollected herself and marched off to her own cubicle.

Mr. Shotworth turned to Louisa and remarked, 'My wife and I used the last drop of our last year's Christmas Cordial in October, Miss Wyatt, and we are sorely in need of the new bottle.' Mr. Shotworth did not add that he had used the last drop of the Cordial topically, applied it to his own throbbing head after Mrs. Shotworth (fed up with his moping, his morose mooning over the Explorers' Club) had flung the *Oxford Companion to English Literature* (old edition) at her husband, not really intending to hit him, only hoping that the thump of the book would rouse him from his sad torpor. The *Oxford Companion,* however, had hit Mr. Shotworth squarely in the temple and the repentant Mrs. Shotworth had hastened to the kitchen cabinet where they kept the Christmas Cordial, taken the near-empty bottle and her own handkerchief and applied it to the bump rising on her husband's head, crooning *Go ahead, Harry take the last swallow, dear, no don't let's look for the spoon, just drink it up, there's only a drop left and it will help you. It always has.* Kneeling together on their sitting-room floor, Mr. and Mrs. Shotworth shared the last swill of the Cordial, their arms around each other, her gray head on his shoulder, the warmth and equilibrium of their long marriage restored. Mr. Shotworth was not about to impart these dreary domestic circumstances to Miss Wyatt. To Miss Wyatt he said only that they had used the last of the Christmas Cordial when they felt the chill of autumn creeping over them, on a night when they both shivered and sniffled. 'We were perfectly fit the next day,' he concluded, considering that this was, in fact, the truth.

'"The vertues of this water are many,"' Louisa recited, chapter and verse from Lady Aylesbury's own notations. '"It comforteth, helpeth and preserveth. It balanceth the bile and the blood."'

Agreeing with this, Mr. Shotworth went off humming 'The Holly and the Ivy,' and Louisa closed up her cubicle. She met Diana again at the porter's desk where Mr. Taft put down his racing paper and handed the ladies their coats, hats and scarves. Louisa sat down on the huge chair (upholstered in crocodile skin) in the shadow of the polar bear and pulled on her galoshes while Mr. Taft bemoaned the paucity of explorers actually staying in the club this holiday season. Only three. Total.

'Perhaps the Explorers' Club is too exclusive,' Diana Dufour offered. 'Perhaps we ought to open our membership to the masses.'

Mr. Taft was aghast at this. In his own way Mr. Taft was the most consummate snob among them. He pointed out that the Explorers' Club had indulged in quite enough democracy by admitting scientists and anthropologists (who, in the opinion of Mr. Taft, were not explorers in any sense) and travel writers who were a dubious lot at best. Besides these individuals, the Club had extended membership to any and all blood relations (and descendants) of the Club's once illustrious founders, as well as the descendants of Sir Matthew Curtis, slayer of the famous Pip.

'It's a pity,' Louisa observed, 'that we can't charge the animals for residency.' She nodded toward Pip, which was the incongruous name accorded the outraged polar bear for as long as anyone could remember. 'Or the ghosts,' she added, alluding to the long-held, perpetually dismissed and never-quite-laid-to-rest notion that the ghosts of those illustrious

Imperial explorers Sir William Barry, Sir Clive Rackham and Sir Matthew Curtis lingered amongst the parquet and wainscoting in the library, rattled the cases of memorabilia lining the halls and uneasily tenanted the spartan rooms overhead. 'If we tithed the ghosts and animals,' Louisa added, 'our coffers would be very full indeed.'

Bidding good night to Diana and Mr. Taft, Louisa walked, as quickly as her three-quarters of a century would permit, across Hyde Park to Bayswater Road, there to await the Number 12 or the Number 88 bus. The Tube would have been faster of course, but she disliked the Tube. Going down down down into the bowels of the city, deep into the Underground stations reminded Louisa inevitably of the Blitz, of hunkering with her parents, huddled there with neighbors and strangers as the city shuddered, and they knew not what was being destroyed overhead. Never mind all the intervening years, Louisa could not bear the Tube, associating the deep tunnels with those war years, with loss and deprivation and things never being quite the same. Besides, she enjoyed riding the bus, always climbed the stairs to sit amongst the smokers and the cigarette butts, chose a window seat when possible from which to view the city. Though she had lived in London nearly all her life, Louisa Wyatt never tired of the city, particularly at Christmastime when she could watch from the top of the bus and feel herself enfolded into the general celebration, caught up in the throngs of shoppers and overworked clerks; she felt herself imaginatively pulled into shops, even the most modest of which twinkled with fairy lights and the windows draped in shiny ropes of tinsel, and overheard (even if she did not exchange), greetings of good cheer, tidings of comfort and joy piped in over scratchy loudspeakers, the caroling of the bells and voices punctuated by the happy ring of the cash register.

In this general, impersonal sense Louisa Wyatt kept Christmas. Personally she had not had a tree, so much as one fairy light, a sprig of mistletoe or holly, for thirty years. Maybe more. What would be the point? Louisa Wyatt's observances of the season were solitary, singular rites performed over many weeks in her own kitchen where every year she made Lady Aylesbury's Christmas Cordial, bottled it up, corked it, tied the bottles with ribbons and gave them away to people whose lives had touched her own. The list, sadly, had diminished over the years and now only included the people at the Explorers' Club, her solicitor, Mr. Shillingcote, her cousin Enid, plus a bottle each for the milkman, the postman, the two dustmen and reserving always two bottles for herself (one to store and one to use if necessary) and perhaps a couple of extras because one never quite knew.

Did one?

The brutal cold chilled Louisa's old bones clear through by the time she arrived at her own street in Holland Park where the windows of the houses around hers (all long since divided into flats) advertised the multiplicity of the many lives therein. The windows of Louisa's house that fronted the street contrasted sadly; they remained draped, closed, obscured, rimed in the winter with great loops of frost that testified to rooms unwarmed with human breath or bodies, lacking expiration, expectation and voices.

It was, however, a lovely house, one of those fine old homes, spacious and high-ceilinged, suggestive of long vanished comforts and conventions. The house would have looked splendid with a thorough cleaning, the sort of blasting they were doing all over London, using high-powered tools to scrape away the accumulations of hundreds of years of coal fires and wood smoke, exhaust, the grit and granular accretions of time. Louisa, in any event, could not have afforded the expensive cleaning. A satisfactory annuity set up by her father, who had been a prosperous wine merchant in his day, allowed her to keep the house without quite maintaining it. Whatever got broken, for the most part, stayed broken and Louisa simply lived around it. Her paltry, though regular, pay from the Explorers' Club saw to the few necessities of her limited life.

What little she could spare from the annuity she lavished on her herb garden from which she gathered the ingredients for her Christmas Cordial. She figured her expenses right down to the pence, and allowing for the rising cost of bottles and corks.

She put her key in the lock and stepped into the imposing front hall, though she waited to remove her coat, gloves and galoshes till she came into the kitchen which, along with the bath, her own bedroom and the small back sitting room, were the only rooms Louisa lived in or visited at all. All four of these rooms were on the ground floor. They offered a view of the herb garden at the back, and beyond the garden wall to a block of insufferably ugly flats put up in the Sixties.

She fired up the kettle, the cooker, the heater and turned on the squat old radio, took off her outer garments, washed her hands and put on an apron as though she were about to undertake the cooking of a grand meal. However, all she did was heat up the teapot before slicing bread and putting it in the toaster, opening a can of beans and heating it (in the can) for her supper. She surveyed the collection of Cordial bottles lined up on the enormous kitchen table, remnant of another time, like the web-strewn bells above the sink that once connected kitchen lives to other lives. Her work stood before her and she took pleasure and pride in it: the bottles of

13

Lady Aylesbury's Christmas Cordial were all filled, corked, and now wanted only labels and ribbons. The making and bottling this cordial were Louisa's private rite of Christmas, which reflected the singular passion of her solitary life.

The passion of Louisa Wyatt's life was old cookbooks, not of the Nigella Lawson, nor Elizabeth Craig vintage, not even of the Mrs. Beeton variety (though Louisa had nothing personally against Mrs. Beeton and the nineteenth century) but truly ancient cookbooks, two and three hundred years old, sometimes older. She bought them when she could find (and afford) them, and when she could not, she explored on forays to museums and libraries where she copied out the contents of these old books in the same laborious hand she donated to her indexing work at the Explorers' Club. In copying these ancient recipes, Louisa preserved their exact spelling and syntax, taking pleasure in the immediate transcribing, as well as the many re-readings she gave to her efforts. Each book, each recipe opened for Louisa a door to the past, granted her entrance and egress into a long vanished world she came to know intimately and vicariously. Indeed, over the many years she indulged in this passion, Louisa came to know and understand the past as few other people did. Her knowledge of sixteenth-and seventeenth century diction, her careful research into the meaning of their terms, her understanding of the methods, ingredients and the beliefs that underlay cookery in the past made her an expert, though in a world shackled to the automatic toaster and the electric kettle, the microwave and the Cuisinart, no one valued her expertise, or even acknowledged it.

Like most people Louisa Wyatt had stumbled on the passion of her life in her youth. In those gorgeous days at Oxford when, as a student at Lady Margaret Hall, she had reveled through the streets with her chums, punted on the river, bicycled vast distances, shared late-night cocoa and confidences. One day, in the august confines of the Bodleian Library, researching a very boring essay due on the dissolution of the monasteries (Louisa was reading history) she stumbled on an indexed listing for an ancient recipe book dating vaguely from the same period. She wrote a ticket and waited, watching the rain pelt the silvery windows and hammer the cobbles below. From somewhere in the vast uncharted capillaries of the Bodleian, there was brought to her a book with thick vellum binding, hand-sewn with thick luscious pages; on these pages she read the thin spidery scrawl of a long-dead hand. The days she spent with that book told her nothing of the dissolution of the monasteries, but volumes about the conduct of life. She learned the ways in which these lost people had lived and breathed and had their being, treated their chilblains and agues and fevers, their palsies and rheumatism, their poxes, small and large; she learned how they grappled with infertility and difficult births, how they wasted not and what they wanted for, the rites by which they marked the passing of seasons, how they stowed the summer against the winter's chill, bottled the blossom against the bare branch, how and what they stewed and roasted, poached and stuffed and laid in a 'pritty hott oven,' how they made 'syder' and ale and 'cockwater,' a 'surfit of poppies' and cowslip wine. In short, how real people in the visceral past spent their daily lives, how they kept their souls united to bodies that had long since turned to dust. That day in the Bodleian was a turning point in her life.

Of course, when she went to Oxford, Louisa had not expected to discover a passion for old cookbooks. Like most young women she expected to come upon a young man at Oxford who would become the passion of her life, or at the very least, her husband. Such a man did not materialize. The War had depleted a whole generation of men, and those who returned were survivors, but they were no longer young; they were somehow set apart from the younger undergraduates. They made the younger ones feel guilty. And, too, though the war had ended, rationing had not, and the pinched and crimped conditions, mend-

and-make-do ways of thinking persisted long after the peace had been signed. Louisa's was not a high-spirited generation. There was one young man with whom she had shared a brief romance, a moonlit kiss at the college gate, a few punting picnics on the river that spring of 1948, but he left Oxford unexpectedly when his father's business failed, and she never heard from him again. In any event, he had failed to make a true impression on her heart.

Louisa's mother constantly inquired after a sweetheart. Surely there must be such a man in Louisa's immediate proximity. Her mother was anxious on her behalf because the First World War had demolished that whole generation of men, leaving women like her three sisters, Tilda, Charlotte and Jane, husbandless. She did not want to see Louisa suffer the same fate. Louisa told her mother there was no one for whom she felt anything approaching passion or love, requited or otherwise. To this her mother replied that one could live without passion, but living without a husband was difficult and unpleasant. *Look at Aunt Tilda, Aunt Charlotte and Aunt Jane living out their days in cramped poverty in Illfracombe, twittering over comforters and hot water bottles and cheese rinds.* Louisa's mother contrasted this grim picture of the aunts' life wordlessly with her own comfortable, connubial existence in Holland Park. She so hoped for a son-in-law.

Certainly Louisa's parents would never have daughters-in-law. Both Louisa's older brothers died in the war, one in Burma, and one in the North Africa campaign; Alone of her siblings, Louisa remained in the Holland Park house, her thirties looming before her and no husband in sight. Like it or not, she accepted the lack of husband. Certainly her fate was shared by many other women of her generation. But a lover? Truly someone who would stir her heart, her passions? Surely she ought to have that much. Like other women, she had expected that love would make a foreordained stop in her life, rather like a train one waits for on a crowded platform for a long time till the crowd thins out and one waits alone.

Louisa found herself—gradually, guiltily, furtively and certainly not intending to tell definite lies—making up a lover: a man compounded of the might-have-beens, a man who though he lacked substance, eventually came into a name. *Julian.* Julian seemed a good sort of name for one's lost lover, a musical, evocative name with a dash of the stately. She began alluding casually and in glib conversations with strangers to 'Julian,' and over the years the allusion coalesced into anecdotes that highlighted Julian's David Niven wit, his Leslie Howard charm, his cleverness and thoughtfulness, and how

18

he had died in the war. Since everyone had someone who had died in the war, she was accorded a measure of patriotic sympathy that also tended to give Julian, as it were, weight and girth. Moreover, as the people closest to her (those aforementioned friends and family who thought Louisa ought to have 'done something' with her life) died off, Julian's vivacity (so to speak) increased commensurately. Diana Dufour knew the story of Louisa's passionate love affair with poor Julian who had died early in the war. Mr. Shotworth knew the story of Julian, as did Mr. Taft and Mrs. Jobson. Louisa's cousin Enid never questioned the existence of Julian, nor did Mr. Shillingcote. How could they? On those rare occasions when they came to call at the Holland Park house, they saw Julian's picture on the mantle of the back sitting room, amongst the gallery of other framed family photographs. At first Louisa had put Julian's picture at the back of the gallery, inching him forward, year by year, till he now occupied the central situation: the hub, if not the husband.

Louisa had stumbled on Julian's picture one memorable day in the spring of 1963 when she had gone up to Oxford (this in the days when she drove and had a car) to further research old cookbooks at the Bodleian. On Saturday the library closed at noon, and as it was the first bright day of the daffodil spring, she decided to drive to Woodstock before

19

returning to London, perhaps to have a walk around the grounds of Blenheim Palace and a look in Featherstone's Rare Books. Featherstone very often had old cookbooks in his dusty collections, and in fact he sometimes kept the really ancient ones aside for her.

She was alarmed that spring day in 1963 to drive into Woodstock and discover that Featherstone's Rare Books sported a new sign: YE SPINNING WHEEL: ANTIQUES AND RARE BOOKS. Mr. Featherstone was rather shamefaced about the change, but launched into a long catalog of causes (mostly having to do with tourists) that had brought him to this change. As he was talking, Louisa's eye fell on a silver framed photograph. The frame was for sale. Very expensive—but then Mr. Featherstone added, noting that Miss Wyatt's eyes were riveted to it—it was, after all, sterling silver and very old and look at the workmanship and—

'That's not an old photograph in it,' Louisa observed.

Mr. Featherstone put on his glasses and regarded it more closely. 'Rather old,' he remarked optimistically, 'but it's the frame, Miss Wyatt, just lift that frame and you'll see—'

Louisa did lift the frame, but the opulence and intricacy of the worked silver was not what had arrested her attention or held it now. Inside was a photograph (neither quite

20

snapshot nor quite studio portrait) of a man without any background visible behind him. He was a young man, well-dressed in a suit with wide lapels. He had broad shoulders and thick unruly dark hair. He was smiling, not just his mouth, but his eyes. His expression, the jaunty position of the shoulder suggested the wit of David Niven, the dash of Leslie Howard, good manners, good morals, good upbringing combined with irresistible impertinence and cheer. Dark eyes, dark hair, fair skin, the man was saved from conventional cosmetic beauty by his mouth that was a shade too small for beauty. Clearly and without doubt: this was Julian.

'Who is the person in this picture?' Louisa inquired affably, still hefting the frame and pretending to be impressed with its every sterling quality.

Mr. Featherstone shrugged. The frame, photo included, had come with a huge consignment from some warehouse or another, crate after crate of goods from a number of estates all puddled and muddled together in catalogs on which Mr. Featherstone had successfully bid, though he could not remember particulars on any of it because, as he reminded Louisa, he was new at the antique business. But he assured her they were very old families and very old estates, and he waxed on at some length about nothing being the same, the war, hard times and all the great estates breaking up, its being rather akin to the dissolution of the monasteries and so on. Then he added that he could certainly take the picture out; he only had left it in because it showed the frame off to such good advantage.

'That won't be necessary,' said Louisa, plunking down her chequebook and uncapping her pen.

'Don't you want to have a look at the cookbooks, Miss Wyatt?' Mr. Featherstone inquired. 'I've got one very old one, hand-written in fact that came in with that consignment, an old library now broken up. I've been saving it for you, hoping you'd come in.'

'That's very good of you, Mr. Featherstone.'

'I should tell you, though, it's very expensive.' (And seeing that she was in a spendthrift mood and the book was not yet marked with a price, it instantly became more expensive yet; if she balked, he could always bring the price down. Just for her.)

Louisa did not balk. She paid. She would have paid twice that for the photograph of her dead lover, Julian, and for the handwritten cookbook of Anne, Lady Aylesbury, who, from that day forward, became, in a manner of speaking, Louisa Wyatt's best friend.

At first Louisa approached dreary genealogical libraries trying to dig up information on Anne, Lady Aylesbury, trying to locate her in vast family trees. But it was difficult going, confusing and unrewarding. She gave it up. In a cavalier fashion she decided to take Lady Aylesbury at her word, that is, the words so beautifully transcribed in the hand-sewn cookbook, written in a hand so elegant, so clear, it seemed to have the ring of a flawless soprano. Louisa spent the long evenings that summer in her rank, untended and overgrown garden reading and rereading Lady Aylesbury's cookbook.

It had been carefully divided into *Cookery, Sweetmeats* and *Remedies,* the recipe for the Christmas Cordial granted its own singular place on a leaf of paper between *Sweetmeats* and *Remedies.* Bringing her historical expertise to bear on the internal evidence, Louisa surmised that Anne, Lady Aylesbury, had been married, the mistress of a vast household and the mother of many children. (This latter conclusion drawn from listings of sovereign remedies for childhood afflictions, the sheer number of which further suggested that Lady Aylesbury might have seen a good many children to the grave.) Clearly Lady Aylesbury was a consummate gardener—this fact supported by the intricate and elaborate herb garden Lady Aylesbury laid out at the back of the book with space for nearly every herb that would grow in Northern Europe (and some that would not). Louisa looked up from the diagram, and regarded her own weed' overgrown plot. She contemplated.

That summer she broke into her savings to hire some men to do the initial, difficult digging, pulling up, tearing out, and hauling in of topsoil, raised beds and brick. The following spring, Louisa planted her own herb garden, according to Lady Aylesbury's design. While she was not always successful, she comforted herself that Lady Aylesbury, too, must have known some measure of failure, but persisted nonetheless. As did Louisa.

Louisa's expertise further allowed her to estimate that Anne, Lady Aylesbury, had lived in the mid-eighteenth century. Louisa's twenty-some years of pouring over ancient cookbooks enabled her to date some of Lady Aylesbury's recipes from much earlier eras, Stuart England, Elizabethan Tudor, some recipes even wafting the odors (rosewater, saffron, and almond milk) of the Middle Ages. The presence of these earlier recipes indicated that Lady Aylesbury's family was a very old one, a family that had managed to maintain its lands and superiority over hundreds of years. Louisa further deduced that the family was enormously wealthy, given the luxuries prodigally lavished throughout: the currants and cloves and pomegranates, butter and sugar and dates, the nutmeg, ginger, musk and ambergris, Sevil orringes and lemons, olives, capers and a cornucopious number of vegetables, all of these in various exotic combinations to be sauced, tansied, tarted, put into pastry 'coffins,' and used in 'sallets.' The grandeur, expense, the lavish generosity everywhere abundant in the cookbook conjured in Louisa's mind a sprawling manor with opulent gardens where, even in winter, the smell of boxwood floated on the fogs and crackling fires the rooms. At Christmastime Louisa pictured prickly holly protruding from huge vases set on inlaid tables in each bedroom, and along the portrait-lined halls. The drawing room, hung with yellow damask and satin drapes the color of caramel, would boast a pianoforte, a harp and violin before the ten-foot windows. The dining room at Christmas would be warmed by charcoal braziers and lit by a million vanilla-colored candles strewing golden light on Lady Aylesbury (beaming at the top of the long, polished table) and all her guests: portly, well-fed wigged and waistcoated men taking snuff, women in satin, sniffing pomander balls, young men, perhaps impecunious younger sons, paying court to marriageable young women with dowries and doting papas, married women flirting with gusto and impunity, heavy-breasted dowagers, their white hair further powdered white, casting knowing glances on all these goings-on. They all feasted on pastries and peacock, on legs of lamb stuffed with sweetmeats and sparrows stewed with oranges, on tansies and syllabubs and marchpane cakes and all of it washed down with 'ye best gascoyne wine,' the whole gorgeous edifice supported by a bevy of eager, well-cared-for servants: thumping good natured wenches and blustering boys, cooks who wielded ladles with the authority of scepters, ruddy men who smelled of straw and leather stamping their cold feet by the roaring kitchen fire, servants in livery darting up and down the stairs, laden with trays and silver serving dishes, stone-faced before the gentry, amiable over a fireside flagon of ale once their duties were finished.

All this—memory and imagination—along with twenty-five different herbs and spices laid up in faire water, steeped over days then dried and bruised and shredded and added to ye best gascoyne wine to be distilled finally into the Christmas Cordial. This was Lady Aylesbury's recipe which Louisa followed faithfully each year. The process took six weeks. At the end of that time, she poured it into bottles, corked them, labeled and be-ribboned them to give away at Christmas. The vertues of this water were many, and each time Louisa gave the Cordial as gifts to her friends, the hundreds of years between herself and Lady Aylesbury seemed to contract with a snap: she saw herself in the same beautiful, bountiful light and imagined that Lady Aylesbury, too, had offered Christmas Cordials to each individual, not only as a token of the season, but assuring them of her recognition of their unique qualities, her understanding of their

26

secret hurts and ills, comforting them with whispered promises of the cordial's efficacy against whatever ailed their bodies, whatever unhappiness unbalanced their minds, whatever loss or hope-denied troubled their hearts.

*   *   *

Louisa pulled the can of beans off the cooker and burnt her fingers in the process. She sucked on the burnt fingers of the one hand while, with the other, she dumped the beans over the slice of toast on a plastic plate. She was about to eat them when the doorbell rang and she mentioned (to no one in particular) that it was probably Enid. She took off her apron and went to the door.

It was Enid with the youngest of her brood in tow, a girl. 'How good to see you, Enid,' cried Louisa, genuinely happy to have her intuitions validated.

Louisa led her guests down the cold hall to the back sitting room where she flicked on the electric fire and gave a secret connubial smile to Julian. He smiled back at her from his frame on the mantel shelf. In their years together Julian had become as much husband as lover. She remarked to Enid how Margot had grown.

'No, Louisa, this is Molly. My youngest. Margot is the—'

'Of course. How stupid of me. Let me get

27

you a cup of tea, Enid. It will take the chill off till the room warms up.'

'No, thank you just the same, Louisa, I must get back. Jack expects his supper.' However Enid and her daughter sat down on the sofa. Louisa took the chair across. 'Molly and I were just on our way home from some shopping, and we thought we would stop by and invite you for Christmas instead of ringing you on the phone. Please do come Christmas Day— unless you've another invitation.' Enid always offered this last caveat with some trepidation, fearful lest someone else might have wormed their way into Louisa's affections, to say nothing of the possibilities of her last will and testament. Moreover Enid never phoned with the Christmas invitation, but always delivered it in person so that she might see the house she hoped to inherit. She glanced now around the sitting room with its boxy television, its chintz-covered chairs from the days of Louisa's parents. Inwardly Enid re-decorated while she made inconsequential conversation. Down would come those velvet drapes. First thing.

Enid was perhaps forty-five, her clothes, her hair a sort of moth-brown, her nails nibbled, not to the quick, but nibbled nonetheless. The girl was about twelve, entering into the gangly cocoon of adolescence from which she would emerge a plain young woman. All Enid's children were plain, though when they were little, Enid believed them to be winsome moppets, but as they grew up, even Enid had to admit that they had inherited her own air of nervous desperation and their father's shambling sloth. Still, Enid eternally hoped that one of the children might kindle affection in her cousin's childless breast and thus, Enid's family would inherit the house when the old lady passed on—which she showed no inclination to do. Enid could not help but wince every time Louisa remarked that her Aunt Charlotte had lived to be ninety.

'Your garden's looking very ghostly this time of year,' Enid offered with a glance out the velvet-draped window.

'All gardens look ghostly this time of year— it's the frost and ice on all the cobwebs, don't you think? Makes the plants look bearded and hoary, especially with everything skeletal and frostbitten, reminds you of a graveyard.'

'Hmmm,' replied Enid, whose powers of imagination were easily taxed. *Hmmm* managed to sound both neutral and positive at the same moment.

'But my herbs did rather well this summer and I think the Christmas Cordial will be especially good.'

'Hmmm.'

'In fact I feel certain Jack will find the Christmas Cordial especially helpful this year. Still suffers from Troubled Tummy, does he?'

Enid smiled wanly, unwilling to discuss her dyspeptic (and consequently surly) husband.

'"The vertues of this water are good against the bloat of ye bellye and the winds of flatulence,"' Louisa quoted from Lady Aylesbury who (lady though she was) did not shrink from being physiologically precise. '"It helpeth the wamblings and gripings of the bellye and killeth the worms in ye body."'

'Yes,' replied Enid, ' we've used our last year's Cordial all up. By August,' she added, hoping to flatter her cousin. In fact Jack (he of the wambling, griping bellye, propelled by the winds of flatulence) not only would not touch the stuff, but instructed his wife to chuck it out on Boxing Day. Enid could not bring herself to defy her husband, but neither could she obey him. She had twenty-five bottles of Christmas Cordial stuffed at the back of her closet, kept there, even when space was so much wanted for other things, in the superstitious belief that they amounted to a kind of account, a middle-aged hope chest. Enid lied ably. 'The Christmas Cordial has been very good for Jack's dyspepsia, Louisa. He's said so. Many times.'

Molly gave her mother a sneer of wonderment and was about to lisp some cute morsel of childish truth when Enid gouged her in the ribs and admonished her not to fidget. 'Molly, show you Aunt Louisa' (Enid instructed the children to call her Aunt Louisa, hoping to call forth maternal feelings from those unused breasts) 'your new

30

orthodontic work.'

Molly bared a mouth full of metal in an expression that reminded Louisa of Pip the polar bear. Louisa remarked on the equivalent of How Nice Dear while Molly and Enid waxed on in virtual unison about her orthodontic saga. Louisa reminded (without a flicker of a smile) that according to Lady Aylesbury, the Christmas Cordial also 'Helpeth the stinking breath' which effectively closed the subject.

Enid rose. 'Shall we look for you then, Louisa, Christmas Day?'

'Thank you very much. Yes, of course.' Louisa was grateful for the invitation (since it spared her the Women's Anti-Nuke Coalition) but she did not relish the thought of a meal with the flatulent Jack. 'You're the closest thing I have to family, Enid,' she added.

Enid's whole face lit, her fatigue and pinched desperation eased under the glow the way a candle illuminates frost crystallized on a frozen pane.

'Shall I bring anything?'

'Oh, you needn't, Louisa. Just the Christmas Cordial.' When her children were little Enid cherished the dream that Louisa would come with a good deal more than a bottle of Christmas Cordial, hoping Louisa (whom she thought to be rich) would arrive in Shepherd's Bush laden with be-ribboned, bright-wrapped parcels of toys to delight the moppets. Enid

31

saw Louisa as a female Scrooge and cast her own family as the Cratchits, though she mercifully had no lame children, and her husband, Jack, could not by the remotest stretch of the imagination, pass for good-natured Bob Cratchit. Besides, as her little children grew up into dispirited youths, the vision paled, staled and crumbled, leaving Enid with no fodder for her starved imagination, save for the hope of inheriting the Holland Park house. 'We really ought to get together more often than just on Christmas,' Enid said shyly,. 'Being family and all.'

Louisa was touched by Enid's offer. She put her thin arm around Enid and squeezed her. 'Isn't it amazing how time gets away from you?'

'Yes,' Enid concurred, smiling and feeling altogether better than when she'd arrived. She and the heavy-metal Molly stepped outside into the lamplit dark with many wishes for the season and sage observations on the brutal cold.

After they left Louisa turned off the electric fire in the sitting room and hurried back into the warm kitchen. The beans and toast were cold, as was her tea. She made a fresh pot of hot tea, but ate the beans and toast as they were. Food, that is the food she actually ate, mattered little to Louisa and reheating the beans would be too much trouble to take for herself. As she ate her solitary meal to the tune of Christmas carols on the radio, she reflected that if Julian had lived, everything would have been different; they would have had lovely meals and Louisa's reputation as a great cook would have gone far and wide among their many friends; she would have been renowned for gala dinner parties, each one gleaming for years ever after in the minds of her guests. She often sat up late at night reading ancient cookbooks in bed, and fell asleep dreaming of the meals she might have fixed for Julian, their children, their many friends, these feasts mingling with Lady Aylesbury's: all the guests, eighteenth century and contemporary alike, arriving with anticipation and good cheer and leaving surfeited with excellent food, brilliant hospitality, bright wines, bonny ports, glowing sherries, taking their leaves in moments imbued with conviviality, affection and memory.

Louisa Wyatt read cookbooks the way other women read novels; she kept them by her bed and in a basket in the bathroom. For Louisa these well known recipes had the vivacity of characters from a much-loved novel, people one could go back to again and again, savoring their novel lives, pitying their squandered loves, weeping for their renounced affections, rejoicing when their passions and principles were rewarded, enjoying over and over all those gambles that may safely be taken on paper, but not in life.

Lady Aylesbury was the foremost of Louisa's heroines and she had fallen into the habit of chatting with Anne, Lady Aylesbury, night after night. Their discourse was talk between equals (while Louisa ate cold beans on toast) of 'How to Make a Lettis Tarte' and the techniques needed to perfect 'A Capon Roste with Oysters,' the amenities of 'A Gruelle of French Barley' (which they agreed would stir the invalid's wan appetite), discussion between experts on the intricacies of 'Rice Florentine,' the art of fritters and furmenty, of possits and fools and cheesecakes and syllabubs and (oh, can you imagine!) 'A Creme Made of Fresh Snowe.' While Louise fortified her body with cold beans on toast, she fortified her imagination with Lady Aylesbury's cookbook and the multitude of dishes that she made from it, dishes she served to Julian and the children they might have had, and indeed, to the grandchildren they might well have hugged, all of whom Louisa imagined as golden-haired moppets: eager, bouncing girls, and shy, serious little boys, or sometimes, as suited her fancy, she imagined them as beautiful young men and women, about to go up to Oxford, to embark on lives of wonder and achievement, passion and requited love. She never imagined them any older than that. She could not bear to.

*　　　*　　　*

The next day she waited, teeth chattering in the front hall, for the post to come through the slot and then stuck her head out and asked the postman of the weather.

'It an't a day for man nor beast, Miss Wyatt,' he replied, clapping his cold hands together and inwardly cursing the bleeding cold. He was a dim, fraying man of about forty with a wreath of graying hair around a bald head which he always kept covered with his hat. 'It an't day for you to go out.'

'Oh, I must go out today. The Club has its Christmas party.' Always on the day before Christmas Eve, she, Diana Dufour, Mr. Shotworth, Mr. Taft and Mrs. Jobson celebrated the season in the Captain Cook Library. Notes were put into the boxes of any guests at the club who might wish to join them. Inevitably these guests were men whose inclination to explore and habits of travel and denied them the pleasures –and pangs– of family, and they were usually grateful for the invitation, and joined the staff for a sip of sweet wine, a bite of cake and a bit of Christmas cheer. The party at the Explorers' Club might be all the cheer they got.

The postman hadn't any idea what sort of club Louisa might be referring to, guessing it to be a bridge club or knitting party, something of that sort, and because of the cold, he didn't stop to inquire. 'Have another bottle of that

Christmas Cordial, do you, Miss Wyatt?'

'Tomorrow,' she assured him.

'You can't buy a better remedy for the bunions.' He pointed to his feet and shook his head. 'I'm looking forward to it, I am,' he added with a grin and a wave, not admitting that he had squandered his last year's bottle in June when his wife had left him.

When it was time to go to work, Louisa took the postman at his word and indulged in the unwonted luxury of calling a cab. Not simply due to the cold, but she had her box full of the bottles of Christmas Cordial to transport. She had wadded newspaper between the bottles to protect them. She directed the cabby to the Explorers' Club in Belgrave Square, hoping he might think she was an explorer, and not a mere indexer of journal articles.

They arrived at the club, and the cabby (a young man with a total of five gold rings in his ears) hopped out and opened the door for her, held her ancient arm up the marble steps and then went back to the chugging car to get the box with the bottles of Christmas Cordial to be given to the staff. Mr. Taft himself carried them to the Captain Cook and placed them on the library table.

The newly cleaned animal heads dotting the walls of the Captain Cook Library still stank of wet hair, but the fire was cheerful and the room almost warm and certainly pleasant when they assembled that afternoon, the staff

36

and the three club guests: Colonel Stanhope, who was associated in some way with Africa; Mr. Thrumley whose connection with the club was of long standing, having done something wonderful (no one could quite remember what) in the days of the Raj; and Mr. Turner, an American travel writer who was between travels (and between advances from his publisher) and who, as he explained to Louisa, was staying in London a while to recover completely from jet lag.

Seasoned and experienced traveler that he was (Mr. Turner informed Miss Wyatt), jet lag never much bothered him in the past, but lately it seemed to attack him. He suffered grievously, inexplicably. He was a man of about fifty (Louisa reckoned as she nodded her white frizzy head and sipped her sweet wine) who must have recently made the dreadful discovery that his body was beginning to echo with the muffled creaks and cranks of age, who had recently recognized that a half-century had passed over, or around, or beneath him, that his past was irrevocably gone, his continuing future no longer assured, and his present a good deal less pleasant than it had been prior to this baleful illumination. 'I find the jet lag affects more than my body,' Mr. Turner confessed. 'It gets to my mind. Lately it just undoes me. I get depressed and forgetful,' he added with a contradictory laugh, 'Depression and forgetfulness are things no traveler can afford.' He laughed again to further trivialize the discussion and quoted from one of his own books, ' "Depression is *not* in the wise traveler's budget!" '

'Melancholia, would you say?' inquired Louisa.

He shook his head somberly. 'Clinical depression. That's what my doctor in America says. He gave me a prescription to treat clinical depression.'

'You must fly through a good many time zones,' she observed, listening with one ear as Diana's voice grew shrill in her efforts to convert those two old servants of the Empire, Colonel Stanhope and Mr. Thrumley, to her views regarding the Family of Man.

'To pass through time zones is part of the traveler's package and privilege. It's just that I find I can't take it like I used to,' Mr. Turner added glumly.

'I've never been out of England myself,' Louisa returned her attention to the American. 'I could have traveled, I suppose, after Oxford, but, well...' She did not want to say that her father had died, her mother soon after, that she had only the house and a small annuity, that she spent such money as she had on old cookbooks. 'I can't remember just now why I didn't travel, but I didn't. And of course now, at my advanced age, the opportunity's passed me by altogether, hasn't it?'

'Advanced age?' Mr. Turner inquired gallantly. 'You don't look a day over sixty.'

At this Louisa revised her initial sour impression of the man. 'Perhaps I can help you,' she offered as she led him to the library table where the box of Cordials sat. She always brought a few extra bottles with her each year so that the club guests (if they wanted a bottle) should not feel excluded. 'Every year I make a Christmas Cordial from an ancient recipe,' she explained to Mr. Turner. 'I follow it exactly. The book I got it from was transcribed by a beautiful hand in the eighteenth century, but the Cordial, I know, is a good deal older than that and I feel certain this Cordial has been helping hundreds of people for hundreds of years.' She smiled at him reassuringly. 'Take it sparingly, Mr. Turner. A scant teaspoon at a time, I should think. No more. The vertues of this water are many, "it comforteth the vital spirits. It draweth away melancholy, lethargie and the phlegm. It comforteth against the ague and wardeth off all plagues and pestilences," and though Lady Aylesbury says nothing about jet lag, I'm certain it can help that too. "It restoreth the humours and whosoever shall drink of this water, it preserveth their health and causeth them to look young."'

'Did you make all of that up?' he asked, abashed.

'I'm quoting from the cookbook.'

'I see Miss Wyatt has offered you one

of her famous Christmas Cordials,' Mr. Shotworth interrupted them genially. In these Christmas gatherings, Mr. Shotworth's best nature bloomed; he made himself personally responsible for the cheer and comfort of everyone, from Mrs. Jobson to Colonel Stanhope. 'You are a lucky man, Mr. Turner.'

'I am?'

'Oh, yes, I can attest personally to the efficacy of Miss Wyatt's Christmas Cordial. It does everything she says it does.'

'It's not mine, Mr. Shotworth,' she corrected him. 'It's Lady Aylesbury's.'

'A family recipe?' inquired Mr. Turner.

'In a manner of speaking,' Louisa replied confidently. (After all, she had met Lady Aylesbury the same day she met Julian.)

'I don't doubt that you're skeptical, Mr. Turner,' Mr. Shotworth continued. 'But we here at the club, we swear by it. My wife always tries a shot of the Christmas Cordial before she takes so much as an aspirin,' he added truthfully.

Mrs. Jobson, after discreetly filling her wineglass once again, joined them at the library table, adding her praise. 'I give the Christmas Cordial to my daughter when she started her—you know—and it worked. She takes a scant sip every month. So do I. For the PMS. Well, a sip of Miss Wyatt's Christmas Cordial and it's *PMS—good-bye!*' she added with a yellow-toothed grin. Mrs. Jobson was a woman in her late thirties, perhaps overfond of the bottle, but understandably so; she was either widowed or divorced, certainly the deserted mother of three children whom she was raising on her own. The Explorers' Club staff's pity for her was absolutely unanimous after her eldest boy showed up to demand money from his mum; he had a bright green mohawk and a bullet shell hanging from a ring in his ear. Whatever Mrs. Jobson's fondness for the bottle, she had never in eight years missed a day of work due to hangover. While she might have shared the woes of her menstrual cycle with the assembled company, she did not deign to add that she had also used the Christmas Cordial successfully against the hangovers which had crippled her in the old days. 'A tonic, sir!' Mrs. Jobson addressed Mr. Turner authoritatively, 'that's what this 'ere Christmas Cordial is. No mistaking. Why, Miss Wyatt might've been a rich woman if she'd bottled it up, but it's better like this, if you know what I mean.' (Clearly Mr. Turner did not.) 'I mean, it's more exclusive like, makes you feel you've got something special, like you've something all your own to cure whatever ails you and no one else.' She regarded the bottles lovingly. 'Is it the ailing that makes you call it Lady Aylesbury's, Miss Wyatt?'

'No. It was written in her hand.'

Mrs. Jobson again turned to Mr. Turner.

'Well, sir, whatever's got at you, the pain in the gut, palsy in the hand, the bad bowels, you can take it from me, you can, the Christmas Cordial is the very ticket. The very one, Mr. . . . Mr. . . .'

'Turner,' replied the American, annoyed at having his innards discussed. Clinical depression. Jet lag. That's what he had in mind.

Mrs. Jobson wandered away to refill her glass yet again, and get the last bit of cake. She took a roundabout route to avoid Diana, Colonel Stanhope and Mr. Thrumley, whose discussion had escalated (and their voices correspondingly elevated) to the rights of individuals versus the rights of nations, the argument gathering such verve and acrimony that even Diana glanced wishfully at the library table with its bright be-ribboned bottles of Christmas Cordial.

Mr. Taft put down his wineglass, bid adieu and Happy Christmas to Mrs. Jobson, and ambled in his military fashion over to the library table to say his goodbye's and wish them all the best of the season. Louisa gave him his bottle and in accepting it, Mr. Taft's blue eyes sparkled and he turned to the American. 'Now, Mr. Turner, I don't know what Miss Wyatt puts in her Cordial, sir, but I'd swear it was a bit of the season itself. Whenever I've lost at the ponies, or my luck's run down, or the old war wound,'(he patted his thigh affectionately) 'acts up, I take a bit of this, and I can't explain it sir, but it brightens me right up. My old lady, my wife, Mr. Turner, I think she hit on it. Bertie—the wife says to me—Bertie, that Miss Wyatt's Cordial, it's like a nip of Christmas—whenever you need it during the year. Any old time. You can just close your eyes, Bertie, drop a teaspoon of this down your gullet, and hear 'The Holly and the Ivy' singing in your veins.'

*   *   *

'The Holly and the Ivy' was on Louisa's lips as she put the key in her lock, closed the door behind her and hastened down the passage to the kitchen where she remained shivering, bundled against the cold until the cooker and kettle and heater had all warmed up. Despite the cold, she was in a cheerful holiday mood, full of gratitude and affection for her friends at the Explorers' Club, convinced that no other job could have afforded her such friends and such pleasures—to say nothing of allowing her to continue working part-time long past retirement age. Then she laughed out loud to think of Diana Dufour and the two old servants of the Empire, Mr. Thrumley and Colonel Stanhope. 'Oh, you should have seen it,' she said to no one in particular (as there was no one there). 'Diana had poor Mr. Thrumley by the lapels! Diana

43

the huntress indeed! That girl ought to have run for Parliament,' she remarked, knowing full well that thirty years stood between Diana and any girlhood she might have enjoyed. As the warmth percolated through the kitchcn, Louisa's account of the afternoon's festivities grew more animated and precise, as though reconstructing the event for the entertainment of people intimately involved, but who could not have been at the Club, people whose presence seemed to gather without quite coalescing, to dissipate without quite disappearing. 'And Colonel Stanhope, when I gave him his bottle of the Cordial, he called me Dear lady and said I should have labeled the Cordial "Spirits of Christmas." And well, naturally I told him it was *your* cordial, the recipe in your hand, my dear, of course. And did you remember we'd given Colonel Stanhope a bottle the Christmas of 1973? Neither did I, but Colonel Stanhope did. Oh yes, and he told everyone there that he'd taken the bottle with him to Angola, and that the Christmas Cordial–and that alone–had got him through the war. No, I don't know which war. People like Colonel Stanhope are always getting through one war or another, aren't they? Yes, of course I'm hurrying. I haven't forgotten Mr. Shillingcote's coming to tea. One cannot forget Mr. Shillingcote, can one?' And then Louisa bit back and smile and silently concurred that one wasn't allowed to.

She surveyed her tray: teapot, cups, saucers, cream, sugar, a plate of shop-bought vanilla biscuits (shop-bought so long ago they looked to have been cut from stucco). She was in the midst of relating the woes of Mr. Turner, the American travel writer, when the doorbell rang. 'Clinical depression indeed!' she concluded with a sniff. 'Melancholia, that's what ails Mr. Turner, and of course the vertues of this water will—'

The bell rang again. Mr. Shillingcote, for all his bonhomie, was not a man to be kept waiting, but a man for whom time was money, and he treated both with equal respect. Indeed, in bestowing his time upon Louisa Wyatt, he considered himself to be giving her a gift that could not be ribboned or wrapped.

After the usual pleasantries in the freezing front hall, Louisa led him back to the frosty back sitting room where she flicked on the electric fire, chagrined not to have done so earlier. He lowered himself into one of the chintz-covered chairs and shivered. He had the big, ramshackle frame of an athletic schoolboy whose prowess had gone lumpy in all the predictable places. He had a long horsey face and a thick mane of hair that was once blond, but turning gray now and coarsening in the process. He chafed his hands and looked around. No wonder the old girl didn't keep the place up. It would cost a fortune to heat nowadays. Still, he offered his thoughts aloud, 'This old house must have been grand once.'

'Comfortable, Mr. Shillingcote. Hardly grand. Not, certainly, on the order of Lady Aylesbury's.'

The solicitor colored slightly. 'Well, I'm sure this house would have some tales to tell if the walls could talk.'

'Do you think so?' Louisa glanced at the green velvet drapes, the fraying furniture, the stolid television (c. 1961), the boxy radio (c. 1948), the doilies and antimacassars and table scarves and china dogs that still testified to her mother's fastidious tastes. 'I rather doubt it. It's a staid old house, I should think. No ghosts whatever—certainly none in all the years I've lived here. There weren't any scandals in our family and—'

'I never meant to imply—'

'Of course not. I mean, my brothers both died very young and far away, and my mother and father were very ordinary, upstanding sorts of people, and so, I believe, were the family previous to ours, and no doubt the family previous to that. I rather wish there were ghosts here. Sometimes I like to think that miscreant merrymakers from the old Holland House might have reveled on these grounds. You know, the Holland House from oh, the seventeenth century, the one that was bombed during the War and then demolished.' He nodded, and she went on pleasantly, 'I like to think perhaps they left some morsel of their youth and gaiety, some bit of the seventeenth-century here. I like to think of recklessly extravagant young men cavorting with young women who had been married off to husbands too old for them, and being very much in love, even if was hopeless, squandered love, even adultery. I like to think...' Louisa smiled primly, aware, from the look on Mr. Shillingcote's face, that she had said too much. 'Well, ghosts are unreliable at best, aren't they, Mr. Shillingcote? Life is far more comfortable without them. What if one had a weepy, morose ghost, some Roundhead from the Civil War, or a displaced priest bemoaning the dissolution of the monasteries?' Behind closed lips, Louise put her tongue between her teeth and bit down hard, resolved not to let up till Mr. Shillingcote spoke, and not to go on in that vein in any event. She blamed the wine at the club this afternoon.

'Of course one would prefer ghosts of one's own class and religion,' he offered drily and to this Louisa nodded, still biting her tongue. He went on in a lighter fashion. 'Perhaps it's just as well then that there are no ghosts, Louisa. That way, when they tear the place down, there won't be anyone chucked into the street!' He laughed in his horsey way.

'I don't intend to sell,' she reminded him.

He gestured broadly about the room. 'But really, Louisa!' He always took this informal line with her, though his predecessor had never called her anything but Miss Wyatt. 'Keeping all this up, why, it must ruin you!'

'I don't keep it up, as you know very well. Saving for the garden. I do my best with the garden. But I only use these few rooms, and all the rest of the house is sheeted and cold, and I never have any cause to go upstairs.'

'Surely you'd be more comfortable in a cosy little flat. Certainly you'd be warmer,' he added with a glance to the electric fire whose glow had not yet permeated the sitting room.

'I shan't be moving anywhere. Cosy or not. This is my home.'

Seeing that he had once again suffered his annual defeat, Mr. Shillingcote took it manfully like the good sport he was, and after making his customary remarks about a small fortune being better than no fortune at all, he contradicted himself entirely and emphatically stated that indeed, this *was* her home and she not think of moving and he would never *dream* of urging her to do so. He brought his hand down upon his knee as if to close the deal. 'Well, Louisa, Margaret and I are hoping you'll join us on Christmas Day. Come in the afternoon.'

'Thank you very much, Mr. Shillingcote, but if my health permits, I shall go to my cousin Enid's in Shepherd's Bush.'

'Your health, Louisa? Surely you haven't been—'

'Oh no, Mr. Shillingcote. I'm quite fit, more fit than a woman my age has any right to expect. Now you wait here and let me go fetch the tea and your bottle of Christmas Cordial.'

She vanished into the kitchen and left him there with his mental calculations, turning square feet into pounds and pence, thinking that perhaps, in gratitude for all his years of service and his friendship, perhaps Louisa Wyatt would leave the place to him. After all, he had always shown her not merely courtesy, but generosity of spirit in asking Louisa Wyatt to join them for Christmas, offering this friendless old woman the considerable pleasures of his table, his wine cellar, his own stellar company, and that of his lovely wife, Margaret. He did this every year, his convictions of his own munificence bolstered by the fact that he knew Louisa would decline. She had come once, in 1978, early on in their acquaintance and not since. After the 1978 debacle, Margaret had vowed to divorce him if he ever again brought that thankless, potty, garrulous, insufferable old hag home with him again. *And,* Margaret sniffed, *I don't care if the old girl owns an entire block of flats in Westminster Abbey!* On her 1978 Christmas visit, Louisa had criticized the cooking at every turn, not in a nasty fashion, only as a disinterested cookery expert. Nothing was quite right, none of the flavors quite balanced, nor was the skin on the goose quite as crackling as it ought to have been, and the oysters hadn't that salt water tang, the taste of the sea, which was impossible to come by nowadays anyway because everyone knew all waters were polluted and God knows what oysters fed on nowadays, though once they must have seemed like slimy little surprises to the taste buds, dashed with a bit of salt. Just imagine . . .

Mr. Shillingcote had watched Margaret's features pinch around her nose, and he dove into the conversation, striving for equilibrium. He asked if Louisa did much cooking. The old woman had rolled her eyes and said Never, adding that she was expert, just the same, from reading old cookbooks. Then she launched into a long disquisition, beginning with her chance discovery that day so very long ago at the Bodleian Library and culminating with her 1963 purely serendipitous foray into Woodstock, to Ye Spinning Wheel which used to be Featherstones' Rare Books in Woodstock before the tourists came and changed everything, and her discovery there of Lady Aylesbury's hand-transcribed cookbook. She had gone on and on.

It was the wine. That's what Louisa was thinking now, in the kitchen as she gathered the tray and remembered that dreadful 1978 Christmas with the Shillingcotes. She'd drunk far too much wine. She was unaccustomed to drinking at all and somehow in a dithery and inexplicable way, had confused the drinking of wine with the reading of drinking of wine, enjoying the Shillingcote's wine as though it were Lady Aylesbury's, not realizing that one may read of drinking as much as one wishes with few ill effects, but to actually put it into practice in one's life. Well. That was a wholly different matter. Rather like squandering love, she thought, as she placed the bottle of Christmas Cordial on the tray and went back to sitting room. One might read of squandered love with nothing more than few pangs and sniffles, but to endure it . . .

She set the tray before Mr. Shilingcote and he regarded the bottle of Christmas Cordial with the relish he might have donated to a perfectly grilled chop. 'We are looking forward to our Christmas Cordial, Louisa,' he said with a wink. In fact since 1978 his wife had dumped each bottle of Christmas Cordial on the houseplants, and though she had remarked to her husband that very morning at breakfast that the philodendron had grown a five full feet since she'd doused it last year, he thought it best not to submit this fact in evidence of its efficacy. 'Excellent tonic, your Cordial.'

'The vertues of this water are many,' Louisa began as she poured his tea and passed him a stale biscuit. ' "It provoketh urine and preventeth the gravel and the stone. It helpeth against the pantings and swimming of the braine. It cureth contractions of the sinews.

It preserveth the heart against envy", Mr. Shillingcote. ' "Whomsoever shall drink of this water shall be made content and to knoweth the manifold pleasures of life.' ""

*   *   *

When Basil Shillingcote finally left, Louisa saw him to the front door, closed it after him and stayed there, just for a moment, bracing herself against its comfortable solidity. Mr. Shillingcote had overstayed, she thought, walking slowly back to the sitting room and hefting the tea tray. Seeing the tea still warm in his cup, she wondered if her estimation were correct. Had he overstayed? She wasn't certain. She was about to say something to Julian when he reminded her (in his husbandly way) that she had best turn off the electric fire before returning to the kitchen. 'Oh, yes,' she said absently. 'A pity to waste all this warmth, dear, but it is the night before Christmas Eve and I have work to do. The bottles for the milkman, the postman, the dustmen and Enid.'

She carried the tray back to the kitchen and considered the possibilities for supper. Frozen fish fingers presented themselves, but the very thought made her queasy. A cup of tea. That's what she needed.

The cup of tea did not quite have the restorative effect she had counted on, but she busied herself with the bottles just the same, flipping through her ribbon box and mentally designating colors: two blues for the dustmen, a yellow for the postman, green for the milkman. The milkman's green-banded bottle (labeled with a small card wishing him holiday best from Miss Wyatt) she took to the front door and left it on the porch for him to collect in his early morning rounds. The bottles for the dustmen and the postman she would give them personally the next day. It was her tradition. She took a bottle and put it on the shelf beside the sink, glancing at herself in the darkened window, her own familiar features somehow oddly awry.

She returned to the table, picking through the ribbon fox, fancying a red ribbon for Enid's bottle and not finding any. She must have used them all up for the bottles she took to the Explorers' Club. She remembered that her mother kept a ribbon box in the bottom drawer of her vanity. For the jaunt upstairs Louisa bundled up, buttoning her cardigan and throwing the mothy scarf around her neck and took with her the bottle to store.

Every year Louise kept two bottles of the Cordial for herself. One bottle she left by the kitchen sink in case she should need it for some momentary infirmity or failure of spirit. (She had used it in 1978 to ward off the hangover resulting form the disaster at the Shillingcotes'.) And one bottle she stored in the armoire of her parents' bedroom, the armoire in which her mother's wedding dress still hung, as though there might yet be a bride to wear it. Her mother's wedding dress always seemed to Louisa to be appropriate company to the many bottles of Christmas Cordial that had accumulated over the years. The bottles constituted a sort of record of her life, the milestones she had marked off since she had first read Lady Aylesbury's gorgeous script and heard—in a manner of speaking— her cool, cultivated voice telling of the vertues of this water and her precise and elaborate rendering of the twenty-five different herbes and spices to be laid in faire water and then dried, bruised, stamped and shredded, added to ye best gascoyne wine and let steep before distilling a limbeck with a gentle fire. As Louisa made her way laboriously up the stairs to her parents' room, she found she could not remember a single thing about any of the Christmases she had so carefully stored and laid away; they all seemed to mull together silently, leaving her with the sort of gummy sadness the one feels at the sight of ribbon and wreath frozen in a January gutter.

Of course, she told herself, as she flipped on the overhead light in her parents' front bedroom, everything might have been different if Julian had lived, even, she reasoned, if her brothers had lived, if they had come home from the war, if they had married and had families, if there had been children and grandchildren and perhaps even a fat baby great-grandchild, if— 'Pull yourself together,' she commanded herself, 'before your humours get unbalanced and the melancholia—' Her breath came in short swift stabs, slicing between her ribs like a knife, her pulse raced, her head pounded, pounded, and she gripped the pineapple-topped poster of her parents' bed, hugged and clung to it as though begging it to dance, as her feet slid out from underneath her and she tumbled sprawling senselessly to the floor.

Pull yourself together. She could not speak. She could not move. But she could think. Slowly. *I can think* and in doing so she thought of the telephone a full flight down. She thought of tomorrow, the twenty-fourth, when no one would miss her at the Explorers' Club because no one worked that day; no one worked for another three days. She thought how Enid would not miss her till Christmas Day; she thought how she might die and not be missed at all, and how her stockings had holes in them, and her underwear not the freshest, and her skirt splotched, the hem pinned up. Thinking how she would die, splayed on the floor of her parents' room like a tiny rag doll carelessly thrown down by a pouting child, and how she'd not accounted for an heir to the house and how she would be the only ghost here when the wrecking ball came through and chucked her into the street. *Pull yourself together,* she wept before succumbing again to the darkness in her head.

The clock in her parents' room was of the winding variety and had not been wound in thirty years and so Louisa Wyatt hadn't any idea how long she'd lain there on the floor, except that when she next blinked, she could see it was still dark out and the blaring overhead light burnt into her squinting eyes and hurt them. Slowly she issued a series of commands to her body, some of which it obeyed and some it did not. She was aghast to discover that her urine had been provoked, but she assured herself she was not only not dead, but not about to die. *Not Yet. Not now. Oh please not now not now not now no now* Though why *not now* she could not say. Was it that she hadn't yet 'done something' with her life? Because it was Christmas?

Death heeds no holidays and seemed intent on prying Louisa Wyatt's bony fingers from what little life she had left, but she silently struck a bargain: if Death would allow her to get up on the bed, at least to be found like a lady, in bed, composed as a lady ought to be, then she would go quietly. She had no intention whatever of keeping this bargain, but thought it prudent to make.

With a monstrous effort of will and using only the right side of her body, since the left side had died already, Louisa dragged herself along the floor beside the bed. She saw that the bottle of Christmas Cordial lay directly in her path, and as she inched and heaved forward, she considered the many vertues of this water, and thought it a shame she hadn't the strength to pull out the cork and take the proverbial swig against what ailed her, assailed her and would doubtlessly defeat her. *But not yet. Not just yet. Not just now.* She clutched the bottle in her right hand, just for comfort and considered the most efficient way to heave her bones from the floor up to the high, beckoning bed. She raised herself to a slumped sitting position, resting her back against the bed, and then it occurred to Louisa that she had teeth. Her own in fact. Most of them. She raised the bottle to the right side of her mouth, and urged her lips to open, to bare her teeth much as Molly had bared her gleaming orthodontic work. Louisa's teeth obeyed; she shoved the cork between those teeth and commanded them to close. Her teeth seemed to hold a conference to decide if they would do this or not. Then, reluctantly they clamped around the cork. Louisa realized she was confronted with a difficult choice, indeed, a gamble: she probably did not have the strength to yank this bottle open with her teeth *and* get up on the bed, to die like a lady, to rise to the occasion. If she opted for the bottle, she might well die sprawled on the floor like a bug. She considered the possibilities for a time, knowing she might not have much time in which to make her choice.

Like the heroine she had never been, Louisa took the gallant path, used her every morsel of strength to yank on the bottle while imploring her teeth to keep their grip on the cork. The Cordial burbled out, over her sweater and down her collar and stained the rug before she could get the bottle to stand upright in her hand. And spit out the cork.

Haltingly Louisa raised the bottle to the right side of her mouth (which she consciously, carefully opened) and the Christmas Cordial, splashed the whole contents of the bottle over her lips, the liquid ran down her chin, washed over her teeth and tongue, or as much as she could feel of her lips and teeth and tongue. She swallowed as best she could. Again and again. She prayed that the vertues of this water were such that it would give her the strength to cast her body up on the bed in which she'd been conceived and brought forth, a squalling infant more than three quarters of a century ago

Before she could quite focus—the overhead light pricking her eyes the way Lady Aylesbury advised pricking cracknells before putting them like mackroons in a pritty hot oven— Louisa was besieged by sounds of crashing buckets and tinkling harps, the playing of the merry organ's sweet singing in her ear, along with the rustle of satin, a whiff of coriander, clove and orange, a spray of ye wilde thyme brushed under her nose while the glow of a million golden candles melted the frost that wept its crystalline way down down down into the bowels of the city to escape the bombs, to huddle with strangers, with thumping good-natured wenches and blustering boys, footmen and handmaidens, with Anne, Lady Aylesbury, her voice graceful and cultivated as her handwriting, turning to a portly, well-fed, wigged and waistcoated man beside her and asking if the Cordial wasn't just a bit tart this year and he, taking a pinch of snuff and eyeing his marriageable daughter, (who was enjoying the attentions of an impecunious younger son) applies the snuff to his nose and begins in stentorian tones that the vertues of this water are such that he sneezes, and Mr. Turner, the American, sitting there beside him, completes his thought in saying jovially that whosoever shall drinketh thereof shall be caused to look youthful, Mr. Shotworth contributing that it comforteth the vital spirits and restoreth the humours to their proper balance, easeth the swimming of the braine and Mrs. Jobson, refilling her glass yet again from the decanter of ye best gascoyne wine, laughs and adds it cureth the contractions of the sinews, the hangover and (Mrs. Jobson rising unsteadily, lifts her glass w/a rousing hurrah) *Goodbye PMS!* which nets her some cheers from the women while Aunt Charlotte, fingering a stalk of candied angelico, inquires discreetly of

Aunt Jane, what exactly *is* PMS, and Aunt Jane, giving a nudge to a quaking jelly of damson plums beautifully unmolded before, remarks to Louisa's mother that living without a husband is difficult but not impossible, calls on Aunt Tilda to corroborate, but Tilda is smitten unto speechlessness at the sight of Lady Aylesbury's gown, textured and compounded in the bittersweet hue of Sevile orringes, a string of pomegranate seeds beaded with currants around her neck, gleaming like jewels in the candlelight, and the reflected warmth of the charcoal braziers, while twenty-four carat Jordan almonds drip from her ears, as Lady Aylesbury wordlessly instructs a bevy of eager servants, their cheeks made ruddy from the kitchen, to bring up steaming silver platters and lay them before the guests, to see to their comfort and joy, such that Diana Dufour turns to the famous Imperial Explorer, Sir William Barry seated beside her, marveling that *this, clearly this* is the Family of Man as it was intended to be, and both Sir William Barry and Sir Clive Rackham rattle their goblets—as they rattled the parquet and the wainscoting in the Explorers' Club for years—they rattle and nudge Sir Matthew Curtis (the slayer of Pip) and all laugh heartily, reminding Diana that it is the Family of Man and *thensome* with a nod and a knowing snort to Pip, sitting beside Sir Matthew Curtis (who is cracking his knuckles

60

and walnuts, the shells of the latter dropped without ceremony into his amber port) and Pip roars his agreement, the expression of outrage softened by years of acceptance, and wreath of holly strung rakishly over his polar bear brow, the wreath slipping as Pip's laughter bellows, gusting the candlelight before them and the holly and the ivy threading down the long table to the uncomprehending, certainly irritated and vaguely outraged Shillingcotes, Margaret Shillingcote describing in a shrill voice Louisa's disgraceful conduct that Christmas of 1978 for the edification of the bewildered Enid, the sneer or wonderment highlighting Molly's heavy metal mouth, till Lady Aylesbury's cool cultivated voice interrupts Margaret, gently but firmly reminds Margaret, reminds all of them all that it is all very well to read of these things, drinking wine and squandering love, but do to them is quite another fa la la la la altogether just before she directs her beneficent attention to the flatulent Jack and inquires after his wambling belly, asks if he hasn't found the vertues of this water to be such that it cureth the griping belly, the lethargie, the frensie and madness of the war in Angola, Colonel Stanhope is saying to a lady who sniffs a pomander ball in manner at once coy and suggestive, offering the old soldier a muskadine comfit which causes the admiring Mr. Taft, sitting nearby, to rise to his feet and raise a toast to luck with the ladies and luck with the horses, a proposal drunk with much gusto by everyone save for the displaced priests, upset and uprooted by the dissolution of the monasteries on whom Lady Aylesbury lavishes, extolls her most calming grace, her skin the color of a honey of roses, her gown spun from sparkling loaf sugar, a necklace of candied violets ringing her neck and tiny brittle mint cakes gleaming on her fingers, she smiles says, God rest merry, gentlemen and ladies, it came upon a midnight clearly we've not welcomed our guest of honor, she adds, rising, the whiff of her compounded court perfume combining with the smoke spiraling form a million vanilla candles and the steam off a capon roste with oysters and a peacock roasted and draped agin in its own finery set fragrantly before Louisa's proud father (claret glowing ruby in his appreciative hand) and Louis's still lovely mother, her brothers in their unstained uniforms who sit beside the dustmen in their blue uniforms and the milkman in his and the postman (his fraying ring of hair covered by his cap) in his, all of them smiling and stuffing marchpane cakes in their cheeks and pockets as they laugh to the tune of the music wafting over them, as they wax on about the vertues of this water while Lady Aylesbury addresses them all—priests and polar bear alike—to tell them of the things Louisa Wyatt hath done with her life, of those she helpeth and preserveth, of those she comforteth and restored, of all the time zones she had passed through, and at this Mr. Shotworth (seated nearby Mr. Featherstone and an eighteenth century dowager with bosoms like two enormous boiled puddings) Mr Shotworth drops the bones of the roasted plover upon which he has been nibbling and leaps to his feet, glass in hand, to announce that Louisa Wyatt, in recognition of her explorations into the past, is hereby granted Honorary Membership with All Privileges Appertaining Thereunto in the Explorers' Club while a great cheer goes up and people say: *Here Here!* And some say *There There* as one would to a pouting child, to a golden haired moppets, a bouncing girl in a dress of jolly holly green sitting beside a small boy with his father's dark eyes, long lashes and small mouth, both restless and listening as the guests exuberate upon the vertues of this water and their mother, their mother who loved the beautiful young people they would become when they went up to Oxford and embarked on lives (Lady Aylesbury was saying) of reckless virtue; *in Louisa Wyatt,* Lady Aylesbury's voice rings out over all, *I give you a life of reckless virtue, of gallant service, of unstinting imaginative energy, rendered lovingly, generously and cordially* (the guests all laugh) *to those who were closest to her, and those who were not* (a chilly glance bestowed on Margaret Shillingcote), *to the living and the dead, to my friend, Louisa Wyatt, who did not make those vulgar distinctions between what might have been and what was, a woman who, in this joyous season, offereth comfort and joy to all,* continues Anne, Lady Aylesbury, whose dress has turned golden and light as puff pastry, the billowing sleeves elaborately beaded with caraway and anise seed, with bayberries and gooseberries, the bodice escalloped in perfectly sliced peaches preserved from some long-past summer, flounced with caramel ribbons in the style of a long time ago when she turns to Julian and smiles at him, Julian rises. And as he does, the music slowly stills, the last notes gleaming at the edge of hushing voices because Julian gives them all his wonderful grin, impertinent and cheerful, and he addresses them with a flash of David Niven and a dash of Leslie Howard and says to the assembled company that *We are come here today to celebrate what Louisa Wyatt has done with her life, to celebrate Louisa Wyatt, who, with equal parts of joy and love has protected us all, the living and the dead, against the brutal hand of Time which would have seen us cast into the heap of the unremembered, Louisa Wyatt, who, with the most skillful of hands, each year combines that delicate elixir of memory and imagination and twenty-five different herbs and spices, laide in faire water bruised, shredded, dried and combined with the best gascoyne wine, steeped over days and then distilled on a gentle fire, to be brought forth every*

Christmas season in a cordial, the vertues of which are manifold, a water to dispel! the soot and grime of compromise, my friends, the accretion of smoke from dreams long snuffed out, the exhaust of idling lives, the dust of fear, of hope denied, oh my dear Louisa—Julian turns to her, his too-small mouth poised in its beautiful, familiar smile— *oh, Louisa, I love you so*

*   *   *

'It's so! I tell you she an't missed a Christmas in fifteen years and the bloke before me said she an't missed a Christmas with him either, so I'm telling your bleeding bobby lordship, there's something wrong, and you have to go in there!'

'And I tell you, I can't. Not without a warrant.'

'Bugger the warrant!' She's old. She must be ninety! She gives me a bottle of this stuff every December twenty -fourth and she an't there today and it ain't there today and something terrible's a gone on.' The postman mopped his face against the choler and unexpected anger.

The police sergeant behind the desk regarded the postman indulgently. 'She might have gone away for the holidays. Think of that, did you? Lots of people leave on December twenty-fourth.'

'Not Miss Wyatt.'

'Fancy yourself a friend fo the family, do you?

'Look, she an't got any family. She's a hundred years old, see? She's got no one and she's all alone in that big house and while you're clacking your jaws, she might be on the edge of life and death, she might be drawing her last while the London police diddles their doorknobs over warrants and—'

'The law's the law.'

'Oh, that's a good one. Tell me about the law. You'd see it different if she was some punk in the Tube station shot full of—'

'That's enough,' the sergeant announced, heaving his bones out of the chair and adding that he would be right back. The postman took off his cap and ruffled his fraying ring of hair, his fraying patience which was tried to the last when the sergeant returned and said the London police could do naught about an old woman who always left a bottle with a ribbon on it on the porch for the postman every December twenty-fourth. He advised the postman to get back to his rounds if he knew what was good for him, but just then the two dustmen burst into the station and hurried to the desk and said their bottles (ribbons and all) had not been left in the alley for them and at that the sergeant threw up his hands and called the hospital and eventually an ambulance wailed through the streets of London, braying its way toward Holland Park, to the only house not cut up into flats, where they found the postman and the two dustmen awaiting them on the steps. The police came too because a crowd gathered, and it was necessary to contain them so that a half dozen men could force the door of the woman known to them only as Miss Wyatt.

Amidst the haste and commotion, the confusion and excitement, no one noticed that in the upper floors, the windows fronting the street, all the frost that usually ringed them had melted, as though the heat and hope and human expiration of a great many people had combined to warm those otherwise empty rooms.

READING WITH MY FATHER

I was either an afterthought or a big surprise, my parents never would say which. By the time I joined the Nolan clan, my parents were middle aged, and my sisters, were in high school and middle school; Mary, Margaret and Susan were far too sophisticated to pay me any mind, but old enough to begrudge the babysitting I required. I might have grown up in the family shadows had I not been a prodigy, displaying my genius when I was just a toddler, not yet two. According to the family story, I was sitting in the grocery cart in the vegetable aisle, while my mother picked over the turnips, I astonished everyone in listening distance by pointing up above a door and shouting out, 'Exit!'

My mother raced home to call my father at work. Rose could read! My father was a printer at the St. Elmo *Herald*, so reading was of great consequence in our family. He was awestruck When he came home, he said seriously, 'Is this true, Rose? Can you read?'

'Exit!' I said, since it had been such a hit just hours before.

My father read to me every night, but after my display of genius, his ink-blackened fingernails would follow each word. We read the picture book classics, *Madeleine,*

Blueberries for Sal, Make Way for the Ducklings, and the like. However, early on he began reading to me real books. Chapter books. We spent months with *The Wind in the Willows, The Railway Children,* the *Oz* books, *Hans Brinker, Little Women.* I was so young that frequently he had to stop and explain things to me, like why wasn't Jo's father at home, and what was the Civil War? I remember sitting close to my own father, Frank Nolan, smelling the ink-and-oil metal-and-sweat smell that never left him, and being glad he was not fighting far away like Jo's father.

The St. Elmo *Herald* was a morning paper, and his working day began at four in the morning, but he got up at three. My father and I got tired about the same time of day, sort of between seven and eight, so when I was little, our schedules meshed. He'd read to me, stretched out on my bed, Dad in his stocking feet, me curled beside him, his finger following each word. Sometimes a chapter. Sometimes just a few pages. He would kiss me goodnight, and then I'd hear him singing in the shower. Ours was a small house. After this, there was quiet. Even if Mom and Mary, Margaret and Susan watched TV, they had to keep the volume down. Certainly there was no rock and roll for the Nolan girls. My older sisters felt the pinch of these restrictions, and resented them. They usually went to their friends' house where the noise level might merely irritate the parents. At our house my father's getting enough sleep was crucial to the small universe we lived in. Frank Nolan, veteran printer, prided himself on a shop without accidents and a paper without errors.

He prided himself too on finishing the books we started. And I did learn to read very young, though I must admit I was lazy prodigy and much preferred being read to. In truth, *Sesame Street* deserves the credit for my recognizing Exit, but I inflated the legend, and I knew how to dazzle teachers. Whispered word went round Fourth Street School, *Rose Nolan could read at the age of two!* No other kid at knew the classics like I did. Inevitably at the annual school pageant of *A Christmas Carol*, I corrected the other students' diction. 'No, no,' I'd tell them, 'you have to say it slowly. Like this,' and I would roll my eyes heavenward, and raise my arms high, using the intonation my father used, and declare: 'I-Wear-The-Chains-I-Forged-In-Life!'

A Christmas Carol was certainly one of my father's favorite classics. Our copy was a dog-eared paperback, the spine much-weakened, the pages coarse to the touch and aged to a sepia color. Every year after Thanksgiving dinner, while the scent of pumpkin pie and turkey still lay heavy on the air, our tradition never varied. My mother would retreat to the livingroom and put her feet up for a well-deserved rest. My sisters would be in the kitchen doing the washing up. My father would say to me, 'Well, Rose, now where did we put Mr. Scrooge last year?'

This was a ceremonial question because he always put the book on the same shelf in the hall bookcase. I would bring it to him along with his reading glasses. My father would place a bookmark to mark the pages of whatever novel we had been reading up till then, and put it aside. He would clear his throat, point to the words, and say, ' "Marley was dead, to begin with." '

And so, year after year—as certain as Friday's turkey tacos—we began *A Christmas Carol*. I listened to the wintry depiction of Old Man Scrooge, his gnarled fingers grasping after money, his heart frozen against goodwill, his soul and life shriveled up. I recognized, as the story progressed, that a connection with community, with the past and present— and of course, the terrors evoked by Ghost of Christmas Yet To Come—thawed and restored old Scrooge so that he knew how to keep Christmas well. Indeed, to keep it all year long.

My father gave himself over to the telling, and he did the voices, especially Marley's ghost, with spirit and precision. We read *A Christmas Carol* every night between Thanksgiving and New Year's Eve. On New Year's day, no matter where we were in the story, he put it back on the shelf, and we returned to the book we'd been reading before Thanksgiving.

A Christmas Carol was the only book we never finished.

* * *

My father Frank Nolan was a tall rangy man with long legs, long arms and a boney face that I alas, have inherited. He was a serious man, practical, not given to mirth, nor joking. My father had gone into the St. Elmo *Herald* press room at age sixteen as a copy boy. He had learned his trade well, but the presses roared in his head long after he had left work. He was slightly deaf. If he had been high spirited in his youth, nothing was left to testify by the time I came along. My mother, Sara, was petite, quite lovely as a girl, hardworking, fiercely loyal to Dad and the family, but not especially lively or cheerful. I always envied my friends whose parents were young, vivacious, even funny, active in Scouts and sports. By the time I was nine, my parents were pushing fifty; they had flecks of gray hair, and worked too many hours to have enthusiasm left over for Scouts and sports. Mom sewed my sisters' prom dresses, and made most of their clothes, so I wore nothing but hand-me-downs, and when I think of my mother, I think of the whirr of the sewing machine.

Sara Nolan valued Clean and Neat as

72

entities in themselves, though after she went to work, breakfast shift at the Wagon Wheel Café, she was too tired to live up to these standards on a daily basis. She left precise lists of the housework assigned to Mary, Margaret and Susan. As the baby—and the prodigy, of course—I was spared much of this, but my sisters, in addition to looking after me, had before school chores, and after school chores. Mother was never too tired to criticize their efforts.

My mother's critical faculties relaxed only once a year, as soon as she donned the Santa hat my father gave her. Though ours was not a lighthearted household, the Nolan family Christmases were flamboyant, a long ongoing season of excitement that I associate with the Fezziwigs' Christmas party, with the anticipation of the Cratchits' Christmas goose. Now I know, as I did not then, that my parents did have a streak of lightheartedness, even high spirits that had been dampened down in their youth, and obscured by the worries of everyday life. Only at Christmas could they release merriment, and dispense with their usual prudence. My mother wore the Santa hat at a jaunty angle. My father would tuck a fiver or a ten dollar bill under our plates at dinnertime and pretend to be surprised when we found it, blame it on the Christmas elves. Sometimes the elves would visit two or three times before Christmas. We girls did lots of shopping and kept many secrets. We barred our bedroom doors as we wrapped gifts in the leftover Sunday funnies which the *Herald* printed in color. Each present was then be-decked with cascades of ribbon; the sound of scissors curling ribbon seems to me one of the most poignant I can imagine. Slowly the presents under the tree would spill across the bedsheet around the bottom, and out on to the floor. The season itself licensed what Frank and Sara kept locked up all the rest of the year— hearts that delighted in the happiness of others, prodigal spirits.

On the 24th of December (even if he had to work that day) my father always made his Christmas Fudge in the afternoon. I loved to help him. Susan, Mary and Margaret no longer thought this was an exciting moment, so there was no one to fight me for the ultimate honor. As soon as my father poured the hot fudge into the deep dish, I got to drop the money in, four quarters and a fifty cent piece. My father would wash the coins, boil them, and then pluck the four quarters from the boiling water. On his command, 'Have at it, Rose,' I commended these coins to the deep, the thick, the glorious sea of chocolate.

For the rest of the day, I liked to stand near the Christmas Fudge just to smell it. Susan said I was a stupid to be so eager, so dazzled at the prospect of a quarter.

'I can't be stupid, I'm a prodigy.'

74

(Susan swears I said this. I probably did.)

Since the Wagon Wheel Café took up much of Mom's time, she left her Christmas recipes out for The Girls to follow. Mom's recipes were written in her neat, rounded hand, on notebook paper splashed with old batter, stiff with flour thumbprints, and faded. Though Mary, Margaret and Susan griped about having to cook, there was something about all four of us in the kitchen, following Mom's directions for Rice, Sausage and Sage stuffing that created a bond between the Nolan girls. Even me. My job was to cut the sage from the bush outside and tear the leaves over the bowl.

We had to have the stuffing all ready to go into the turkey, and a pumpkin, an apple and a Cranberry Apricot pie all made by the 23rd. The cranberry relish took the whole morning of the 24th. The relish (so easily made now in a food processor) was laborious beyond words. My sister bolted the food mill to the table, and the four us turned the crank till arms ached. Susan says I was a terrible whiner and begged off after a few minutes, and in this, too, I'm sure she's right.

Christmas Eve, we went to Midnight Mass (Mary and Margaret both sang in the choir), and we also had to attend the early mass because of the kiddie pageant, in which I was invariably a shepherd and wore the same shepherd costume till I outgrew the kiddie pageant. Between church services, we ate,

Mom's pork roast with onions, followed by Cranberry Apricot Pie. But not the Christmas Fudge. No, that was reserved for the Christmas Day.

At our house, opening our presents on Christmas morning took hours and hours, not because we had so much, we didn't, but each present got opened one at a time. No one could open anything till everyone was in the living room—and my parents each had a cup of coffee and a few cookies on a saucer delivered to them. I stationed myself by the tree, and poked through the presents, choosing who would come next, reading out everything written on the box, even if they were silly poems, parodies of Christmas carols. Each gift, from the handwoven potholder, to my rocking horse, got equal time, if not equal delight. (I don't think anyone—ever—was as delighted as I was with that rocking horse). Even Mary and Margaret and Susan let go of their sophisticated ways and were known to jump up and down with delight. My mother's exacting housekeeping standards relaxed for this one day, the colorful funny papers billowing across our living room like clouds. With four kids and two adults, opening the presents could take hours, everyone *oohing* and *ahhing* to watch, especially as we have been known to wrap the smallest stocking stuffer, a key ring, a teatowel. Sometimes we'd have to take a break and eat a quick breakfast or we couldn't continue, so vast and opulent was our Christmas.

My parents never had a dinner party (as the term is usually understood) in all their lives, but Christmas was always crowded. It was the only time we put both leaves in the kitchen table, and every chair and bench in the house pulled into use. Usually we had an aunt and uncle or two, and their families (though not grandparents, Mom's parents had moved to an Arizona retirement community, and my dad's parents had died before I was born). But every year, different kinds of people came to Christmas dinner. My mother might invite the Wagon Wheel waitresses or cooks who had been through rough times, Delores who had been widowed in April, or Esther and Stan when the railroad laid him off. There came to our Christmas dinners Susan's English teacher, Miss McTavish, and Mary's science teacher, the bachelor Mr. Wells. (We went to their wedding, the following year, Mary and Susan proud as if they'd been bridesmaids.) My parents would often invite young couples new to St. Elmo, young men just out of the service who worked at the *Herald*. The young husband, his hair slicked down, uncomfortable being uncomfortable would call my mother Ma'am, and my sisters Miss. The young wife (sometimes with a baby at her breast) was grateful to talk about 'back home,' wherever that might be.

One year I sat beside Mr. Giddings, from the print shop who had been injured in an auto accident. His arm was in a huge white cast; he was useless to the paper, and not working. I watched him eat everything else, the stuffing, the sweet potatoes, the little creamed onions. 'Mr. Giddings,' I said, 'would you like me to cut your turkey?' I was afraid he would cry.

I don't remember who all came all those years, but I knew they were grateful and delighted to be part of the Nolan Christmas. My sisters basked in the praise of a pie well done. My father would inevitably touch his lips with his napkin and declare the Rice, Sausage and Sage stuffing was just as good as if Mom herself had made it.

'I think you're right, Frank,' Mom agreed. 'It might be even better.'

The Christmas Fudge was the last thing at dinner. I carried the deep dish to the table. Mom explained to the guests, on behalf of cleanliness, how Frank boiled the coins before putting them in. My father, a smile tugging at his lips, cut the fudge into squares. Everyone had to take one. 'There's four quarters,' he announced, 'and they're good luck for the whole year. But that one fifty cent piece, well, whoever gets that, that person's probably just lucky forever.'

I never did get the fifty cent piece. I was annoyed, of course. My prominence as the prodigy ought surely to have entitled me to endless good luck. But now, when I look back those Christmas dinners, I see the faces around our table—the impoverished young couples, the dazed look of the recent widow, the grim unemployed, the prim Miss McTavish, Mr. Giddiings and his huge white cast—and I see their slowly savoring the Christmas Fudge, looking for that promise of luck, of happiness. Young as I was, I had the sense of both the giving and the getting, that seasonal quality that had saved Scrooge's withered old soul.

Naturally I took all this for granted. I did not think of Christmas itself as a creation. I believed that such Christmases simply happened. I never asked how.

*   *   *

My father was paid once a week on Fridays. In those days, before direct deposit, he came all the way home, tooted the horn of the pickup truck and I ran out and got in. Then he drove all the way back downtown to the bank. All the way back is relative, I guess. St. Elmo California was a pretty compact city, and we lived in an old section. On summer afternoons we would have ice cream after the bank, on fall and winter afternoons, we might stop at the bakery for a donut (half price late in the day) before going home.

79

I loved these Friday jaunts, not just for the donut or ice cream either. I loved the bank. Strange as it sounds, the bank seemed to me like a vast theatre where significant events took place, where important papers shuffled, and typewriters clattered and rang, where adding machines rattled. I felt certain that behind the frosted glass doors, and amongst the frosted glass partitions, there must surely be authoritative adult undertaking momentous tasks. The bank itself was a somber institution, the flooring, huge squares of black, white and gray, a high-ceilinged temple to money. None of your contemporary free coffee, Muzak and comfy chairs. You were not invited to linger. You stood at high marble tables in the center where you wrote out your deposit ticket, choosing from a row of pens stuck in a wooden rack that also held the date. I know this because my father would often hoist me up to sit on this table, my legs dangling over the edge.

One year, the Friday before Thanksgiving, I was eight or nine—I remember what I was wearing, a maroon coat with lambs wool trim, hand-me-down, of course, but very pretty— we drove to the bank as usual. Besides his usual ink-and-oil- metal-and-sweat smell, I caught from my father, another whiff that I recognized but could not name. Fatigue,? Worry? Gnawing anxiety? Anyway, he didn't ask me if I wanted to sit on the marble topped table while he made out the deposit ticket, and so I wandered around the bank. The lines were longer than usual that Friday.

The bank in those days was so austere, their single nod to the season were two large wreathes on either side of the wall clock. However, draped overhead were banners that implied all sorts of excitement. Tied with thick, red velvet ribbons, these banners read: JOIN OUR CHRISTMAS CLUB in bold letters flanked on either side by a man and a woman. The people each wore jaunty Santa caps on their well-groomed heads. They both grinned, great toothy smiles, beaming at wads of cash-money they held in one hand. The man winked at the woman. At the bottom the sign said, HAPPY SANTAS HAVE MONEY. The woman gave him the big OK! sign.

The Christmas Club must be a lot of fun, I reasoned. Where was the party where they were handing out money, and everyone was happy? This banner hung over a low swinging gate that separated the bank's private offices from the great public spaces. I pushed through the gate and wandered around, past frosted glass doors, and frosted glass partitions between which women were typing furiously, keys pounding. No one was having fun or handing out money. On the contrary, it was all rather grim and forbidding.

'And where might you be going?'

I was all but yanked off my feet by an

enormous woman with cats' eye glasses and hugely bouffant hair. She seized my arm and held it tight, high, my elbow up in the air.

'I'm looking for the Christmas club,' I explained. 'I want to join.'

'Children are not allowed here. I don't know why parents don't look after their kids.'

'I'm looked after,' I protested, 'I just thought—'

'Where is your mother?'

'Home.' Her eyes narrowed and she growled, and I quickly added, ' but my father's over there. In line.'

She only let go of my arm when we'd reached my father. As the line shuffled forward, Mrs. Bouffant chided him for allowing me to run wild.

'I wasn't running wild,' I finally interrupted her. 'I was looking for the Christmas Club.' I pointed the banners overhead. 'I want to join.'

My father didn't smile, but his blue eyes softened and his lips twitched. 'Well I'm sure there's no harm done. Is there?'

Everyone in line was laughing. The teller was laughing. Mrs. Bouffant colored and marched away. But, by the time we got to the front of the line, bank manager himself came out, all smiles, and and pinned upon my coat a little round button that read: *Join Our Christmas Club*.

I was the heroine of the hour, but I still didn't know what a Christmas Club was.

In answer to my question, once we were safely in the truck, my father said, 'A Christmas Club is a special kind of saving account. Every month the bank moves some money for you, from your regular account into this one, and then, say, a year or so later, why, you go take it all out and you have lots of cash money for Christmas. That's the theory.'

'What does that mean? Theory?'

'Means it's a good idea. Even if it doesn't work out that way, it's a good idea.'

'I know there's no Santa, so you don't have to treat me like a baby.'

'I don't treat you like a baby.'

'Do you belong to the Christmas Club?'

'Oh yes. I wouldn't miss the Christmas Club for anything.'

'Do they have a party every year?'

'Well sort of. I guess you could call it a party.'

'Like the one they have at *Herald* where the managing editor hands out candy to the kids?' We had quit going to the *Herald's* Kiddie Christmas party the year before. The peppermints were always stale, as if they'd been on the original journey with the Three Wise Men. 'Or is it like the Fezziwig's Christmas party?'

'Oh, not like that,' my father smiled. 'That's immortal. No, this is where you pick up your savings and the teller says, *Merry Christmas!* and you go home knowing it will be a wonderful Christmas for your family.'

He sounded sad, so I reached over and patted his hand. 'We always have wonderful Christmases, you don't need to join the Club.'

*   *   *

The notion of a Christmas Club now seems quaint as Scrooge's counting house, doesn't it? Now, so ubiquitous is the credit card, it seems downright laughable that you might join the Christmas Club in January, so that the following December you could have your own money back. You could look smug and happy like the people on the banner, plenty of cash and a big OK! sign. Merry Christmas! That is, if you were nice. If you were naughty, and withdrew money early from your club account, the bank penalized you, as if to scold you for snatching from Santa.

My parents joined the club every year. But they never did have any money in December. Instead, my dad took out loans. He spent the next year paying off the loan at whatever interest. And then at Christmas, he took out another loan and we all had a fine time.

What happened to the Christmas Club money they socked away? Well, Mary, Margaret and Susan all needed braces. My teeth were fine. But Margaret and I both needed glasses. Susan needed expensive corrective shoes and then refused to wear them. (For which stubbornness she has paid for thirty years, by the way.) Mary went to San Diego State where the tuition was reasonable, but her books, the dorms, the lab fees, all the rest of it, that strained the family coffers. I contributed a few dents to my parents' hearts too. One night I took my parents' truck out, joyriding with my high school friends, and I managed to run it into an irrigation ditch out in the orange groves. One friend had a broken arm, one friend no injuries, and I broke off my tooth on the steering wheel. The old truck was considered totaled. The insurance skyrocketed, and Frank and Sara pulled the money from the Christmas Club to buy a used car. I was humbled.

*   *   *

That particular afternoon when I had *Join Our Christmas Club* pinned to my maroon coat, my father said, 'Let's skip the donut tonight and just go home. 'We want to be there when Mary comes home from college, don't we?'

I personally would have preferred the half price donut, though I could not say so. When Mary came home from college, everyone made a tremendous fuss, lavishing applause and attention on her just as if she were a prodigy.

'An education is great thing to have, Rosie. No one can ever take it away from you. San Diego State,' he always said the name wistfully.

'Just think, Mary will be the first Nolan to graduate from college.'

We pulled in the driveway in early winter dusk. 'That's odd, isn't it? The house is dark. Where is everyone?'

My father moved swiftly from the truck, and I had to hurry behind him, coming into the unlit kitchen. Margaret and Susan sat in the dim light, staring at each other across the kitchen table. From the bathroom, I heard my mom crying, long jagged sobs.

Mary had called a half hour before. From Vegas. She had eloped with her new boyfriend, a marriage from which she would extricate herself with some difficulty a couple of years later. And that too, her divorce, came out of, was paid for from the Christmas Club.

You wear the chains you forge in life.

As it turns out, I got a partial scholarship to UCLA, and I was the first Nolan to graduate from college. (Mary and Susan both went back later and got their degrees.) While I was at UCLA in the Eighties, the St. Elmo *Herald* moved from their old downtown location to a vast new building in a light industrial park. And they made the big transition to computer printing. They hired technicians whose faces glowed blue with the luminescent light of production. The *Herald* management placed one of the old metal presses (gleaming now, not inky) behind a red velvet rope at the main entrance of the new headquarters. A museum piece. An artifact. A relic of another age.

And the old printers? Those guys who smelled of ink-and-oil, metal-and-sweat, their inky palms so veined and traced they looked like road maps? The *Herald* honored those men (and make no mistake, they were all men; the pressroom was an entirely masculine enclave) with a retirement farewell at the annual Christmas party.

The party was held at the Elks Club, a big windowless barn of a room with a fake tree in the corner. There was bar against one wall and a long dais with a podium at the other. The publisher and editors all sat there. The retiring printers' tables were right in front of the dais, each family had its own. Ours was pretty empty. Of the Nolan girls, I was the only one who attended. Mary, Margaret and Susan had all married (or, in Mary's case, re-married) and moved away. Across from me, my parents both maintained expressionless faces— neither Frank nor Sara Nolan would betray an emotion in public—but their eyes were not empty. With a stab of understanding, I remembered the eyes of all those guests at Christmas dinners: the still-stunned, the lost and the lonely, the injured, the far from home. I wanted desperately to see my father pull a shiny fifty cent piece from the sea of chocolate fudge, to see his face light up, as those face had lit, to watch him savor his guaranteed good luck ahead. In truth, I wanted to weep, but like my parents—oh yes, by then I was a true Nolan—I kept my mouth shut, and my eyes on the podium.

The managing editor of the *Herald*, tapped on the microphone and as it squealed, he announced that the retiring printers should each have a look inside the special Christmas stocking on their table. My father looked in his. He found a gold wristwatch, and peppermint candy, leftover from the journey of the Magi.

*   *   *

I was not a prodigy. At UCLA I was an English major. What else could I be with all those classics in my head? I met the man I married, in a study group for a chemistry class where I was struggling to pull a C. Our paths crisscrossed for a couple of years, and then, at the wedding of a mutual friends, Brett and I saw each other afresh. Really, it was just like putting on glasses, having your vision corrected. We stood there at the reception, punch cups in hand, and he asked me if I wanted to dance. I figured he was asking me to marry him since there wasn't any band.

Ours was a small wedding, and yes, I wore Margaret's hand-me-down wedding dress. Mom walked me down the aisle. At first she wouldn't hear of it, but I insisted. Someone has to give me away, I told her. My father had

88

died a few years after the *Herald* gave him the gold wristwatch. He went quietly and without fanfare. One morning when my mother got up she found him slumped over the kitchen table where, every day, still rising at four, he sat to read the paper and check for errors.

*   *   *

'"Marley was dead to begin with, dead as a doornail,"' I began.

It was the Friday after Thanksgiving. Brett was downstairs watching afternoon football. I plumped the pillows on our bed, all ready to begin the first annual reading of *A Christmas Carol* to my two little boys, Frankie, eight, and Joe six. After all, my dad read it to me when I was younger than that. 'This is going to be so much fun,' I promised them as they snuggled in on either side of me. 'My father read this book to me, every year. Just like we're going to do.'

I started to read aloud, but the voice I heard reading was my father's. I sounded like Frank Nolan as I read about the deadest piece of ironmongery, the doornail, as I described Bob Cratchit's frozen fingers, and the cheerful nephew telling his uncle 'Merry Christmas,' and the indignant Scrooge declaring of the poor, '"Then they should die, and decrease the surplus population!' But as I moved through this first chapter, I winced; I could sense my boys were restless, and in truth, my reading slowed. I stopped where old Scrooge is about to eat his lonely evening gruel before Jacob Marley returns to him. I closed the book, and looked at my sons' sweet, expectant faces. 'Shall we finish some other time?' I asked, and both boys bounded off the bed and out of the room.

I sat there with the book in hand. Why had I never noticed that, even from this opening chapter (that I had always thought so delightful) the heavy hand of mortality is everywhere in this tale? Why was I, at age five, not terrified in Scrooge's wretched chamber? Had I been frightened when my father read to me? I don't think so. No. Whatever else my father gave us—or, for that matter, didn't give us—we were never scared. Not of dying and decreasing the surplus population, not of Marley's ghost and the phantasms that swirled with him. Frank Nolan gave us a gift that could not come wrapped in the funny papers. My father must surely have known, too, how terrifying the book, especially the conclusion, could be. That's why we never finished, but put it away on New Year's Day, always leaving the bookmark in the same spot.

That afternoon, I found that place, fittingly, just as the Ghost of Christmas Present is about to leave Scrooge shivering and alone. I read to the end. How different is the Scrooge in these pages from the various movies and take-offs, from the Muppets to a musical. In those incarnations, he is a dismal geezer at the beginning, and a cheerful geezer at the end. The miser Scrooge has been morphed and re-mottled into the Ghost of Christmas Presents. More, always more! Join the Christmas Club! Have lots of cash and a big grin! But in the book, Scrooge watches ragpickers selling the very clothes he died in, with no more thought than of the money they will make. In the book, he is terrified not simply of death but by Ignorance and Want as well. This is a book is about death and regret. About creating Christmas, snatching life from the fear of death, evading the long, sharp fingers of regret, so that they shall not pluck at you from the future. About wearing the chains you forged in life.

I heard my children's voices, one whining that the other had taken his Legos. I would not be reading this book to them. At least not till they were older. I could imitate Frank Nolan's voice, but could I do what he had done? I thought about death and regret. I thought about love and luck. I blinked back tears. The Nolans are not a demonstrative clan, but I so wanted to thank my father for the gift he'd given me, not just as a little child, all those Christmases ago. But today. Now, as a grown woman. I recognize Christmas as a creation. I recognize childhood as a creation. Our sons will grow up, no matter what Brett and I do, but their childhood will be our gift to them. As my childhood was the gift of Frank and Sara.

I heard my husband's footsteps coming up the stairs. He stopped in the boys' room and settled their little spat amicably. I got off the bed and went to the dresser where, in a small box I habitually put fifty cent pieces when I find them. They're rare now. That kind of luck is rare. I opened the bedroom door and called down the hall, 'I'm going to make some fudge. Anyone want to come help?'

THE LAND OF LUCKY STRIKE

Dikran Agajanian stepped back from the mirror, and with the pale green tiled splendor of the bathroom for a backdrop, regarded himself critically. The new shirt collar irritated his freshly shaven neck; the tie was slightly crooked. He adjusted the tie and smoothed his crisp, dark hair, freshened his mustache, checking that the ends stood up pertly. Very nice indeed. His face was old enough to have character, young enough to express enthusiasm. Today, the first day of his new job, both the character and the enthusiasm were visible. To the figure in the mirror, he said: 'Cigarette? Cigar? Chewing gum? Candy bar/ Thank you. You are welcome. Which one? Lucky Strike.' Pleased with himself, he re-arranged the towels (borrowed from his brother-in-law) on the rack, and surveyed the gleaming bathroom. The bathroom was his favorite room in the new house. These Americans, they thought of everything.

He heard a knock at the front door and his wife's heavy step. She moved slowly these days; she thought the new baby would arrive very soon. His brother-in-law's voice shook the bathroom door. 'Ha! Ha! Little Armenoui!' (Dikran thought that probably Harry was pinching his wife's cheek.) 'How you doin'' today? How's that big baby, Jack? When's he gonna come out and meet his old Uncle Harry? Huh? Huh? Hey, Dikran! You ready for the big day?'

'Would you like to drink some coffee, Harry?' Armenoui Agajanian asked in her still pristine, book-learned English.

'Sure, sure, we got time for some coffee. Dikran, come out here and have some coffee.'

When Dikran entered the little dining room, Harry was pinching the fat cheek of the three-year old, Ahngah who sat quietly eating her breakfast.

'Hello, Snooky,' he said, blowing his cigar smoke away from the child. 'What you want Santa Claus to bring you for Christmas, huh? You want a big doll? You want a model train set? Your Uncle Harry get you anything you want, Snooky.' The child screamed with delight, and banging her spoon down on the tin dish in front of her, sent cereal flying around the room. 'Hey, Armenoui, come get this kid. She gonna mess up my nice suit. Hey, Snooky, you cut it out.'

Delighted, Snooky sprayed more cereal. Armenoui lifted the child from the chair, removed her bib and told her in Armenian to go wash. Then she picked up the cereal dish and took it into the kitchen, re-emerging with two small cups and a long-handled brass coffee pot. Another tin plate was tucked under her arm.

'For your ashes, Harry.'

'Sure, sure. We gotta get you some ash trays. Who can work in cigar business with no ash trays in the house, eh Dikran?' Harry pronounced it biza-neece, clearly enjoying the word itself.

Dikran put a small amount of cream and sugar in his coffee and stirred. Harry always made people happy, he thought; Harry made them laugh. They had only just arrived in Los Angeles after a harrowing journey of more than four months. Harry, the husband of Armenoui's sister Martha, gave Dikran this job. Harry found this little house for them and paid the first month's rent. What a fine man Harry was.

'Well, Dikran, you know all you gotta know today? Let's hear it.' Harry struck a match and re-lit his cigar.

'Cigarette? Cigar? Chewing gum? Thank you. You are welcome. Candy bar? Which one? Lucky Strike.'

'Very good. You remember that Lucky Strike, don't you?'

'I remember *Lucky*.'

Harry heaped sugar and poured so much cream into his coffee that it slopped over the rim and splashed into the saucer. 'You right, Dikran! You stick with me, you gonna be lucky all right. We make you rich man in no time. Next year this time, I bet you have car—what you think? Send word to old country: 'In 1924

95

Dikran Agajanian Buys Car!"

Dikran smiled. The thought of owning a car was beyond his imagination—the little house, with its cool tiles in the bathroom, its blue hydrangea and stately palm in the front, that was enough for him. The hunger for the car was Harry's and that hunger trebled when Harry's daughter drove off with a young American donkey in the donkey's own car.

'You look real good, Dikran. You handsome man—good thing too. I don't want no ugly babies in this family. That baby, Jack, he better be beautiful before he calls me Uncle Harry, that's all I gotta say. Hey, Armenoui, you hear that? Good thing good lookin' woman like you don't marry no ugly mug!'

Dikran laughed inwardly. Harry loved American slang; he had probably thought all the way over here how he would use that new one—*ugly mug.*

'I hear you, Harry,' Armenoui called from the kitchen. She came into the dining room since she had been taught by the Congregational missionaries in school that only urchins yell. 'What if the baby is a girl, Harry?

'A girl,' he blustered. 'You ain't gonna have no girl. You already got one girl. What you want another one for? You have a boy. Girls nothin' but trouble. You take my word for it. My daughter, we name her Shushan, after her own grandmother, and what she does? She change it to Ginger. Now we all gotta call her Ginger. I say to her, why Ginger? Why not we call you Eggplant?'

Armenoui laughed. She was a handsome woman, Dikran thought, in spite of her swollen body and tired face. Her usually smooth olive skin had a yellow cast to it, and she was puffy. She would be handsomer still when the baby came, and her face could assume its old, fine planes and contours, the firm mouth, the clear, intelligent eyes, the strong chin. He was a lucky man, he thought, and then he laughed out loud: it was the first time he had thought the American word.

'Well, Dikran, we gotta go,' said Harry, wiping his mustache with the back of his left hand. With his right he dropped some cigar ashes in the plate Armenoui brought him. 'You wanna make money in this country, you gotta get out and catch the early worm. You ready?'

'Yes.' Dikran rose and walked toward the front door.

'Hey, wait a minute. Ain't you gonna kiss her good-bye?'

'Kiss?'

'Yea, you know—*kiss kiss*—listen, Dikran, I gotta make an American outta you. When you got to work in the morning in America, you kiss the wife goodbye. Everyone does. Me, I kiss Martha every morning. It's good for you. Good for the wife too.'

Dikran demurred. He and Armenoui had never kissed in front of anyone in their lives; his wife could not bear for him to kiss her before another person. Armenoui blanched.

'Hey—what's this? You two don't like each other? You have a fight or something? Armenoui, he treatin' you bad. You tell me, you just tell me.'

'No, Harry. Dikran is good to me always.'

'Then, what—Dikran, go on, kiss your wife,' he urged Dikran toward her.

Dikran bent his face down to hers. He did not touch her with his hands. She closed her eyes and raised her lips to meet his; it was a dry, soft kiss.

'Aha! That better. Let's go now.'

All the way to the streetcar, Harry sang a song called 'Jingle Bell.' It was his favorite Christmas song. He sang with such gusto that people would smile at him as they passed on the street. On the main boulevard, the streetcars clanged and thumped, going in all different directions. They all looked alike, however. Dikran dreaded the day he would go to work by himself; imagine catching the wrong streetcar, ending up in some strange place without the language to tell where he wanted to go. Dikran could speak Armenian, Turkish, French, some Arabic, some Greek, but not English. English he was learning only very slowly. Armenoui could speak the English. she had been taught in the school run by Congregational missionaries. The school had taught her English and saved her life.

Harry sensed his confusion. 'Dikran, you ever get on the wrong streetcar, you just to the driver and say: I work Santa Monica Beach—you remember that? Say that.'

'Santa Monica Beach.'

'Right. You never get lost.'

He went on singing 'Jingle Bell' in the streetcar, and the woman behind them said 'Merry Christmas' as she rose to leave the car. The December sun was behind them; Dikran could feel it intensified through the glass, shining on his shoulders. Everywhere he looked out the window as the rode through the town, there were red and green decorations, streamers, and bells and bows and figures of angels. From the streetcar Dikran watched the store owners righting their goods, the clerks bracing themselves behind tills for the onslaught of shoppers who were already poised before the glossy windows, clutching bags and the hands of small children.

Harry poked him in the ribs. 'We get off next.'

Beyond the conductor, Dikran craned his neck to see the shining expanse of the bright Pacific. 'Pacific,' murmured Dikran. *Pacific Ocean* and *Lucky Strike* were Dikran's favorite English words.

'You gotta get off quick. They don't wait for no one. They gotta a schedule to keep, you know.' The driver said 'Merry Christmas' to Harry as the two men alighted, and Harry tipped his hat.

The beach was bordered by a ragged sidewalk, and it was on this sidewalk, facing the ocean, that Harry's four tobacco and candy concessions stood at half-mile intervals. 'This is Number One,' said Harry proudly, as if the stand were a son. 'My first,' said Harry hitting the wooden stand painted to the brilliance of a banana yellow. 'Number Two, she is blue. Number Three, she is red. Number Four, she is yellow too, for the Golden State. Number Five gonna be green. Nice huh?'

Dikran agreed, but Number One was less impressive than Harry had led Dikran to believe. It was about as tall as a door frame, as deep as a pantry and a little longer than Dikran's outstretched arm span. Harry no longer worked in any of these four concessions, though he had up until last year. He now had a small office in Santa Monica with an impressive sign on the door, HARKER CONCESSIONS in orange lettering on a red background. Harry now hired the men to work in the concessions, as well as a Miss Felton part-time to type his letters (and not incidentally, clean up his spelling and tidy his English). Harry collected the money, did the accounts, the ordering, and looked for new business opportunities.

From his pocket Harry drew an impressive-looking key ring and set about opening the stand's four locks. Two holding the wooden shutters closed in front and two locking the Dutch door which allowed access to the inside. An orange and red sign in front said CIGARETTES AND CANDY. Number One was decorated with picturers of attractive young women advertising candy and handsome young men advertising cigarettes. When Harry opened the front, Dikran saw shelves that held a brilliant panoply of colored cellophane, candy and cigarettes in shiny gold, red, brown and yellow.

'C'm'ere, I show you all you need to know for the first day.' Behind the counter there was a small folding chair and some newspapers. Under the counter were more boxes of goods, some rags and cleaning fluid. The stall was too small for the two men to occupy together comfortably, especially since Harry was portly. Grunting, Harry pulled forth a small cash register from underneath the counter and set it up. 'Now, I show you all this the other night, but here it is again. Easy. The five. The ten. The twenty, and so on. You just push the one you want, and bang—there she is!' The ten popped up in the window at the top of the cash register. 'But if you need, I got it all writ down for you.' He handed Dikran a piece of paper with money equivalents and cash register procedures written in a graceful-looking language that was more comfortable

101

for Dikran than the sharp, bulky English letters. Harry drew an envelope out from inside his coat, and began to put money in the neat trays. He took two rolls of coins and they splattered into the drawer 'I pick up the money, afternoons, evenings, whenever I get by. You don't worry about that, Dikran.'

A customer approached the stand, an older, well-dressed man. He did not look at Dikran or Harry. 'Cigar,' he said.

'Which one?' said Harry.

'Havana.'

Harry expertly picked one out. The man tossed a coin on the counter and walked on. Harry said, 'Thank you.' He turned to Dikran. 'You see? Easy. Now, where you gonna put this coin?'

Dikran was stricken with terror. All his life he had worked behind a counter, measuring out tea, coffee, spices. How could he do it now, though, in a language he could barely speak, with coins he hardly knew?

Harry clapped him on the shoulder. 'Ah, Dikran—you gonna be all right. C'mon—what you do with this coin?'

Dikran glanced at the paper in his hand and hit the 25¢ indicator on the cash register. The machine chimed, the figure bounced up in the window, the drawer flew open, and he placed the quarter where it belonged with the others.

'Very good. I knew you have no trouble. You just say, 'Which one' to them, get them to point, you know? See—all the cigarettes on this shelf, candy on this shelf, cigars, matches on this shelf. Each thing, I mark the prices yesterday so all you gotta do is look at what they want, and there's the price right underneath it. They hand you the money, you say, 'You're welcome,' and you are fine. Well, I gotta go now, Dikran. I wish I could stay here with you and watch the pretty girls, not so many now 'cause Christmas, but I tell you — in summer, right here, this number One, is the best job in the world!' He laughed. 'I come by this afternoon, see how you doin'. Armenoui didn't pack you no lunch, did she? Well, I'll bring you something today. You gotta tell her you got responsibilities now and you gotta have your lunch. You a working man.'

Dikran politely walked out of Number One: his brother-in-law was too fat to scoot by him. 'Thank you,' he said in English.

'Ha! You learn in no time. You speak English good as me real soon now.'

The morning passed quickly and without mishap. Dikran never tired of looking at the faces of the customers, but most of them ignored the man behind the counter, looking right past him, or perhaps right through him. But most people knew exactly what they wanted, and pointed to it with no difficulty. He imagined, too, that each time he said *thank you* and *you're welcome* his English improved. In between customers he dusted off the stock and leaned over the counter and watched the ocean roll in, long, muscular waves. The winter surf gouged the bright sand. He could see the stunted reflections of the walkers in the wet sand. He had once been a walker on a Mediterranean shore, and he had crossed the Atlantic, and he had always been a lover of the ocean. The sound of the sea. The smell. But to look before him now, he thought, the Mediterranean, the Atlantic, what were they compared to the grand Pacific? He wanted to be the acolyte of the Pacific, to serve at Harry's Number One and stand in perpetual awe, facing west.

Harry came back about one with encouragement, some sandwiches and soft drinks. He ate his lunch there at Number One with Dikran. He brought some shiny red and green paper loops, too, and draped them across the front of Number One. At either side of the counter he placed a picture of the fat, pink-faced gentleman with a full white beard.

'Who is that?' asked Dikran.

'That?—Whew! Good thing you ask me \ that question and no one else. They think you crazy, and lock you up somewhere. That Santa Claus. Look. For Christmas here in America all kids, little ones like Snooky, believe in this Santa Claus. They believe he lives at the North Pole. They believe on Christmas Eve he has a . . .' Harry could not find the word, 'one of those things, and deer pull it through the sky and they go all over the world.'

'Who believes such things?' scoffed Dikran.

'Everyone. Children. Little children say, 'Santa Claus, please bring me dolly. Santa Claus, please bring me—whatever they want, and believe me they always want something you can't afford, especially when they sixteen and stupid.' Harry's daughter, Ginger, was sixteen. 'Then, their parents go to buy it for them, and the parents give it to the children, and say, 'Here, Merry Christmas—Santa Claus bring you this.'

Dikran looked puzzled. Armenoui would probably not like this one bit. She was very straightforward about such things, and he could not envision her telling little Ahngah that this fat man brought her gifts when in fact Dikran's hard-earned money had paid for them. 'Armenoui know about Santa Claus?' he asked.

'Well, if she don't, she's goin' to. We gonna get you a Christmas tree—have real American Christmas for you and Armenoui and Snooky, and Jack if he gets his self born in time. Martha tells me yesterday she gonna get you some candles for the tree. You put the candles on the tree, see? You sing 'Jingle Bell'—what a great Christmas. Dikran, I tellin' you, I'm goin' get that little Snooky the best present in the world, and if Jack get born before Christmas, him too, him too.' Harry popped the last of the sandwich in his mouth and chewed reflectively. 'Well, I be back later, Dikran.'

The trade died down, and Dikran pondered broaching Armenoui with all this frivolity, Santa Claus, a tree with candles on it? She would surely disapprove; she had had so little frivolity in her life, scarcely even a hair ribbon after she was orphaned. He had met her when, as one of the older students from the missionary school in Adana, Turkey, she and another student did the shopping. He was the clerk, working for a Turkish merchant, weighing out tea and coffee and spices. They had fallen in love on these shopping trips, shy exchanges at first. He asked permission to call on her at the school. To his mother's everlasting ire, he declared he would marry her. Orphaned or not.

He asked the American missionary principal, Miss Beller, for her hand in marriage. There was no one else to ask. Miss Beller had gone to Armenoui's mother in 1915, and asked that she become a boarding student at the school where she attended only by day. Miss Beller said the Turks would not dare invade an American school. So Armenoui had left her mother and brother behind. Her father was already dead. She had seen him killed. The Turks had rounded the men up first. Her parents heard the screams from their neighbors in the Armenian quarter. Feet pounded up and down the narrow street.

106

Her mother had overturned the table, and put Armenoui and her brother behind it. Her mother took the girl's index finger and stuck it between her teeth and told her not to cry out, no matter what. Armenoui watched through the slats of the table. She still had the scar on her finger when she had bitten through her own flesh. But she had heeded her mother, and she had not cried out. Armenoui's beauty was dipped in sorrow. She lacked humor, but not courage.

In the distance he watched a woman approach the along the sidewalk. She was the prettiest woman he had ever seen. She came up to Number One and smiled at him. She was blonde, and her glossy hair, cut short, curled around her face; she reminded im of the attractive young women in the ads who framed Number One. She had china-blue eyes and pink cheeks, and a small, red mouth. Probably she wears lip rouge or paint or something, he thought, but she was so pretty it didn't seem to matter. His eyes drifted from her pert, painted face to her body and the loose dress made of some kind of crushable material, and the brilliant green silk stockings that sheathed her legs. Since he had come to America, Dikran had grown accustomed (or thought he had) to seeing women's legs, but not women's legs in green stockings. The girl rested her hand on the counter: her fingernails looked like pale little shells against her smooth skin. She accepted his obvious admiration not as a gift, but as though she were extracting a tax from him for the sheer pleasure of looking at her. She chewed a little gum with which she made rhythmical clicking noises.

'Cigarette? Candy bar? Chewing gum? Lucky Strikes?' he said.

'Chewing gum.'

'Which one?'

'There,' she said, pointing.

'You're welcome,' he said.

Taking her gum, she smiled again and said, 'Merry Christmas' as she walked off.

'Merry Christmas,' he replied.

By 5:30 the beach was deserted, the tide out, the water barely visible form the concession stand, which glowed like a bright beacon on the dark beach. Harry had forgotten to show him where the lights were for Number One, but Dikran looked all around and found the switch at the back of the bottom shelf. Before he turned them on, he watched in the near distance a man and a woman walking along the beach. From his unlit stall, Dikran watched as they stopped and kissed. The woman's head tilted back, the man's arms encircled her. Kissing in front of everyone must be American, Dikran concluded. He asked Harry what he thought as they rode the streetcar home. He asked him in Armenian. Harry roared with laughter.

'So, that was it, this morning, huh? I am

an American so long now I forget about old-country women. Ha!'

Dikran laughed, too; he thought he would like kissing Armenoui every morning before he went to work.

Armenoui did not like it. Not in front of Harry, she protested to him as they lay in their bed that night. He told her Harry didn't care, and that it was very American.

Gradually she adjusted to the kissing each morning when Dikran left for work. Now he carried the keys for Number One himself, and got off the streetcar at the beach. He always said goodbye to the driver. Armenoui packed Dikran a lunch each day. They bought a thermos so he could take coffee with him, because in spite of the warm December afternoons, the evenings were brisk and chilly. He took an extra sweater to work and left it under the counter. His English improved gradually; he became acquainted with the particular brand names of chewing gum and cigarettes. One day he found himself singing 'Jingle Bell' as good as Harry sang it, he thought. And every day to his delight the lovely blonde girl came by the stand, bought some chewing bum, smiled at him, and said ' "Merry Christmas' as she was leaving. Every day she looked more beautiful. Dikran wondered what she would say to him when Christmas was past. One day he noted she wore some little bells and a fake spray of dark green leaves and red berries pinned to her lapel. Holly, Harry told him later, for Christmas. Harry said he couldn't understand it, but they called it holly and who was he to question?

Some days were crisp and sunny, but when it was overcast the sky squatted over the ocean, turning it gray and lavender at the horizon. One day it rained all day. He had hardly any customers, some of the stock got wet, and the girl did not appear. Harry told him when it rained that much, to close up and go home. Just put the money in an envelope, put the envelope in his pocket and take it home.

If the rain beaded on the shiny cigarette packages, and pocked the sandy beach, if it chilled Dikran, it did not alter the tide of shoppers who, unsmiling and intent and clutching their goods, streamed by Dikran's window as he rode the streetcar to and from Number One. My first American

Christmas, he thought, adding the phrase to other favorites, Pacific Ocean and Lucky Strike.

However Armenoui resisted Harry's notion of an American Christmas. He grew very nearly hopping mad, certainly he was hopping around their livingroom when Armenoui insisted (just as Dikran knew she would) that Santa Claus was not necessary for Snooky's Christmas, and that the tree of lighted candles would set the house on fire. Martha sat quietly in the livingroom, but Harry paced

110

and wrung his hands, extolling the virtues of Santa Claus and Christmas trees until at last Armenoui relented. Then Harry bought the tree in; he had left by the front the door all the time. Martha laughed and brought in the candles and shiny, opaque glass balls. Harry and Martha showed them how to decorate the tree. They lit the candles, turned off the lights in the livingroom and watched the tree. The room smelled wonderfully of fresh pine and dripping, sweet wax. It was so quiet that they could hear the candles splutter and hiss. Martha and Armenoui began to cry softly, no wracking sobs from these women, but tears nonetheless. Then they stopped.

One afternoon Harry and Martha made a date to take Snooky to meet Santa Claus. Armenoui was too heavily pregnant to enjoy the outing on the bus, so Snooky went alone with her aunt and uncle. At a big store Snooky held Harry's hand, and watched as the other children climbed up in Santa's lap. She seemed dubious, but Harry encouraged her 'Go Go.'

Santa Claus listened attentively, but Snooky spoke in Armenian, so Santa could only smile and look at her strangely. He handed her back to her uncle with a pained expression on his face.

'Hmmph. Next year she talk English good as you,' said Harry to Santa.

It didn't matter to Snooky; she was enthralled. The packages began to pile up under the Agajanian Christmas tree, lots for Snooky and some for Jack, no matter what he was.

Two days before Christmas Harry showed up at Number One. 'You gotta present for Armenoui yet? Two days! That's all. You better roll it,' he said, savoring the slang. 'I'll stay here close up. You go get a present for your wife. That boy gonna be here any day.'

Dikran took the bus into back into Santa Monica, stood on the street with the shoppers he had so often watched. He let them jostle and move him as though he stood waist-deep in the Pacific's breaking surf; he liked the electricity generated by their bodies and the static in their uncrushed bags. As the afternoon waned, the lights grew everywhere more brilliant. The very streetlights seemed to conspire with the season as they blinked red and green. Dark-bonneted women clanged bells on the sidewalks, the wonderful and unrelenting cacophony of Christmas.

Dikran wandered from store to store, looking for something for his wife. Everywhere he looked the merchandise beckoned, begged to be touched, stroked, bought. He bobbed with the crowd's rhythm people were pushed, like complex musical notes on a staff, between waist-high wooden counters where soft pairs of gloves lay in repose and new umbrellas stood at attention. There were long aisles of silky slips and stockings and fragile underthings

112

which embarrassed him and found another department of the store in which to browse. He circled the cosmetic counter where a woman whose face had to be peeled off at night guarded an unctuous galaxy of creams and pots and potions which wafted a cloying fragrance into the stale air. He went outside to breathe, and then wandered through shops with rows of copper cookware, and gleaming china dishes, frail glassware perched in triplicate on mirrored shelves. A lovely scent wafted to him, and he found a young lady sitting in a booth demonstrating an electric toaster. She put the bread on either side of a the unit, and snapped it shut, then turned on, then took them out and toasted the other side. A marvel. He passed through stores where substantial looking furniture and lamp fixtures spread out in panoramic living rooms, and rugs hung, draped over low bars, and rows of pianos stood upright, ornate and respectable. How could he ever decide? What could he buy for his wife? A man with a waxed mustache stood guard by a slick icebox in a room where iceboxes outnumbered the people. Dikran saw a young couple whose rapt and happy attention was riveted to a machine that made an awful noise and sucking noises along a carpet. Sewing machines stood like troops awaiting inspection. What could he buy for his wife? His dilemma wasn't simply that he didn't have much money, even with the money,

113

what could he get? How could he choose? He explored a sporting good store that smelled of metal and leather, of wood, full of items for which he could imagine no earthly use. The odors and the fabrics and the people and the sounds of cash ringing and paper crunching and customers barking at salespeople melded, could no longer be distinguished individually. His senses rebelled, then revolted, then ceased to record, and the crowd moved his body like he belonged to them. A woman thumped his back and asked him a question he did not understand. She asked only once. She was armed with a tin breadbox; she forged past him, and he watched her back retreat as the packages of others crushed against his shoulders. A vast network of pneumatic chutes hissed and spat and sped the money on its way to distant coffers. His eyes dried out and began to hurt; he squinted in the artificial indoor ligh; his lips desiccated and his throat parched. His brain pulled away from his skull; he lost his balance momentarily and tumbled against a nearby ambulating overcoat which withdrew from him before he could regain his stance, and he fell. People offered him a hand to rise. 'Thank you,' he mumbled, 'You're welcome. Lucky Strike.' He looked for the door, out to the street, but the great commercial bin seemed to have swallowed him whole. He felt like Jonah struggling, swimming to the mouth of the leviathan till finally he saw the door and made his way to the noisy sidewalk. He dashed out, moving too swiftly to see he'd pushed beyond the sidewalk and into the street. A horn sounded and he jumped back before an automobile nearly ran him down.

Dikran turned to the bonneted woman ringing her bell. 'Santa Monica,' he said.

'Yes?' She never quit ringing.

'I work Santa Monica beach.'

She pointed him west. He walked without stopping, without looking around him.

When at last he came to the beach, he sat in the cold sand. It was not the beach by Number One, but there was the dark water, the Pacific. Soothing and merciless, the sea rolled in and over mere mortals, mere time. By the time he caught the streetcar for home, nighttime had cleared the streets and lit the windows of Los Angeles.

Armenoui was pale with worry when he arrived. Martha was with her. When he saw his wife he realized he had no present for her. 'The baby?' he asked.

'Not yet. Not now. Where have you been?'

Dikran could not say. He had not the words. Not in any language.

'Well,' said Harry the next morning, 'what you get your wife?'

'Nothing.'

'Nothing? What you mean nothing?'

'Nothing.'

'What's wrong with you, Dikran?'

115

Harry's bushy eyebrows shot up. 'Tomorrow Christmas. What you gonna give your wife?'

He knotted his fingers together. 'Too much,' he said in English.

'Too much? Too much what? You makin' good money now, well, all right, not great, not yet, next year, yes? But enough for a nice present for your wife.'

'Not money. Too much. Too much. Too much. Too much...' Dikran's knuckles went white. He cleared his throat; he clenched his teeth.

'Dikran, I know. I am new here once. How to understand? But you must. You know?' Harry's shoulders sloped forward; he stared silently at the gum wrappers and cigarette butts on the floor of the streetcar.

The car made two stops before Harry's shoulders straightened, and he brought his right hand down into his left with a resounding clap. 'You know what I do? When I go to work I telephone Martha, and I tell her go downtown and get Armenoui the best Christmas present ever, from Dikran—good idea? Martha, she's got good taste. Like they say, she knows things. Armenoui will love it. I promise you. Ha ha —you gonna be a lot happier man after that baby get born. I'm sure on that!'

Without commenting on Harry's estimation of his domestic life, Dikran thanked him. 'Tell Martha I will pay her back tomorrow,' he said in his familiar tongue.

'No—not tomorrow. No payin' back on Christmas. Day after.'

Dikran nodded. Harry always made people happy.

Late in the morning Dikran rested his arm on the counter and his eyes on the Pacific. Then his eyes ceased to rest. He stood up straighter; he smoothed his hair. The beautiful blonde was walking toward Number One with several other girls, all pretty, but not as pretty as she. She looked even prettier today, with red stockings and a green dress and the same now-bedraggled sprig of fake holly.

But this time she did not look at him. She was engaged in an animated conversation with her friends. 'So what'd you tell him, Ethel?' The four arrived at the Number One, ignoring Dikran

Ethel laughed. 'I said, you musta confused me with some other girl. I let you buy me dinner. That don't mean what you think it means, buster.'

The young women all burst into laughter at this.

'What'd he do then?' asked the beautiful blonde, leaning her arm on the counter.

'He says he oughta get a kiss at least and I says, oh yeah? Who says, and he says Rudolf Valentino.' Ethel let the flurry of their laughter die down, 'So I said, well who am I to resist the Sheik?'

Dikran understood the tone and mood, and the sound of *kiss*. Did young American women often discuss their intimate lives around strangers? 'Cigarettes? Candy/ Chewing gum?' He knew the blonde would want chewing gum. He took out the kind she liked and put it on the counter in front of her.

'Gum for me,' said the blonde without looking at him. 'Get this for me, willya, Ethel? I haven't got a cent.'

'Got any Luckies?' asked one of the women.

'Lucky Strike,' he said.

'Get me a CocoNut bar, willya?' said another.

'Hershey? Baby Ruth?'

'CocoNut Bar,' she replied, digging in her purse.

'Which one?' He stood back so she could point.

'CocoNut. Are you deaf?'

Dikran swept his arm across the candy shelf and grinned at her.

'Are you deaf?' she hollered. Finally she pointed. 'You blind as well?' The girls all laughed again.

He handed her the candy bar, and took her money. He could feel himself flushing.

'Gimme some change for this fiver,' said Ethel pushing a bill toward him.

'Cigarette? Candy? Chewing gum?' he said.

'All I want is some change.'

Dikran stepped back so that Ethel could

118

view the whole panorama of the candy and cigarette counter to make her choice. 'Cigarette? Candy. Which one?'

'You dumb-bell,' she said.

'Come on Ethel,' said the beautiful blonde, already walking away. 'Come on. He'll be all day.'

Ethel's gaze narrowed. 'Dumb-bell.' Then she left, ambling away with her friends.

Dikran stared out to the Pacific for along time. He tired to think what dumb-bell might mean. Perhaps it was some relation to Jingle Bell. He would ask Harry. The bead of Ethel's gaze still seared him; a metallic taste formed at the back of his throat. For the first time since he had been in America ambition gripped him, not merely to do well, to support his family, but ambition alloyed with bitterness: Dikran had been a foreigner all his life, born to it; he did not want to die a foreigner too. Though his family had lived in Turkey for generations, as long as anyone could remember, any Armenian in a Turkish city never forgets he is a foreigner, a stranger to his own land. Any Armenian is taught swiftly and while he young: do not speak Armenian except among your own kind, speak Turkish when you must talk to them, say little in any event, tread easy, fade inconspicuously, count on nothing, not your safety, not your friends, not your wits, not your luck, not finally even on God. And yet, how could he account for his

119

own life, for having lived, except that God had somehow protected him, protected his whole family? True, they had crouched and hid and paid enormous bribes, but most had lived. They had all left Turkey, but Dikran alone had come to America. Dikran alone had the wife who could speak English. The wife who had a sister and brother-in-law living in Los Angeles. Of his own family, mother, father, sisters, he would never see any of the rest of them again. So be it. He was here with Armenoui, their children. His family. He faced the Pacific. Knowledge began to crystallize in his brain; he realized what his life as a perpetual foreigner had deprived him of; he knew it in a groping, inarticulate way that defied language. It rose up out of his guts like love. He had lived his whole life without a so much as one tendril of a root to bind him, to make him wince when it was pulled up, to make him groan when it was transplanted in yet thinner soil. Not one white root bound him to the past. There was no old country for Dikran Agajanian. He would never sigh for it. He would never drape the past with the veil of nostalgia and the sense of something lost forever. There was no past. There was only the present. The future. The new home. The new country. And, if he had to divest himself of the old ways, of the old language and the old understanding, then so be it. Dikran wanted the rich, rolling tide of America to pick him up and take him too. Let it be too much. Let it be anything at all just so he was part of it. He hated the beautiful blonde.

Harry bustled up to Number One around three. 'C'mon, close up,' he said. 'We goin' home. This is Christmas Eve Day. Anyone wants cigarettes have to buy them from the Jews. This is a Christian holiday, and by God, the Armenians are Christian. The first Christian nation. For a thousand years! What, Dikran, why so sad.'

'Nothing. Nothing. Yes, let's close up.'

'Wait! You and me better take some cigars in case Jack is born in the next day or so— you don't want to come back here for cigars.'

'Why?'

'Dikran. In America when your wife have baby, you pass out cigars to all your friends. You say—Here, have on me. My wife just have baby. I am new father.'

'No friends,' said Dikran in English

'What you mean, no friends? You got me. You got Martha. You got—' Harry's hands waved through the air. 'You gonna have plenty friends next year. And Christmas, next year, 1924, you have new car too. Me too. Let's go. What's wrong with you, Dikran? You sick?

'No.'

'Well when that boy born, you give me a cigar and I give you one and we both smoke. That's good, yes?'

'Good.'

They walked to the streetcar stop and stood with the sun at their backs and their shadows stretching out into the street. 'Harry, what means *dumb-bell*?'

'Dumb-bell?'

'Yes.'

'Hey, you learnin' the slang already. I told you so—you pick it up easy with this job. Dumb-bell mean stupid. Why? Someone call you this?'

'No, no. I just heard it. I ask you because you know American slang.'

'You bet I do! But dumb-bell, you wanna be careful who you call dumb-bell. It's like being a donkey. Only worse.

The streetcar came, and for the ride home Harry talked about the Christmas dinner, the American Christmas dinner that Martha and Armenoui were cooking for the next day. 'None of this old country stuff,' he promised. 'Turkey. Ham. Potatoes.'

'Good,' said Dikran.

Christmas Eve Dikran lay in bed next to his wife. 'Are you asleep' he asked in their old familiar language. No matter how well he learned English, he thought, he would always use Armenian in bed.

'No.'

'When will it be?'

'Soon. Maybe tomorrow. Christmas. Would you like that?'

'A gift.'

122

'But maybe not. Maybe a day or so. Soon, though I think. Soon.'

'Merry Christmas,' he said in English.

'Merry Christmas,' she replied.

Leaning over his wife, he kissed her mouth tenderly. He laid his ear on her swollen belly and listened to the heartbeat of the unborn American child.

FIGGY PUDDING

At seven each morning, I take my place like a conductor at Balboa Central at the hub of the hallways, and make certain that all the parts of my orchestra are performing. We call it Balboa Central, rather than a nurses' station because the residents on Balboa Wing aren't sick. They're old, they're slow, they may be cranky and occasionally lose their train of thought, but they're ambulatory, and for the most part, sociable. By eight each morning we've made certain that everyone's had breakfast and their morning meds. The TV in the commons room is on, with its cascade of laughter, and there are board games and big unfinished picture puzzles laid out. The staff put up a huge Christmas tree last Sunday, and with the residents' help trimmed it, so the fragrance of Christmas permeates. Muzak floats overhead, all the Christmas songs played too fast and jingly. Despite the wreath, the twinkling lights, red velvet bows and bells draping the hall, the staff here always dreads the holiday season. I think our residents do too. Some, especially those without nearby family, wilt. Many just stew in a sour holiday broth. Sometimes I think it would be kinder to the men and women of Sunrise Villas if we just allowed Christmas to slide past without drawing their attention to the past and its contrast with the present. However much we try for cheer and Christmas ho ho ho's, the residents are still on Balboa Wing of Sunrise Villas, and Christmas here is not to be envied.

Christmastime or not, at ten o'clock, daily, Mrs. Schwarz emerges from Room 308. As always, she is wearing her pantsuit from the Seventies, bedroom slippers a pink hat with a veil. Mrs. Schwarz is one of my special residents. I am always ready for her. 'Where are you off to today, Mrs. Schwarz?' I always ask, falling into step beside her.

'I'm going downtown to meet my daughter.' She pushes the walker and waves into the open doors of her neighbors' rooms. 'The cab is at the door.'

'Well, let me walk you down.' By the time Mrs. Schwarz and I reach the end of the Balboa Wing hall, we've agreed her daughter is coming tomorrow and I walk her back to her Room 308. She never seems to hear Amanda Day call out the door of 312 that Mrs. Schwarz probably last saw her daughter in 1972.

I always say to Amanda Day, 'That is uncalled for, Mrs. Day.'

'True, though,' she remarks in her chirpy fashion. She waves to Mrs. Schwarz who waves back and calls her Sarah.

Amanda Day, plump, sallow, blue-eyed, disapproving, reminds me somehow of the

125

elderly, indomitable Queen Victoria. She has the same fat face, her lips set in unsmiling rectitude. Add to that, Amanda's upper-crust British accent. She is one of our most difficult residents, though she is in good health for a woman in her eighties, and could conceivably live on her own. But then—as her son once pointed out to me without cracking a smile—she'd have no one to criticize. And too, she'd have no audience. Amanda Day likes to talk about herself, never tires of telling her World War II stories, how Amanda—daughter of an Earl—scandalized her social set by marrying a Yank. She had two more Yank husbands after that one, but they left no particular inroads on her memory, though they left her financially comfortable. She still carries herself like the daughter of an earl, and and condescends to the rest of the world. She hasn't a kind word to say about anyone, except that first Yank husband. He must have been something. She never tires of recounting their affair in opulent detail, how they danced in Mayfair cafes during the Blitz while bombs fell all around them. It's hard for any of us here to imagine Amanda in love or vulnerable, even to bombs. She is imperious, used to getting her own way by any means. She must have been a fearful mother. No sooner had she moved to Sunrise Villas than both her sons got divorced and moved away, to the East Coast. Her grandchildren never visit. She declares she doesn't like them anyway. I expect the feeling is mutual.

So given that Amanda Day takes few pains to endear herself to anyone, I was not surprised to see her stand conspicuously apart from the general female flurry of excitement late in October when Mr. Knight arrived. When the Balboa Widows heard that a man was moving into room 316, they called in the hairdresser, freshened up their faces, pulled up their stockings, prepared to charm and be charmed. Men are scarce on Balboa Wing, perhaps four of them to some twenty widows.

The Balboa Widows are a lively troupe. I always thought they could wring a smile from a stone, but Mr. Knight remained impervious, blind to their charms. Indeed, he was outright blind, taciturn, hunched, and lived in a funk from which all their efforts could not rouse him. And yet, he was very careful about his appearance. He never wore sweats like some of the other old gents. Each morning he came to breakfast clean shaven, his wispy white hair smoothed flat. He wore pressed pants held up by suspenders, a ironed white shirt with buttoned cuffs and a bow tie clipped to the collar, always lop-sided. He ate breakfast without chatting, then bestirred himself, tapping with his cane, to the common room, finding a chair that sat in a patch of sunlight. He could hear the TV, but paid it no mind.

127

He kept his sightless gaze on the floor, and seemed to me to be attending to some internal radio. He'd smile occasionally, his head would bob, keeping time, and now and then, his gaunt, doughy face would suffuse with pleasure. When absolutely pressed to respond to the ladies' common-room conversation, Mr. Knight would sometimes look up from his funk and warble out a chorus from some old, long-forgotten ditty. Rather than quashing the Balboa Wing Widows' interest in him, this always spurred fluttering, fruitless inquiries into his past.

Which, in truth, was odd. He was an entertainer, so said his file. The great-niece, Tina, who moved him into Sunrise Villas, made a special point of saying he was an entertainer, and not a bartender, though that had been his job for many years in Medicine Hat, Alberta.

'Day and Knight, don't you know,' Amanda Day remarked to me shortly after his arrival. 'Roland Knight and I are fated to fall in love.' She had wobbled up to the nurse's station and insisted on my attention. 'Day and Knight. Sounds like an old music hall routine, don't you think, Michelle?' She broke into a few bars of Cole Porter's 'Night and Day.'

'I didn't know you could sing, Mrs. Day.'

'Of course I can sing! Don't be ridiculous, Michelle. The truth is,' she lowered her voice into ripe confidentiality. 'Mr Knight and I have

128

a lot in common. He's British, you know. Who else would he fall in love with but me?'

'I thought you only fell in love with Yanks.'

'There's something to be said, at a certain time of life for returning to one's roots, the voices one knows, the familiar, the old home, old associations, the—'

'He's Canadian. He came from Medicine Hat, Alberta.'

'He might have come from North Pole where he once lived among the penguins,'retorted Mrs. Day, 'but I'm telling you, he's British, and I know every song that he knows.'

'Well why don't you go on into the common room and sing with him?' I nodded right across the hall to the open doors. Mr. Knight sat, sulking in his patch of sunlight, alone while the Balboa Widows watched Oprah. 'If anyone can bring Mr. Knight out of his funk, you can, Amanda.'

Clearly she didn't hear the tinge of sarcasm in my voice. No, she looked pleased with my vote of confidence and moved along to the common room, took a chair beside him and I heard say in her sweetest, almost intimate tone, 'Were you ever on the wireless, Mr. Knight? It seems to me I remember a Roland Knight on the wireless. During the War. Was that you singing?'

He turned his unseeing eyes slowly toward the sound of her voice. She asked again, in a rather more chirpy tone about Roland Knight and the wireless. He cleared his throat, and his thin voice cracked with lyrics that had something to do with jolly good luck to the girl who loves a soldier.

Weeks passed, and even Amanda Day with her Grand Dame manner and accent could not rouse more than the oblique response from Mr. Knight. His isolation was clearly a matter of choice. The Balboa Widows, for their part, left him to his patch of sunlight, sunk in silence, his head upon his chest, nodding off, tunelessly humming himself to sleep. The Balboa Widows smiled at him, and then at each other, as though he were their baby, sleeping at last through the night.

His great-niece Tina came once a month on Tuesday. She was a barista and Tuesday was her day off. She collected his white shirts and brought them back, washed, ironed and on hangers. 'Least I can do for the duffer,' she told me. 'It's the only thing he cares about, the shirts.'

'Surely there's something else,' I asked. 'Isn't there some way to help him connect to the living?'

'When you find it, let me know,' said Tina. 'He was my grandmother's only brother, and she begged him to come down from Medicine Hat and keep her company after Gramps died. How could she ever think Roland would be company for her? But she doted on him,

130

and when she died, I moved him here. Gran's estate pays for it. It was in her will.'

'Did he never marry and have a family?'

'Oh sure, but I think they're all dead too. Gran was all he had left. Anyway, I wanted to let you know early on, at Christmas my boyfriend and I are going skiing, so Roland will be here alone.'

'I'm sure there'll be lots of company to cheer him up,' I offered ineffectually.

'You could have all the elves from Santa's workshop, and Dasher and Dancer and Comet and Blitzen. You could have the little drummer boy doing a tap dance on Rudolph's nose, and it wouldn't matter to Roland. He is one sour old dude. But I'll bring him some clean shirts before Christmas.'

A few days later there a delivery man brought by Balboa central an enormous, fancifully wrapped basket, the annual basket of fruit for Amanda Day. Big bows bristled atop red green cellophane, the whole stuck about with holly sprigs. Amanda's sons sent it. I thanked the delivery man, and one of the aides carried it down to Amanda's room. One by one, all of us on the day shift, nurses, aides and workers went into our small lounge and into an empty coffee can, we put dates and times scribbled on a pieces of paper and a dollar. This was our annual betting pool for Amanda's hugely ostentatious fruit basket: we bet on the turn around time. How long it will take Amanda to throw away the gift card, and put her own embossed cream colored paper in the envelope, write her little inscription, call an aide to take it back to the nurses's station? Her message always reads something like *Happy Holidays to the staff, yours affectionately, Amanda Day.* She's shameless about it. Within hours she will waddle up to the central desk, and ask us, pointedly, 'Did you all enjoy my lovely gift?'

What can we say but *Thank you, Amanda.* Some say it with gritted teeth. Some say it with saccharine sweetness. She never notices. Like Queen Victoria, she graciously accepts our acknowledgment.

This year, the turn-around time was about fifty-seven minutes. Kelly, the aide won.

An hour later, Amanda rambled down to the nurses' station and asked how we liked her gift, and after waxing on how she was happy to something nice for the staff etc. etc., she turned to me and asked me to take a turn with her.

'A turn?' I thought for a frozen moment she knew about the coffee can.

'A spin, Michelle. A walk. Is that so very hard to understand?' She left her walker at the desk, and took my elbow so I could not escape. I made small talk, inquiring if her sons, or her grandchildren were coming at Christmas to which she scoffed. More like snorted. She lowered her voice to a cosy confidentiality.

'Mr. Knight and I have had a some nice long chats.'

'Really? You got him to talk?' This was news to me.

'Oh, a bit of this and that, don't you know. A little night music, as they say.' She tittered. I said nothing. 'I know exactly how to bring him from his—what did you call it, Michelle? His funk.' We walked a little longer. 'Well, aren't you interested? Don't you want to know what needs to happen?'

'What needs to happen?'

'He and I will be coming to your house on Christmas Day, and we will have Figgy Pudding for dessert.'

'And what exactly is Figgy Pudding?' I side-stepped the larger and more appalling issue.

'What!' she cried alarmed. 'You don't know the old Christmas carol?' She let loose in her wavering contralto, 'We wish you a Merry Christmas, we wish you a merry Christmas, we wish you a Merry Christmas, and a Happy New Year!' She regarded me as though expecting a round of applause. 'Now you do you remember the second verse?'

I confessed I did not.

She belted out the second verse. 'Now give us some figgy pudding, now give us some figgy pudding, now give us some figgy pudding, and a cup of good cheer!'

I gave her a round of applause, but I still didn't know what Figgy Pudding was.

'Never mind, Michelle. Ignorance is not a crime or a vice, and it can be corrected.'

'Amanda, my family has plans for Christmas.'

'Of course you do, my dear, and we're very pleased to accept.' She smiled, the close-lipped smile of a woman accustomed to getting what she wants. 'Think of as a gift.' She left me, and tottered back to the nurses' station chuckling.

*   *   *

My teenage daughters, Becca and Lucy don't object to my being a nurse, though they've often remarked that they wished I worked in ER or ICU, or some dramatic venue where I was saving lives. The emotional stress and physical strain of saving lives is exactly why I don't work ER or ICU. On Balboa wing, we have a emergencies, of course, but no one requires intensive care. Most of our patients need their meds, a little TLC, and some watching over for their safety. Most, though occasionally cranky, do their best to be cordial, to be part of the little world that is Balboa Wing. All but Amanda Day. Her Grand Dame ways, her insufferable arrogance were all the stuff of dinnertime anecdotes at my house. That night, however, the story I told was not funny. Amanda had invited herself and Roland Knight to my house for Christmas Day.

My husband, Myles, shook his head. Myles is a middle school special ed teacher, and has certainly earned a break at Christmas. 'She nailed you for having a soft heart, Michelle.'

'A soft head, you mean!' Becca and Lucy went into a froth, railing against Sunrise Villas refugees as guests for Christmas. Their attitude didn't reflect anything against Amanda Day and Roland Knight in particular, just the ordinary prejudices and priorities of high school girls.

'She tricked me,' I said in my own defense. 'I don't think I can get out of it.'

'It's just one day,' said Myles. 'It won't kill us. They're both alone. Why not?'

But Becca and Lucy wouldn't let it go. Cleaning up the dishes, they rampaged against Day and Knight. They rattled on, fulminating against the old folks and their old folk families who thrust their care and feeding on the staff. Their attitude really started to annoy me. Becca and Lucy were peevish and difficult, complaining, fault-finding and surly. As these were the very traits that Mrs. Day is renowned for, I figured they would all make good company. I told them to shut up. I wouldn't hear another word about it.

'Oh,' said Myles with a laugh as we lay in bed that night. 'You'll hear more about it. Count on it.' He patted my behind and went to sleep. He knew.

My colleagues on Balboa wing were aghast. Maybe even more so than my daughters, but for different reasons. *Amanda Day will put on white gloves and test for dust. She'll criticize everything in your house. She'll bore your daughters, and flirt with your poor husband. She'll tell you how to do everything better. She'll make you wait on her hand and foot.*

Just then the buzzer of room 312 rang, and Amanda asked for me particularly.

I went to the door where I found her literally powdering her nose in a vanity mirror set about with warm glowing lights; she reminded me of an overdone confectionary piece of cake.

'I just wanted to tell you that I need to come early, Michelle. I'll come on the 24th and spend the night.'

'Amanda—really, Amanda. That isn't possible. We have no guest room.'

'Ta-ta!' she said, swiveling away from the mirror to face me. 'You have daughters, don't you? Let them double up. When I was a girl we slept three to a bed. Warmer that way.'

'I thought you were the Earl's daughter, Amanda, with the big estate in Sussex or somewhere.'

'Summers on the Isle of Wight,' she replied. 'Now, here, have a look at this. These are the ingredients I will need to make Figgy Pudding.'

She handed me a shopping list with everything specifically noted, weights, measures brands. She gave me as well a fifty dollar bill. I glanced at the list. Weird ingredients, dried figs, orange flower water, certain kind of marmalade. Not exactly your supermarket fare. I said I didn't think I had the time to get all this stuff.

'You want to help Mr. Knight, don't you?'

'I do help Mr. Knight, Amanda. I'm a nurse here, remember?'

'Oh, don't be tedious. Look at the poor man, sitting there in the common room, blind, miserable, alone with his memories. I know what I'm doing.'

Yes, I thought, I'll bet you do. But all I said was, 'I think you're overdoing it, Amanda.'

'My finest trait,' she replied, turning back to the mirror.

*   *   *

That night, lying, exhausted beside Myles, I said, 'I can't do this after all. I'd have to go all over town to get this stuff.'

'Send the girls,' Myles advised. 'They like to drive.'

I chuckled.

And, on Saturday, I gave them the list, money for gas and told them don't come back till they'd found everything on it.

'Why are you doing this to us?' wailed Lucy. She was seventeen, already planning out her

137

drama major at any number of universities, all far from home. She is not a great beauty, my Lucy, but I suspect she'll be a success at drama. She can exude prickly silence so well, you'd think she learned her technique from Katherine Hepburn. 'Why should we spend our time going all around to weird delis and groceries for that old woman,' she complained.

I turned my attention to the crossword, mumbled something inconsequential, but I was thinking: bad attitudes will reap a lot of inconvenience, girls. Get used to it.

Becca's objections were less indignant, but just as strenuous. Becca said she'd do it, fine, but only if she could bring along three or four of her best friends and go the mall afterwards. If I find Lucy sometimes exasperating, Becca saddens me. She is smart, very smart, but hasn't the social backbone, so to speak. Becca finds it easier to be like all the Other Girls, who I realized were a youthful version of the Balboa Widows.

'No. You'll go together, just the two of you, and do the shopping and bring it home. Think of it as a gift,' I advised the girls.

*　　　*　　　*

The Balboa Widows scoffed among themselves and behind Amanda's back, pitying her for the fruit and flowers that her family sent in lieu of actually spending Christmas with her, and of course her bad taste in recycling the gift. I don't think they had a betting pool, but they always nodded knowingly to one another as they walked past the central desk and saw the fruit basket, unwrapped now, each piece so perfect, the fruit looked waxen.

However, they were not scoffing when, in the days following, Amanda escorted Mr. Knight in to meals, and sat opposite him, chatting away, as though they were having an intimate tete-a-tete. Mr. Knight hardly ever replied to her. He wore his sad and absent expression. When he finished eating, he rose, nodded courteously to Amanda, sometimes mumbled, but left without further ado.

I happened to be at the central station after lunch one day when Mrs. Day and a few of the widows walked past and pointedly commented on the fruit her son had sent her.

'Oh no. My son didn't send that. That was my gift to the staff. My son wanted, in fact, both of my sons wanted to come here for Christmas. Can you imagine the inconvenience? And all those grandchildren?' Mrs. Day made a face. 'To say nothing of their wives, or girlfriends, or whoever they're living with these days. Unspeakable twits. Really, I couldn't be bothered. with all that. No, Mr. Knight and I are having a quiet Christmas together with Michelle Lance's family.' Amanda smiled graciously at me, and what could I do but smile back? 'Michelle's lovely

139

daughters are giving up their room for us. I mean,' Amanda cleared her throat, 'for me.'

*   *   *

The fateful day approached. Becca and Lucy remained restless, resentful, and sulky. Their attitude was more trying than Amanda Day herself. So I put on a smile and told them they should think of this the equivalent of community service which would look good on their college entrance résumés. As a solution, this did not fly. Myles suggested to me that Becca and Lucy should drive to Sunrise Villas to collect Amanda on the afternoon of the 24th. Predictably, this incurred their wrath.

'We already did her awful old shopping. You invited her! You should go get—'

'I did not invite her. She invited herself and Mr. Knight. But they are invited and she needs a ride.'

'This is going to suck. Big time. These awful old people—'

'How do you know they're awful, Becca?' I heaved the Christmas turkey into the sink and giving it a good rinse-out. I'd heard enough. 'You've never met them. It just might be, Miss Drama Queen, that Amanda Day has something to teach you.'

'Like what' Rank disdain dropped from Lucy's lips.

'She's going to ruin Christmas and it's all
140

your fault,' Becca said.

'Well, you're always saying you wish I had a nursing job that was dramatic, ER or ICU where I saved lives and brought people back from the brink of death. Maybe that's what we're doing here.'

They glared at me and at each other. Clearly I was too obtuse for words. They snapped their cell phones to their ears and went out to the car.

Our home is a modest split level, furnished, rather than decorated, stuff Myles and I have acquired over the years. Our Christmas tree was up and glittering and Myles had lit a fire which danced and warmed. Still I braced for a barrage of criticism when Amanda Day walked in, for her cool patrician superiority to put me in my split-level place. But as Lucy and Becca ushered her in, she shuffled right up to Myles, shook his hand, said something nice about our tree, waxed on how nice it was we had a piano. She tinkled a few keys. Broadening her Grande Dame British, she complimented Lucy on her driving. Both girls grimaced, and then quickly fled to the room they now had to share for the night.

She gave me one of those utterly insincere pecks on the cheek, said something stale and conventional, and then added, 'I hope you have plenty of aprons, Michelle.' She wore a green pants and a bright red sweater that further drained her face of color. She smelled oddly of mothballs. 'I must have an apron. You can't expect me to work in these clothes.'

'Myles made up the fire so you could sit here and enjoy it.'

'I didn't come here to sit by the fire! I came to save Mr. Knight. We have work to do.'

So she followed me into the kitchen and I gave her an apron, and at her request, assembled all the ingredients the girls had purchased from her list. I put them on the kitchen table.

She opened the jar of marmalade and sniffed it, did the same to the other ingredients. She sighed. 'Ah, Figgy Pudding! Nothing like it for Christmas. Nothing at all.'

'You have a recipe?' I asked, tired already. My heart sank. I had fobbed off as much as I could on my daughters, but now, I was here alone with Amanda Day, stuck in the kitchen.

Amanda tapped her skull. 'My grandmother's recipe. It's from Queen Victoria.'

I was tempted to tell her she reminded me of the aged Victoria, but I didn't. 'The Queen herself made this?'

'Don't be a goose, Michelle. Not with her own fair hands. My grandmother was one her cooks on the Isle of Wight, a sort of undercook actually, but she wrote everything down over the years. She knew she wouldn't stay in service forever. One day she would have her own nice little tea shop.' Amanda made a face.

'It was a tea shop, though I must say it wasn't nice. I certainly bolted at the first opportunity. Not for me, thank you, sloshing out the dirty cups and slops of others. I had a career! I was a stenographer. I worked for the BBC, the wireless, the radio as you say.'

'What happened to the Earl? The daughter of an earl? The country estate in Sussex? The servants scurrying at your command?'

'All lies and botheration! So much easier to play the duchess, even with my own children. Why should I tell them my poor old Granny ran a failed East End teashop. Do they have to know that my that my father gambled, and Mother wept? Of course not. All I needed was a change of accent. Easily done. I have talent.' She all but executed a little bow. 'And, after I'd told the story so often, why, it became true!'

I noticed Amanda did not say she had merely believed it. No. It was true. 'And the Yank? Dancing through the Blitz?'

'That was true. Is.' Her prim, pursed lips softened. 'I loved him. I married him. I came to California as his bride, and forty-four months later, I was his widow.'

'I'm sorry to hear that.'

'Oh, all a long time ago. Can't matter to anyone but me. My sons are from my second marriage. Another Yank. A good man, but not . . . Well, quit lollygagging, Michelle. Get out the mixer and a big bowl.'

143

'And Roland Knight?'

'I actually met him a few times when he came into the BBC to record. He was a famous song and dance man! Dashing in his day! Older than I, naturally, but he was often on the wireless during the war. Roland Knight's voice went all over Britain. However, the sort of thing he sang, well, he was straight out of the old halls.' Seeing my confusion, she added, 'The music halls, dearie. "A Little of What You Fancy Does You Good." You know?'

No. I didn't. Amanda sang the whole song, a ditty full of charm and innuendo. She did all this while she cracked eggs in a bowl and beat them.

I said, 'His great-niece said he had been a bartender in Medicine Hat.'

'What does she know?' snapped Amanda, back to her old tart self, 'If he ended up a bartender in Medicine Hat, it's only because his song and dance routines were already passé, even before the War. *The Man Who Broke the Bank at Monte Carlo,* that sort of thing.' She sang a few bars for me with its infectious chorus. 'There's more verses, naturally. But oh yes, Roland Knight was quite something. I had aspirations myself in those days. If I hadn't met my Yank, I might have been a singer. Now pass me the kettle and let's soften up these dried figs. Let's put on the kettle. I hope you have real tea,

Michelle, and not mere bags full of sawdust. I do so love Christmas!' Her round face lit. 'There's nothing quite like it.'

'Will you excuse me for a minute, Amanda?' I went directly up to the girls' room where they were flopped on the bed, cell phones to their ears, video games on the television. 'Turn that off, leave the cell phones here and come down to the kitchen. Your help is needed.'

They moaned, and groaned, and fought me, especially Lucy, but I insisted. After all Lucy the Drama Queen might truly learn something from East End Amanda Day who had passed herself off as nobility. And sweet Becca, smart but lacking all social backbone, might well take a few cues from a woman who would dance through the Blitz.

Amanda Day was amazingly competent in the kitchen. She put my daughters to work, doing the chopping and stirring, all by hand, just as her grandmother had. The girls rolled their eyes and wanted to put on their headphones, but I forbade this. I worked on the stuffing for the Christmas Day turkey while Becca and Lucy did Amanda's bidding—as no doubt, Amanda's own grandmother must have followed orders in that Isle of Wight kitchen. Amanda talked of her grandmother's extraordinary skill in the kitchen, her hopes to be independent and not in service, not even in the service of the Queen. Amanda spoke of the East End teashop her grandmother opened, its failure, the family's pinched circumstances and dashed hopes. She spoke of her long-suffering mother and improvident father. The War changed everything for Amanda's generation, and the California Yank took her far away. But she clearly remembered it all with affectionate vivacity. Her grandmother, particularly held a special place in Amanda's affections, as she retold her stories of her days as a royal undercook. 'She started out no more than a scullery maid at the age of twelve or thirteen. She raised herself up. She watched everything the head cook did, and carried it all in her head.' Amanda tapped her temple. 'She was a quick study, just like me.'

Somehow, as Amanda talked, our steamy windows seemed to be those of that vast Isle of Wight kitchen; we could feel the anticipation of Christmas, *We wish you a Merry Christmas* . . . the snowy cold outside, but all of us perspiring from ovens within. As Amanda, Becca and Lucy grated orange peel and nutmeg for this figgy pudding, chopped the softened figs, and lined the big copper bowl with foil, we could all but hear the laughter, the long ago lost voices, the rolling pins' rhythmic thump. *Let nothing ye dismay.*

*　　　*　　　*

Figgy Pudding baked for a very long time and when at last we turned it out from the bowl and foil collar, I was astonished at the creation. Becky and Lucy regarded it with audible amazement. Sweet steam billowed up from the cake, and the color was a rich, deep mahogany, though the mound was not quite perfect. Never mind, Amanda reminded us, Mr. Knight is blind. Taste and fragrance, that's what counts. Becca and Lucy—with no shred of disdain— commented that they had never smelled anything quite like that.

'Wait till you taste it,' Amanda confided. 'Fit for royalty.' She beamed, and sang a quick chorus of *We Wish You a Merry Christmas*. And we all had a cup of good cheer.

I drove to Sunrise Villas to collect Mr. Knight on Christmas Day. He wore usual bow tie and pressed shirt and suspenders, a pin-striped suit jacket and pants. His sparse gray hair was slicked down upon his skull. We folded up the walker and he took my arm. He murmured, 'I look quite like "Burlington Bertie from Bow." But, with all my cheery prompting, he said little all the way to my house.

Once at home, Myles came out to help him from the car and wish him a merry Christmas. My daughters, less sullen than I would have expected, greeted him and shook his hand. He held each one. 'How will I tell you apart?'

'They're girls, Roland, you don't need to tell them apart,' Amanda interrupted, taking his other arm and steering him into the livingroom with her usual aplomb. 'They have a piano. Would you like to play?'

He declined quickly, emphatically, so she gave him the best chair near the fire, and though he was silent, she chatted on about the wireless, the theatre and London, and other things that excluded the rest of us.

Myles, Becca and Lucy left them there, and I finished up Christmas dinner preparations, setting the table, basting the turkey, checking the yams, and seeing to the last of the red-and-green beans. We had all been instructed to say nothing of Figgy Pudding; that was to be Amanda's surprise for the old gent.

The dinner went remarkably well, I thought. Our dining room is small, so we were an intimate group. Myles carved the turkey. I poured the wine. Amanda Day sat beside Mr. Knight, tucked a big napkin into his collar, and served him, nattering all the while. She described for the benefit of my American family, the marvels of those vast theatrical Christmas pageants known as pantomimes, so beloved of English children for two hundred years. Amanda Day, for once, was not talking about herself, but drawing Mr. Knight out, enlisting all my family somehow in this endeavor. She really did intend to save him, I thought. Not like ER or ICU, but an imaginative salvation; she had linked her past to his, united them in the present. Slowly Mr. Knight's face began to glow.

Slowly he spoke, lingering on the words as though they surprised him. The Christmases of his youth had all been spent in theatres. He had been on the stage since he was five, the son of an acrobat family who had always played the Christmas shows. He spoke of quick cups of tea gulped in cold dressing rooms, quick meals consumed in smoky theatrical pubs, of men and women and children in outlandish costumes, wigs and thick makeup, sweat beading on their painted faces. After the performance, on Christmas night, the actors, singers and dancers all gathered at the Knight's flat, and everyone brought some contribution, food, drink, a musical instrument. 'Figgy Pudding was my mother's speciality. How did she do it?' He asked us as though we might actually have an answer. 'How did she find the time or money? I never knew, but she did, and every Christmas, her Figgy Pudding was the grand finale, and oh, yes, my people knew how to make a finale grand.' Mr. Knight stared, as though to his blinded eyes, the corner of our small dining room had velvet curtains, footlights, and unearthly applause echoed.

We all ate silently, respecting his moment. Early dusk closed in upon our windows and the candles burned brighter. So that was the story Amanda had got from him. What an achievement, I thought. She brought Christmas from the past—another time, another country—and recreated it in the present, in our split-level home. I thought how resilient is the human impulse to clutch at the ineffable past. I thought about what is lost when the past can't be shared, when families splinter and the young are consumed with the own immediate lives, and the old drift off. I wondered what Becca and Lucy would be like as old women. I couldn't picture them, of course, but I wondered if one day our Christmases in the split-level homestead would seem precious. And I looked around the dining room and realized that they were precious, fleeting, as condemned to pass as were Roland Knight's tales of acrobats and actors. I wanted suddenly to protect our Christmases together, to shelter them from all the winds of change that would surely blow through our lives, to protect them as you would shield a sputtering candle and pull it near your heart.

When at last it was time for dessert, Amanda asked Myles to entertain Mr. Knight while she helped me and the girls in the kitchen. The girls set the Figgy Pudding platter on the counter while I whipped the cream and Amanda heated up some brandy, along with the last of the fragrant water in which we'd soaked the dried figs. She kept it hot till the fumes burned off. 'To do this right,' she said to Becca and Lucy, ignoring me, 'You would heat and ignite this, pour it on the cake, and bring it into the darkened room while the blue flames dance around.'

'That sounds wonderful,' said Becca. 'Why don't we?'

'Because Mr. Knight is blind, and it won't matter to him.' She poured the sauce over the Figgy Pudding and stuck in a sprig of mistletoe she produced from her pocket. 'You take in, Lucy, and give it to Roland.'

'Me? It's your gift.'

'Just do as I say. Becca, the dessert dishes, Michelle, bring the whipped cream.'

We all followed Lucy into the dining room as she set the platter with the mound of Figgy Pudding in front of Mr. Knight. It steamed slightly, vapors of fragrance wafting visibly up, filling the small room with anticipation. A look of quiet alarm passed over his features, and he frowned as though struggling, as though straining toward some distant sight, sound or emotion, unavailable to the rest of us. Amanda cut him his piece, dolloped it with whipping cream, moved the platter to his left, gave him a fork and guided his hand down to the dessert dish. 'Happy Christmas, Roland,' she said.

We watched as Mr. Knight took a bite. His lips moved slowly. His blind eyes closed. He reached out one hand for Amanda and one for Becca who sat beside him, and caught thus, between the past and the future, he laughed. He gulped audibly. He took up his napkin and daubed his lips, his eyes. 'Did you say there's a piano in the house? Maybe after dinner I could play for you. Songs from the old days. Amanda, can you sing along?'

Amanda said she would be delighted. She knew them all. There are some things you never forget.

THE TWELVE DAYS OF CHRISTMAS

Ah, my wedding! When I look at the family photos of that event, even now, ten years later, I can feel my arteries gently harden. The drama that day was not the bride coming down the aisle, nor at the altar where Colin and Wendy recited their vows. The drama lay in who was sitting on what side of the aisle, and who was given the front pews. Who would get their feelings irremediably hurt? For how long could those slighted nurse their wounds, and clutch their grudges? Colin and I both come from fractured and re-mixed families. (Some people call these blended families, but re-mixed is the better metaphor here.) Not until we actually married—as opposed to the informal living together—did we realize just how contentious and demanding, how lumpy the re-mix could be. Our biological parents and siblings, the various steps, the exes, half-siblings, companions and other assorted hangers-on, are much given to tiffs that often spiral into long funks. They are like a bubbling stew, salted with prickly tempers and peppered with hurt feelings, seasoned with gossip.

My sister Zappa and I (yes, Zappa is named for the immortal Frank; my parents were fans) were unknowingly spared the worst of these family fracases. Our parents divorced when we were quite young, and we stayed on Isadora Island with Mom, going to island schools while she clerked in a marina grocery store that also sold bait and ice cream in the summer, and cords of firewood in winter. My father, Mike—always in search of fulfillment, enlightenment, in search of someone or something that would make him suddenly Whole!—returned to Seattle. There he married twice more, and had several serious girlfriends in between. Zappa and I, on our twice yearly furloughs to Mike-Land learned to tolerate, even like his women, but we always knew he would seek and find someone else. Mom, on the other hand, was not that avid sort of seeker. She preferred to stay put and see what came to her. Mike was like the boat; Annie was like the beach. The tides matter to both, but for different reasons.

Zappa was more like Annie. I was more like Mike: restless, energetic, competitive, stellar in school, eager to get off Isadora Island, though, I now see that my island childhood was a gift that Mom gave me, for which I am belatedly grateful. (And yes, I've told her so.) I graduated cum laude from UW and got a job, both demanding and rewarding at Microsoft, married the man of my dreams, Colin the architect, and set about living the fine life. Our intense working hours were balanced by expensive restaurants, extensive vacations, a sailboat, the *Halcyon*, and sleek, fast cars, and a condo with a view of the Space

154

Needle. Ever fearless, Colin and I waded into parenthood with the same organizational zeal we'd brought to our careers. We moved out of the condo to an expensive Capitol Hill home with a large sunny playroom. We mapped out time frames. We interviewed nannies, and so on. Executive decisions. Unbeknownst to us, the birth of our daughter would forever upend our lives. No doubt new parents have had this experience since Adam and Eve first gazed at Cain and Abel, but it remains forever a surprise. The love we felt for Alexandra, for each other became suddenly, deeply complex, compounded, and for two people accustomed to executive decisions, we fell thrall to the baby. We were her happy, her willing slaves.

Alexandra (my mother named her Button when she was a week old; she was certainly cute as a button) was the first grandchild on both sides of the family. Everyone wanted time with The Baby. More to the point, everyone wanted to have Christmas with the Baby.

Let the games begin.

Since Button's first Christmas, the family feuds and funks and who-cannot-abide-whom, all of this falls on Colin and me. They all wanted time with the Baby, yes, but they did not want time with or near each other. Their gloved vendettas are complicated, on both sides, by political considerations, some religion and a good many passionately held beliefs about how the rest of the world should live. Since nearly everyone in our families lives in the greater Seattle area, or at least within a day's drive, all these visits must be staggered throughout the holiday season. And so, Colin and I endure 'The Twelve Days of Christmas' nonstop, from Thanksgiving till January second. All the lords-a-leaping, the ladies dancing, the drummers drumming, turkey with all the trimmings and the clucking of interminable French hens, gossiping cacklers of both sexes. Day after day, night after night, our relatives arrive and depart in shifts. Like the tides. All through the holiday season Colin and I cannot relax our rigid facial muscles, frozen into smiles; we hardly speak to one another except across a sea of faces. By January 2 we are, metaphorically speaking, on all fours, too exhausted even to make resolutions we could then break. I have PMS crying jags without the PMS.

Colin and I call it the Hell-a-Day season.

On my side, for instance, Mike's third wife Viv is one of those constantly needy people (nice, but needy) who must always be loved best, and first. In Viv, Mike has at last found someone equally seeking, and in need of being made Whole. So they're a good pair, except that Viv is intolerably jealous of my mother, Annie. My father must constantly prove he loves Viv best, and that too, gets tedious. My dad is a better grandfather than he was a father. He delights in Button. However, Viv

156

is very ambivalent about being grandmother. Viv says she was too young to be anyone's granny, though her son and daughter are the same age as Zappa and me. Zappa can't endure Viv or her kids. Zappa and I affectionately refer to them as the Weedeater and Vegissima. The Weedeater is perpetually stoned and Vegissima is so pure about what crosses her lips, you'd think that a piece of organic lettuce was a communion wafer. One Christmas Viv overstepped the bounds of step-motherly propriety and advised Zappa to drop her handsome ski instructor boyfriend, Eric. Zappa snapped back: 'If I need motherly advice, I'll ask my own mom, Annie.'

Annie isn't all that fond of Eric, either, but she remains remains serene, and doesn't offer up a lot of Thou Shalts. Mom actively practices zen and yoga. She can be so zen, sometimes you want to shake her. She is delighted to be a grandmother. She named herself Grannyannie at the same time she named Alexandra Button.

Colin's family dramas are even more complex. His parents' divorce was incredibly acrimonious, leaving in its wake persistent anger. Gordon and Barbara each have a long caravan of steps and exes. Gordon is now married to Sherri, many years his junior; her troubled teenage son lives with them. The boy is surly and he has two DUI's; he's failed to perform the community service the court required of him, and Sherri and Gordon don't know what to do. Gordon will complain to Colin that the boy is not his responsibility, and he thinks it unfair that he should have to deal with the kid's delinquent problems. Colin just smiles and says to Gordon: Well, dad, you did tell Sherri for-better-or-for-worse. Colin's mom, Barbara considers herself quite the Bohemian. She espouses causes, wears dangly earrings, carries an African basket handbag and has lovers. Barbara always says, *lover* with a sort of breathless hush around the word. In general, I like Barbara, though I am not fond of her new live-in lover, Kirk, a gourmet and wine afficionado she met on a wine-tasting holiday a few years ago. Colin's older brother Ted is forever 'playing the field,' an expression befitting the ex-jock and local rugby club champ. His younger brother Hal divorced after two years of marriage, and soon acquired a new girlfriend, Melinda.

In fact, it was Hal who brought Colin and I to the proverbial lightbulb moment. About ten one night—the end of a long day at the beginning of a long week—Hal called.

Colin picked up, chatted a bit, then lay the phone on the bed between us, and said, 'I'm putting you on speakerphone, Hal. Why don't you explain all this to Wendy?'

'Hi Wendy! How's it going?'

'Super, Hal.'

'How's that cute little Button?'

'Super, Hal. What is there to explain?'

158

'Well you know Melinda and I are really looking forward to Christmas with you guys, and I know Ashlee can't wait to play with Button again.'

I let the proverbial pause become increasingly pregnant while Hal nattered on about how much quality time with this daughter mattered to him. Finally, he convinced himself (he certainly didn't convince me) and went on. 'Melinda's little guy, well he'll be great with the girls.'

'Melinda's little guy?'

'Yeah, I told you Melinda has little boy, Sammy. He's two.'

'How old is Ashlee now?'

'Three.'

'So you want to bring Ashlee and Sammy.'

'Don't worry. The kids can sleep on the floor in the family room. We'll bring sleeping bags, but here's the problem. My ex wants to take Ashlee to her folks in Colorado for the Christmas holiday, so I can only have Ashlee for that weekend of the twenty-second and twenty-third. But what I'm worried about is, isn't it right around then that Barbara and Kirk usually come?'

'I don't have the calender in front of me, Hal.'

'Well, can you look it up, because honestly, guys, I just can't stand Kirk. Melinda can't either. Calls himself a gourmet! He's a condescending, criticizing bastard, if you ask me. I don't know how Mom stands him. Always complaining about everything, snide remarks how nothing is good enough for him. The last time Melinda and I went out with them, well, you heard what happened.'

We hadn't, but we did. At great length.

Finally Hal went on, 'So we'd rather come when Dad and Sherri are coming.'

'Hal,' Colin said evenly, 'you know as well as I do, that Dad thought your divorce was a big mistake. And he thought you took up with Melinda too soon. He's pretty judgmental.'

'Well, Dad can just grow up and be nice to Melinda. The twenty-second to the twenty-third, that's the only time Melinda and I and the kids can come.'

Without committing ourselves, we said goodbye and turned off the speakerphone and looked at each other. I had never noticed the gray creeping in at Colin's temples, the deepening parentheses around his mouth. Had he aged another ten years in the last twenty minutes? Had I? I ran my hands over my own face and through my hair.

'It's not like we don't have enough room for them,' said Colin. 'We do.'

'Yes, I said, 'it's a big house. But I want Hal and Ashlee and Melinda and her two year old like I want antlers.'

'I don't even want Barbara and Kirk. Or Gordon and Sherri and Veganissima and the Weedeater.'

160

'Or Mike and Viv and the delinquent.'

'What about your mom? We've thrown all the other names into the pot.'

'I like Grannyannie. I like Zappa. I even like Eric. But I don't want them at Christmas. I don't want anyone at Christmas.' And then, the twinkling light of inspiration lit up the darkness. 'We could leave, Colin. Go somewhere. Have Christmas away from home. Just the three of us. Far away.'

'How far?'

'Really far. Rome? Paris? Venice?' I said. 'Think of it.'

Colin leaned back against the pillows and smiled. 'Vienna. Just think of all that snow and Mozart.'

*　　　*　　　*

All that snow and Mozart! We rented a small apartment in an 18th century building, on a tree-lined *strasse*. It had a modern kitchen, big, deep beds, parqueted floors that creaked beneath our feet, and a small ceramic stove for warmth in the sitting room. Outside snow fluttered down, caught in the buttery glow of the streetlamps. We bought the tiniest tree we could find. We tied red ribbons on the boughs for decorations. We took the bus and walked, and shopped and ate in restaurants whose on-site histories went back to the seventeenth century. We strolled all over the city's bustling

Christmas markets, along the arcades at the Freyung Passage. Bundled up, we wandered along the beautifully lit Kohlmarkt; we ate schnitzels and tortes, and heard wonderful music in drafty churches. We had a sturdy stroller for Button, and found she was a sturdy traveler, sometimes cranky, but usually alert, and then, when she got tired, happy to sleep in the stroller. She also liked coloring paper ornaments for our Christmas tree and we tied them on as well. In one of the stalls at the Christmas markets we bought a splendid angel to sit atop the tree. The wings and robes were fashioned of a shimmery stiffened lace, and the face and hair of porcelain. Though I know angels have no gender, I still thought of it as a she, and she was far too big for our tiny tree. She stood beside it.

Perhaps best of all of our Viennese interlude was in coming back to the apartment in the evenings where one of us read *The Pokey Little Puppy* to Button about ten thousand times till she fell into one of her sweet little open-mouthed sleeps. We put her to bed, and drank wine and nibbled beautiful confections by the warmth of the ceramic stove. We weren't too tired to play Scrabble. We weren't too tired to make love. We congratulated ourselves for our brilliant evasion. Next year, we told ourselves, we'd go to Copenhagen.

But it was not to be. Our son, Zach was conceived on one of those snowy Vienna nights, and made his squalling appearance in this world late the following August. Shortly thereafter, we had not only a five year old and an infant, but Muttley the dog, a new mortgage, two car payments, and an entirely new lifestyle.

When Zach was about eight months old, our wonderful nanny gave us notice. She was leaving us to pursue an certificate as an x-ray technician. I begged her to stay. I had no pride. My whole life was founded on the trust I had in this young woman, on her being responsible and reliable and looking after my kids and my house, so I could be Superwoman. Even in the throes of my begging, I realized I'd been truly reduced in some fundamental fashion that had nothing to do with pride. If I could not be Superwoman without her help, then, what was I? Who was I?

So, I quit Microsoft, we sold our chic Capitol Hill home, and on one income we moved to an eastside house with a lower mortgage. Colin joined the hordes of commuters who rode the bus across the bridge to his downtown office. We traded my sleek car for a mini-van. We sold the *Halcyon*. These were choices were made together, but the changes were hard to get used to. In my new life, the most executive decisions I made concerned carpooling to swimming and ballet lessons. Instead of working out at the corporate gym, I went to the local 'Y' where they had a toddlers' room for Zach. So all that changed. What did not change was Christmas. We ruefully returned to the Marionettes' Christmas, where other people pulled our strings and made us talk, stale phrases offered up with plastered grins. The whole holiday calendar once again became a mass of names and dates and dinners and lunches. The only thing I had to testify that Christmas in Vienna happened at all (apart from Zach naturally) is the beautiful wide-winged angel with the serene face. She's always at the bottom of the Christmas box, and I unearth her like a gift.

* * *

One November morning, just as Button was putting on her jacket to walk to school, she announced, 'I don't want to be Button anymore. My teacher calls me Alexandra. My friends call me Alexandra. You and Daddy should call me Alexandra.'

'Oh, but Button! Grannyannie gave you that name when you were born. She said you were too little to carry such a big name as Alexandra and you were cute as a button.'

'Well, I'm not little now. I'm seven. I can read the back of the cereal box.'

'Well, of course you are a big girl, no doubt of that. But you're still cute as a button and you always will be.'

'That doesn't mean Button should be my

164

name. It's too much like Muttley. Grannyannie named Muttley too.'

It's true that my mother has the habit of bestowing lighthearted names. Witness Zappa. I got named Wendy because she had always loved the story of Peter Pan. Lucky for me she didn't love Peter Rabbit. I could have gone through life as Flopsy, Mopsy or Cottontail. Annie still lives on Isadora Island, and I suppose, like the tides, things still come to her. Certainly my mother is one of the most serene and observant people I've ever known. At one time I despised that serenity, that attention to detail. I had a sort of genial contempt for Mom's boring job, the narrow circumference of her life. I couldn't wait to get off that island, and have a life with some grandeur! In fact, I named my daughter Alexandra because I thought the name had such grandeur. Now, suddenly, this particular morning, I wanted more than anything for her to remain Button. Swiftly, I gathered my little daughter into my arms, backpack and all, and I wondered: would Button and Zach one day judge me as harshly as I judged my mom? Will I one day be just another ingredient in the old family stew? The possibility wavered before me as probability, but then Zachie dropped his un-spillable cup, and milk flew everywhere, and Muttley chased after it, and brought it back proudly, like a dripping Frisbee. I agreed to call Button Alexandra. At least to try.

As usual, this year the Hell-a-days start at Thanksgiving. This year Viv and my dad invited us first, and so we went there. They invited Zappa and Eric too, and Mom encouraged Zappa and me to go. Mom said she had tons of friends, and even on a small island, and she would spend Thanksgiving on Isadora. So Zappa and I and our Significant Others endured Thanksgiving with Viv (assuring her at every turn that her turkey was the best we'd ever tasted) the Weedeater, Veganissima, and my father's brother, Uncle Roger whose politics are somewhere to the right of Attila the Hun.

So that Mom should not feel left out (no matter what she said about the tons of friends) I invited her and Zappa and Eric to my house on Saturday for another Thanksgiving dinner. Mom stayed on for a three or four days. She was there, in the kitchen making one of her famous sweet potato pies when the phone rang. I was feeding Zach his lunch. (Feeding him in a manner of speaking: I put it in front of him, and he ate some, and flung some, and Muttley's caught the flying bits in the outfield.) I asked Mom to answer the phone, and as luck would have it, it was Viv, now feeling terribly upset and unloved that Mom should be staying after Thanksgiving. I soothed Viv as best I could, but her call put me into a wretched mood. I started to tell Mom and about this year's holiday lineup, working myself into a

166

lather, by the time I got to Hal and Melinda and their two brats. 'And Hal's not even the worst!'

'Who's the worst?'

'You mean: who's the worst so far?'

'Who's the worst so far.'

'Colin's other brother, Ted.'

'Was he the one teaching the bridesmaids Welsh drinking songs at your wedding?'

'He's the one. He emails me with his schedule. Really! Like I'm his secretary, or something! He says he's sorry it's so inflexible, but he's such a big shot, you know. Then at the last, he writes, he's looking forward to seeing my little daughter Betty again. Betty! I zapped him right back and told him my daughter's name is Button!'

'Not anymore,' Mom reminded me. 'She wants to be Alexandra now.'

I gulped back tears. 'I'm at the end of my rope and it isn't even December first. I'll spend the whole holiday season cooking and cleaning up, fetching and grinning like a wind up monkey with cymbals, looking after a bunch of thankless relatives. Not you and Zappa, Mom,' I hastened to add.

'Where is written that you have to do this, Wendy?'

'I don't know,' I sulked. 'In the Book of Love?'

'You don't have to do this.'

'But we always have and now everyone

expects it.'

'Does Colin insist on it?'

'No. He's as undone as I am, except I'm the one at home now, and the whole burden falls on me. Everyone thinks that since I'm not at Microsoft, I must be sitting around at home eating bon bons, reading grade B novels. Don't I wish.'

'Then don't do it.'

'I can't escape. There's no going to Vienna.'

'I didn't suggest Vienna. You're not listening. Just tell everyone there won't be Christmas at your house this year. They'll have to make their own plans.'

I pretended to consider this thoughtfully. 'Well, I could say that if there were flash floods, maybe an earthquake, hurricane, high winds, and a few other natural disasters to intervene. Typhoons. Maybe an epidemic of some sort.'

'Guess what, Wendy,' Mom turned her attention away from the sweet potatoes, and gave me one of her serene smiles, 'the heavens will not fall if you just say you won't do it. What is it they used to say? Just say no.'

'Aren't you my mother? Aren't you supposed to be telling me to do my duty?'

'You're not a child any longer. You have a husband and two kids. Your first loyalty ought to be to them. The rest of it is just ...'

She couldn't find the phrase and returned to peeling the sweet potatoes. I watched the skins fly.

'The family stew,' I offered. 'Everyone bobbing and bubbling about, add a pinch of rancor, a dash of humor, a teaspoon of guilt.'

'And a tablespoon of laughter. Why not? Why should you hate Christmas because of all of them?'

'I don't hate Christmas.' But I'd no sooner spoken than I knew I had lied. I did hate it. I hated the everlasting obligation of it, of living up to other people's expectations, and rising to some sort of standard that had been imposed upon me, to strew ho ho ho through everyone else's life when, really, all I wanted was . . . I wasn't even sure what I wanted.

'For starters, you don't have to fit Zappa and me into your schedule. I'm going to spend Christmas at her place up at Snoqualamie.'

'You don't like Eric.'

She shrugged, 'He's a nice guy, but Zappa's something special. Anyway, they've been together four years. Zappa likes him. That should be enough for me. Christmas is a season, Wendy. It's not a record you play over and over again. It does not have to be the same year after year, the same old groove. So, escape! You don't have to go Vienna to do that. Make some decisions and stick by them.'

'And offend everyone?'

Mom shrugged. 'They'll get over it. Just be sure that Colin will stand by you. It's like anything else in a marriage, you have to stand together. To back each other up.'

I wanted to ask how many times my father had failed to back Mom up, but in thinking about my Dad, I imagined myself on the phone telling Viv that she and Mike, and Veganissima and the Weedater can't come to my house this year for Christmas Eve or Christmas Day, or the twenty-third or any date at all. I imagine Viv putting down the phone and calling down the hall, *Mike . . . Mike . . . you need to come talk to Wendy, Mike. She doesn't want us at Christmas, she doesn't like us anymore, . . .* I imagine my father's voice on the phone, *You mean I can't have Christmas with my only grandchildren? My only grandchildren! You mean that Viv and I can't . . .*' As if I just booked him a ticket for the glue factory, consigned him to the fate of the Utterly Unloved.

I imagine suggesting to Hal and his girlfriend, that they should invite Ted to *their* house so he can teach their kiddies Welsh drinking songs. I imagine suggesting to Barbara that she and Kirk take a culinary cruise to Napa or New England or Neverland. I imagine telling Gordon and Sherri that they should take her troubled teen and spend Christmas Day at the homeless shelter, doing community service.

That night, late, as I fell into bed beside Colin, I said, 'We're never getting a divorce. Promise me.'

170

'I thought we promised that ten years ago. There was a big church wedding, remember?'

'I just want us to stay united. I want us to navigate these everyday shoals and currents and stay together and not be one of those busted up families.'

He pulled me into his embrace. 'What's wrong?'

So I told him my mom's plan for evading the Christmas Family Stew. Just say no.

Colin pondered the idea. He always thinks things through. 'We can't cancel. We'll alienate everyone. They won't speak to us.'

'Would that be so bad? We don't have to do this every Christmas.'

'We always have.'

'Not when we went to Vienna,' I remind him.

'Vienna was a dream.'

*   *   *

The November days dwindled down with the leaves. The holidays loomed like the Maginot Line. Deck the halls with hordes of relatives. Accept it, Wendy. That's what I told myself. But even as I sat, pen in hand, considering the intricate social strategies that would give everyone a real Christmas, but not rock their boats . . . I kept thinking, picturing . . . . The four of us, our own little Christmas together, here at home, our Vienna angel atop the tree, looking down while Colin and I watch Zach and Button play with their toys. A Christmas with ham instead of the everlasting obligatory turkey. (There's no stuffing a ham, no trimmings; you throw a can of pineapple chunks over the ham and put it in the oven on low. End of story.) I wanted to play Scrabble with Colin, and drink wine when the children were in bed. I wanted—finally the word came to me!—an intimate Christmas. It didn't have to be Vienna. But it had to be intimate. After all, one day Zach and Button would be Zachariah and Alexandra, restless adolescents, and their idea of a marvelous Christmas wouldn't be reading *Pokey Little Puppy* with us.

That afternoon, while I was folding mounds of laundry, I turned the TV on to an inconsequential TV movie that included a huge party scene with a colorfully contentious family. Far more comic and actually, less contentious than the tribe I was scheduling. The idea—I don't say solution, only the idea— came to me all it once.

'All at once?' Colin asked, blanching, after I had told him my plan.

'Sure. We have everyone over, all at once, a big party, well before Christmas. Then, we have Christmas for ourselves, that whole lovely week between Christmas and New Year's when the working world comes to a halt, generally agreed upon, unless you're in retail. Maybe we could even go somewhere,

172

not Vienna, OK, but out to Isadora island. For a day or so. We wouldn't be exhausted. We could have some adventure instead of obligation, and duty. Just the four of us.'

Zach was covered in mashed potatoes, fussy, and ready for the bath. Alexandra was coloring on the floor. Muttley barked loudly, eager for his after-dinner walk. Not exactly a pristine moment to remind Colin of the pleasures of just the four of us, but I took it nonetheless.

Colin went on. 'All at once? Everyone? All the family factions? All on the same day? The same house? My dad and your dad and their wives and kids, and my mom and the galloping gourmet?'

'Sure,' I said with more confidence than I felt. 'Get it all over with. No one can say we ignored them.'

'It'll be miserable.'

'For one afternoon it will be miserable, Colin, and then we'll have the whole holiday season to ourselves! Have yourself a merry little Christmas. Just us and the kids.' Muttley barked again, and I included him too.

'Our house isn't big enough, Wendy. Why, that could be as many as,' he started to figure on his fingers.

'We'll make room. We'll rent tables and metal folding chairs.'

'They'll be at each other's throats.'

'Or,' I suggested with something of my
173

mother's unflappable cheer, 'they'll figure out that they're all family too, like it or not. We won't put up any mistletoe. They don't have to love each other, but it is Christmas.' Then I remembered something I'd read, and added, 'The season of forgiveness.'

'I don't know, Wendy. I don't think I can take them all in one place.'

'Can you take them day after day, one after another? We've let ourselves in for this. We've never stood up to them and said, we don't want to do this. We've worried and fussed and fretted. We've given up having our own good time because we, well, we've let ourselves in for it, and now we're going to let ourselves out of it. They're the ones with the prickly rash, not us. We're not throwing them out. They can still have Christmas with us and Button and Zach, just new rules. New time. New day. It's a trade off. We have them all in one place, but only one afternoon.'

Colin has a particular sort of throaty growl when he's turning ideas over in his head. I was cheered to hear it.

I went on, ' We'll do the one big party. One afternoon, and then—ho ho ho— Christmas belongs to us.'

'Maybe for a party like that you need someone who can leap tall buildings in a single bound,' he said. 'I don't think I'm equal to it.'

'We don't need Superman, baby. We just need a good caterer, and a little resolve. All

174

right, a lot of resolve.'

'What if we don't have any kind of gathering at all. Just say no. You know, like Annie suggested.'

'Here's what's wrong with that plan: we'd have to explain ourselves to each of these people over and over.' I went through the various scenarios I'd already imagined. 'They'd all get their feelings hurt, because we're individually turning them down. This way, it's completely collective. They all get invited. They can come or not. It's up to them. No one person can get their feelings hurt. No one can take it personally that we invited someone they don't like. We're inviting all of them.'

Colin kissed my cheek, put on his jacket, and picked up Muttley's leash. 'Well, Wendy, I'm game. We'll give it a try. And when it's all over, we'll have ourselves a merry little Christmas. Or we'll be crazed and blubbering and on really heavy meds.'

*   *   *

I sent an email—with all the addresses showing, so they'd know it was collective undertaking. I wrote with a lot of exclamation points, beginning with 'Hello All! And Merry Christmas!' I went on: *Colin and I have a wonderful new plan for this Christmas that we cannot wait to share with you! Anyone who has*

175

pencilled in a date for Christmas with us this year, it's off! Yes, all invitations already issued are now invalid! None of that will be happening. Instead, Colin and I have decided to celebrate a family Christmas with a big party! Yes, you're all invited to come to our house on the afternoon of December 18th! We're so looking forward to seeing ALL of you Sunday, December 18th. No gifts, just bring your own sweet smiling selves. Merry Christmas! See you on the 18th!'

Results, responses were almost instantaneous.

Predictably, my mom wrote back an enthusiastic 'What a good idea! One afternoon! Then they're gone!' Zappa wrote: 'You've finally lost your mind, I see. Have you been hanging out with the Weedeater? I'll come early and help set up.'

Viv's email insisted my father had elevated blood pressure, and was under doctor's orders to stay clear of stress. Seeing Annie would stress him. If I cared about my father's health, I would not subject him to a huge party which would tax him. In my newly exclaiming style, I wrote something to the effect of: Tell dad we'll have an oxygen tent where he can go whenever he needs to!

The rest of them all weighed in, too, with bits of family gossip and the usual untidy undercurrents. Did I know that Sherri had a spat with Ted last summer? A major spat and they hadn't spoken since? Did I know that

176

Barbara's boyfriend, the gourmet Kirk, liked to drink while he cooked, and had a teentsy little alcohol problem getting worse by the day? Did I know Uncle Roger's politics wouldn't allow him to be in the same football stadium with Barbara? Hal zapped me back a note saying the 18th wasn't good; he didn't pick up his little girl till the 21st and his girlfriend wasn't off till the 22nd. Christmas Eve suited them better. And Big Shot Ted's assistant called and said he would have to reschedule; he was due to be in Palm Springs on the 18th.

I replied to all of these caveats, quibbles, and pettifogging whines with basically the same upbeat reply to all: None of this mattered. Come to the family holiday party on Sunday the 18th or nothing. There won't be any other Christmas gathering here. Colin and I and the kids were leaving after that. Four tickets to Have Yourself a Merry Little Christmas.

And, of course, not all of them came. They had this reason and that. I sprayed myself with Guilt Repellant and said, 'Well, that's very disappointing_____[fill in the name]. I guess we'll just see you next year!'

*   *   *

We chose a Christmas tree that wouldn't absorb the whole room, and put the Viennese angel at the top. We decorated the livingroom and family room and bathrooms with swags of greens, with candles and sprigs of holly, but no mistletoe. Colin and I weren't going to oblige anyone to kiss and make up. However, everyone would be in fairly close quarters; the house isn't that big to begin with. I rented long tables and lots of metal folding chairs and set them all up in the dining room, the family room, in the livingroom, and extra chairs in the kitchen. I rented a huge punch bowl with an ornate silver ladle. We got a good deal on a few cases of wine, some red, some white; we set out tubs of ice with cold pop and juices and sparkling cider and cold beer in the family room. The caterers sent a young woman wearing crisp black and white to serve drinks, and look after all that. I forewarned her about Sherri's troubled son, not mentioning his DUI's, only that anyone with an iPod glued to his ear was absolutely forbidden alcohol The caterer and I conferred on a varied menu that included meat, fish, shellfish, vegetables, salads, rolls, and five different desserts including a pumpkin cheesecake that was divine. We put nonstop Christmas music on the stereo. There were party-favor gifts for all the little kids, Santa hats with little toys in them. And for each couple to take home there was a small poinsettia in red foil with green bows, some twenty of them encircling the base of the tree. Muttley went over the neighbor's. And then, what the hell, we invited a lot of the neighbors and their kids, figuring that they could help dilute the family stew.

Mom and Zappa and Eric came early to help. The five of us cracked a bottle of white wine, and had a small, quick toast to one another and to a Merry Christmas. I felt a sort of unfamiliar rumbling in my heart. Could it be that this was the holiday season, and I was actually happy?

Alexandra tugged on my elbow. 'Can I wear my angel costume from Halloween?'

'Of course,' I said.

Alexandra decided that she must also have a wand, and as the guests appeared, she tapped their backs and shoulders and hearts, I would think, as she turned them into frogs and reindeer and Santa's elves.

December afternoons are short, dark and dreary in Seattle, so we made sure everything was well-lit and welcoming. Colin and I made a pact to talk to everyone there. As I wandered the crowded rooms filled with bubble and boil, steps and exes, neighbors and in-laws, vegans and weedeaters, I reflected that many of these people had not been in the same room since our wedding ten years ago. Ten years is a long time. And though not everyone was full of ho ho ho, no one truly disappointed me. For the most part, those people who were not cordial, were at least careful, not including Uncle Roger whom my mother took as her special Zen mission. Dad did not need an oxygen tent, though he looked distracted and uncomfortable as Viv, oddly living up to her vivacious name, introduced herself around the room as Mike's wife. So as not to be confused with Annie, no doubt. Actually, Dad and Viv looked happier than I had seen them in years. The thought crossed my mind that they might actually be relieved to spared a boisterous Christmas with the seven year old Alexandra, and the toddler Zach who was sweet, but often stinky, and always sticky-fingered.

Barbara dubiously nibbled a catered chicken wing and Kirk drank the wine with a pained look on his face, but he drank it nonetheless. The Veganissima confined herself to those few foods that her purity allowed, and the Weedeater brought a new girlfriend with rings in her nose and ears; she wore a turban, but at least she wasn't stoned.

Assorted teenagers who had come with their parents or parents' partners, sulked, or plugged their ears with iPods, their heads bobbing to intense rhythms only they could hear. Sherri's troubled son played with his Game Boy. What did I care? I talked to him too.

I turned and bumped into Gordon who had just been tapped with Alexandra's magic wand.

'Are you a fairy, Button?' he asked. 'I mean, Alexandra.'

'Of course not! I am the Vienna angel from the Christmas tree whose come down for the

180

party.'

The actual angel atop the tree, the bright-winged ornament, watched the party, the with unblinking eyes. Angels we have seen on high. I imagined the room from her perspective as she looked down upon us. We must all have very much seemed the old family stew, bobbing bubbling, the old human hodgepodge—our lives connected by accident, by marriage, by mistakes, or moments of glory—making merry, seasoned with same old tears and laughter that connect all of us to our intertwined pasts, and to our children's future when these Christmas presents will have become the past, a gift just the same.

UNFORSEEN CIRCUMSTANCES

Jacket buttoned over the Holy Names uniform, lunch bag in hand, resigned, Jig awaited only her grandmother's emergence from the upstairs bathroom. Then she would be on her way to school. Two hours late. She read the note her grandmother had written for her. *Dear Holy Names–Plz. Xcuse Jig from the first three periods of class due to unforeseen circumstances. Yrs., Evaleen Dermott.* If pressed, if some office harpy put her beady little eyes to Jig's and demanded more detail, asked exactly what kind of unforeseen circumstances? Jig had learned long ago to answer: 'I am not at liberty to say.' This line, delivered properly, always shut them up. The circumstances today were that Jig had overslept and Evaleen had let her. 'You must have needed the sleep, or you would have been up on time,' Evaleen said. 'You went to bed on time.' This was true, but Jig had read, flashlight under the covers till the battery died.

Jig folded the note and slid it in her jacket pocket. She took off the jacket and put it over the back the kitchen chair. Might as well get something done while she waited. While the cat, Juno, watched from the throne of her own chair, Jig flung a load of dirty laundry in the machine, started it and stared in the cyclopsian window where it sloshed and gurgled. Sometimes Jig pretended the washer was her own crystal ball and that she could read the future in the soap bubbles kaleidoscoping across her vision. Evaleen said the old machine surely had some kind of magic; she'd bought it second hand in '57 and it had never failed her since. There had been a new fridge twenty years ago, and the other appliances were all sturdy and second hand, crowded together, companionably close in the kitchen where they hummed, chugged, and occasionally groaned.

Jig heard the toilet flush upstairs and the pipes rattle, and the hot water heater in the kitchen corner burped to life. She put more soap and hot water in the kitchen sink, effectively masking the breakfast dishes. Then she sat at the gray Formica table, scuffing her toes on the beige linoleum. She was twelve, slight of build, wary, bookish and bespectacled, diminished at school, dwarfed by the strapping Holy Names girls who roamed the halls in happy packs, sporting their athletic sweaters. Jig Dermott was a sort of small social smudge, and she seemed to many, certainly to her mother, Alicia, irretrievably odd. Alicia had left home at eighteen to be an actress, returned the following year just long enough to have her baby girl, to see her christened Angela Dermott before she returned to LA. When Alicia next saw Angela, everyone was calling her Jig because even when she walked, she seemed to be dancing a little jig. Now Alicia had a steady role on a daytime drama, *Kings Road*, and she faithfully sent money, including Jig's tuition for Holy Names.

A knock sounded at the back door, and Jig opened the door to find Katie McMichaels, slouching with the weight of the toddler on her hip, drenched, and barely sheltered from the sluicing rain. Jig let her in.

Everyone came to their back door because the front steps were moist and uncertain, in need of fixing up. Jig and her grandmother lived on Australia Avenue, in a neighborhood, collectively known as Empire Projects that had been built in the Depression. It still seemed depressed, despite the streets named for exotic and far distant lands. The tracks were not far distant and the trains sometimes rattled windows in their panes and the whistles sounded lonesome in the night. The people who lived in Empire Projects were still solidly working class, mostly very young families or very old people who, like Evaleen, had come here in their youth, and never evinced the energy to leave.

'I need to see your grandmother,' said Katie, a pinched young woman with lank fair hair, sleepless eyes. 'I need her help.'

'Are you in trouble?' asked Jig.

'I just need some help,' Katie maintained. 'I'm not in trouble.'

'Hmmm,' said Jig, 'unforseen

184

circumstances.'

'What-ever,' said Katie, thrusting the baby into Jig's arms so she could take off her jacket.

Outwardly somber, Jig was inwardly joyed. One of Evaleen's house rules was that you couldn't leave, not the house, not even the room, in the midst of someone's telling their troubles. It distracted them, Evaleen explained, and made people feel as if their afflictions were tawdry, uninteresting. Many were. But for Jig, even Katie's McMichaels' troubles, were preferable to Ms. Richards' seventh grade social studies.

'I'm not babysitting,' Jig declared outright as Katie took the baby's jacket off. He was about two, a placid boy who always wore a dirty bib. Lots of the mothers who came here seeking Evaleen's help thought they could have babysitting thrown in for free. Jig refused to be a low rent nanny. She thought of herself as a sort of apprentice, as if she were a nurse, and Evaleen the doctor. 'You'll have to look after little Mick yourself.'

'His name's not little Mick,' snapped Katie with an unusual show of spirit. ' It's Mackenzie. If you call him little Mick again, I'll call you Angela. That is your real name isn't it?'

Jig, who did not admit to Angela, gave the baby back with more emphasis than absolutely necessary.

Katie McMichaels—maybe twenty-three,

married for five years, her husband a bully, her daughter in kindergarten, her son listless—put the baby on the floor, and sat at the gray table nibbling on her fingernails and running her finger under her nose. Tears behind her and tears ahead, that much was clear to Jig. She got a roll of toilet paper and put it on the table. The cat, Juno looked up from her own kitchen chair, yawned and went back to sleep. The confessions of the distraught were of scant interest to Juno. She was not a goddess for nothing. Evaleen emerged into the kitchen like a physical force, vividly displacing the very air, her long gray braid swinging behind her. At the sight of her, Katie burst into sobs, and said she didn't know how things had ever got this bad.

Jig's grandmother was a woman of some girth, well carried, her hair worn in a single, stout gray braid. She had a high forehead and straight nose and a keen sense of smell. She could sniff out fraud, weakness, trouble better than anyone. She had one brown eye and one blue eye, and they looked in different directions. The brown eye had a perpetual squint, and this gave her a sort of piercing and intense vision. Her other eye, the blue eye wandered, gazing at horizons ordinary people could not see. The combination could be very disconcerting, but in the face of unforeseen circumstances Evaleen Dermott was the person to whom everyone turned.

When people came to her, Evaleen created little paper boats to float them away from their troubles. A rift in the family? Evaleen would write you a letter of apology or grievance. A job unjustly lost? She'd write a letter of denial or protest. A character reference for juvenile court? She would craft a letter in which the sender could acknowledge the boy's wrongdoing, but insist at the same time that he was wayward, not wicked. A threat from the landlord? Evaleen invented the Family Attorney, once a figment, now a fixture. (*I have it on the authority of my family attorney that my rights have been breached......*) Evaleen was known all over Empire Projects and beyond as a sort of Noah who could write for you an ark of words. If Evaleen's words could not rescue you, at least she put on paper the phrases and thoughts you could never concoct for yourself.

The baby fussed and Katie took him on her lap, pulled a lint-crusted binkie from her pocket and thrust it between his moist lips. His eyes went round with pleasure. From her purse Katie took a dunning letter and pushed it across the table to Evaleen. The dunning notice threatened legal action against Katie if she did not pay the DVD Depot the $458 in late fees that she owed. She had two weeks. She said again, she didn't know how things had got this bad. 'Mick will kill me if he finds out I owe that much.'

Evaleen, with a complicit look to Jig, let silence be her reply. There would be no syrupy *there there* from Evaleen Dermott, no pious exclamations of sympathy. Evaleen never stooped to gooey phrases. Mick would not kill Katie. But Katie had more reason to fear him than to love him. Everyone knew that. It was fear of Mick, as much as the whopping $458, that had brought Katie here and they all knew it, probably even the baby.

Evaleen lifted Juno into her lap, put on her specs and read the dunning notice over and over, like it was full of holy names. Jig, who knew her role in these matters, put the kettle on the electric stove, poured hot water into the teapot, put the thick mugs on the table. She walked to a small desk behind the door. The kitchen was always in a state of cheerful clutter, but this desk was pristine. Here the computer and printer sat shrouded under a floral sheet to protect them from grease and steam. Jig removed the sheet, turned on the machine and the printer (affectionately known as Camille because it only coughed out the pages in spasms). She folded the sheet and put it on the Spartan wooden chair for a cushion.

With the computer's comforting hum, its audible shallow breaths, Katie managed a smile. Evaleen would make things all right.

Evaleen's gifts, like Second Sight or ESP or playing the piano, were augmented by experience, culled from the forty years she had worked as a court reporter. Day after day—verbatim, making no judgments—she took down the words of the weak, the criminal, the corrupt, the unwashed and the unsung, the victim, the perpetrator, the contrite and the sullen. Even now, old as she was, Evaleen could type as fast as she could speak. She used her gifts on behalf of any old body who asked her. Sometimes, in return, people brought little presents with them, or later sent over meals, home-made bread, or hand-knitted afghans useful for covering up the threadbare living room furniture. The calico skirt around the kitchen sink had been replaced last year with beautiful cabinets, a present to Evaleen from a carpenter over on Kenya Street after Evaleen had repeatedly written, competent, well-argued letters to immigration on behalf of his son-in-law whose visa troubles were finally settled in his favor. Katie's own grandmother lived nearby, on Bombay Avenue, and had first brought Katie to Evaleen with a disputed about a security deposit after Katie and her husband moved from an apartment. Katie's grandmother always acknowledged Evaleen's help with crocheted doilies. They had settled over the livingroom like snowflakes.

'They're bitches, hounding me,' sulked Katie, 'hounding me. I don't know why they're so mad. I took the DVDs back. I returned them. To tell the truth . . .'

The kettle whistled and Jig filled up the

189

teapot, then sat with her elbows on the table. Evaleen, with Juno in her lap, listened like the judges she had watched all those years of being a court reporter, nodding with a judge's gravity and unflagging interest as the dull truth of Katie's situation slowly emerged.

The truth was simple, but Katie told it full of justifications. Wadding the toilet paper into little balls, her thin nose growing pink with emotion, Katie rattled on, how she'd rented maybe a dozen DVDs that weekend when her husband went hunting with his buddies and took the car so she was all alone. Her old friends? Hah. Where were they? Dating. Working. Shopping. No one wanted to be with Katie and the baby and her five year old daughter. No one had time for Katie. So she had rented a dozen DVDs, and yes, some of them were new releases and yes, well she had given DVD Depot a false phone number, but not on purpose. That's what Mick always said you should do. Tell the bastards nothing. But of course DVD Depot had her drivers license number. 'You just know that's how they'd traced me down, even though I returned the DVDs. They're being so mean and threatening me with—'

'When?' asked Evaleen, at last. Her hands splayed across the dunning letter like she was reading Braille, fretting particularly the signature at the bottom.

'When what?'

190

'When did you return the DVDs and when did you check them out?'

Katie sagged and played with Mackenzie's curls. 'I took them out in November. Hunting season. I returned them in March.'

'It's December now,' said Jig. 'Have they written you about the late fees before this?'

'Yes, but they didn't threaten, see? Now, they say they'll garnish Mick's wages. He'll kill me.'

Evaleen pondered this in a silence, the only sound the baby and his binkie.

Jig poured the tea and passed the sugar. Evaleen passed the letter over to Jig who read it gravely. Privately, Jig thought Katie McMichaels a lost cause with a runny nose. Katie was always full of excuses, denials, slumping under her burdens and bad choices. Katie's grandmother had filled Evaleen and Jig in on Mick. His short fuse. Swift to blame and bluster. Mick knew how to use his hands. How to threaten, and glower and instill fear. He hadn't much education, but he knew that. Katie's grandmother detested him, but she stayed out of it, not wanting to make things worse for Katie.

Evaleen rose with the decorum of a duchess and moved toward the old computer. She flexed her fingers and sat down in the wooden chair, and began by asking Jig to whom this letter should be addressed.

Jig said it had been signed by a Mr. Pierce.

191

Juno curled up on the chair still warm from Evaleen's body.

'Such an unfortunate name,' remarked Evaleen, typing away, inquiring further of Jig the correct address and case number and as she entered all this, she said, 'Mr. Pierce, as I see him is about thirty-eight, married, two kids. His collapsing upper lip is concealed by a moustache. He is dyspeptic. He wears wire-rimmed glasses and brown suits and uses too much aftershave to compensate for his perspiring so heavily.'

Mr. Pierce all but materialized in the kitchen, gathered his perspiring self from the steam rising out of the sink where the sticks and spars of dirty dishes stood upraised. Juno squealed and jumped off the chair as though Mr. Pierce had sat down on her.

'Mr. Pierce is outwardly prim, but enjoys his power. He likes pushing people into corners and making them feel his power. He is the same way at home. An unsavory sort of man. I don't think we can appeal to his better nature.'

Oh yes, Jig thought, Mr. Pierce would take, a lot of convincing.

Evaleen rested her fingers lightly on the keys; the computer purred. 'Dear Mr. Pierce– Thank you for your letter. It's true that I kept some few DVDs out past the due date, but you will admit that they were all returned. They were none of them harmed or defaced, or in any way injured. I took them out in November because my husband was going away for a few days, looking for work in Alaska.'

'Alaska?' asked Katie.

'Why not?' Evaleen continued, 'my husband took the car. The children and I would be home all alone till his return. Still, I certainly would have returned these DVDs on time. You'll note my record is good one. I have never before reneged on my responsibilities to DVD Depot. I would not have done so now, but unforeseen circumstances intervened.'

Jig grinned, sipped her tea. She knew that Evaleen's blue eye, the one with distant vision was not on the screen, not on her hands, but seeing possibilities no one else could see.

'Now, Katie,' Evaleen inquired, 'do you have a sister?'

'Sarah. But she won't lend me the—'

'Is she married?'

'She was. She's divorced now. She lives in—'

'Shh,' Jig cautioned Katie, 'you don't want to get between Evaleen and Mr. Pierce.'

No, indeed Katie did not. Mr. Pierce's bristling presence was palpable. Juno stalked round the chair. Mackenzie had binked himself to sleep.

Silently and with her brown, squinting eye, Evaleen consulted a particularly revealing cobweb on the wall festooned between a drawing of Jig's Honor Roll certificate and her last snapshot before braces. After a time Evaleen continued, 'The day after my husband

193

left for Alaska, before these DVDs were due, my sister Sarah called, desperate because her husband of fifteen years, walked out on her and left her with their bills, and two kids.'

'And the ranch,' said Jig. 'The sister lives on a ranch.

Katie frowned, 'There is no ranch.'

Evaleen smiled at Jig, then fastened her gimlet gaze on the young mother, and said, 'There was no Family Attorney when we got your deposit back on that apartment either, was there, Katie? I like the ranch. I can see it now. It's very isolated, up in the foothills, the nearest town is miles away. The ranch has a windmill and a barn and tumbleweeds caught on the barbed wire fences. Sarah, your sister, is lean and lanky, an older, tired version of you, Katie.' Evaleen typed away, and Katie, already an older, tired version of herself, sipped her tea and said nothing.

'The ranch has chickens, some sheep and a few horses,' said Jig.

Evaleen added the animals to the ranch inventory. 'What about a cow?'

'No,' said Jig. 'Not a cow. The cow has to be milked every day, and if Sarah's collapsed, she couldn't do it. I don't know about the boy. Could he do it?'

'What do you know about cows?' Katie demanded.

'I go to school,' retorted Jig.

Evaleen erased the cow. 'We'll keep the

194

chickens, the sheep, and one horse.' She typed away. 'My sister Sarah is not in the best of health, in fact she has chronic illnesses. What does she have, Jig?'

Jig regarded Katie McMichaels chewing on her fingertips. A diet of fingernails would surely give you an ulcer, but such an internal demon didn't really suit these circumstances. An ulcer was interior. Sister Sarah's affliction had to be visible even to Mr. Pierce. 'Asthma. She can't breathe.'

'Yes,' mused Evaleen. 'This is a woman who is being slowly strangled.' She returned to her furious typing and then read out loud, 'When my sister called that afternoon, Mr. Pierce, she was hysterical and she could not breathe. Of course I said I would come to California immediately.'

'How?' asked Jig. 'The husband has the car.'

Evaleen's fingers rippled over the keyboard. 'On the bus.'

'Oh yes. Two kids. On the bus. All the way to California.' Jig could see the journey: the children's faces pressed against the grimy glass. Gum stuck under the seats. The slightly stinky lavatory at the back of the bus. The seats with cracked upholstery and little white tufts sticking to the children's thighs.

'One week before Christmas, I arrived and found my sister paralyzed with asthma, bedridden with a broken heart, the animals untended, the place in shambles, and the children had eaten nothing but dry Cheerios in days.'

'That's overdoing it,' said Katie, 'No one would live like that.'

'Really?' asked Evaleen who happened to know from Katie's grandmother that there were days that Katie McMichaels stayed in bed, unequal to her life, not useful to her children, tearful, sullen, without hope. Immobile. That her children ate nothing but dry Cheerios.

'You owe $458 in late fees for a bunch of DVDs,' Jig reminded Katie, regarding the phantom Mr. Pierce in his chair. 'Why did you wait so long to return them?'

Katie played with Mackenzie's hair. She didn't know why. She just forgot. Then she forgot again. Forgot everything. Then in March she vacuumed the livingroom and found them under the couch.

'Regard for my sister's privacy, her grief,' Evaleen rattled along on the keyboard, 'means that I am not at liberty to divulge her personal, tragic story. But, the situation confronting me, Mr. Pierce, was heartbreaking. I had to nurse her back to health. I had to look after her two children . . .' Evaleen paused; the computer hummed,' . . . ages eight and twelve, and of course, my own who are only seven and five. My sister's husband had not only deserted them, he'd cleaned out the bank account, leaving her with very little money, and hardly

196

any food in the house. I gazed around me at the wreck of my sister's life and health. The children, the ranch, the animals.'

'Coyotes,' suggested Jig. 'Katie should battle coyotes too.'

'What would I do with a coyote?' Katie asked.

Evaleen's blue eye roamed over to Jig and she smiled. 'The morning after I arrived, I found the carcass of one of the sheep there in the barnyard, and loose feathers where the chickens had put up a fight. It was not a pretty sight, Mr. Pierce, but I cleaned it up. What was left of the carcass, I put in the back of the pickup and dumped it far from the ranch. The coyotes come out of the foothills at night, and I had to protect the other animals.'

'Snow,' said Jig. 'There are mountains in the distance, and it's December, and there's snow.'

'There was a stove in the kitchen, but her only other heat was a woodstove in the livingroom where my sister lay on the couch, unable to breathe, unable to move. The wood for the stove was stack outside, but not chopped. I chopped up the logs and sent the children to round up the animals, and shelter them for the night, safe in the barn. I had the younger ones collect the eggs. No one had collected eggs since my sister's collapse. We ate eggs that night, and the next day I took my sister's truck into town.'

' A long ways,' said Jig, 'the ranch is far

197

from town.

Evaleen backed up and re-wrote, '. . . my sister's truck ten miles into town. No one knew me there, but they recognized the truck, and they guessed what had happened. My sister's husband is a bastard and bullies his wife and kids all the time. That he would desert them was no surprise. The grocery store clerk threw in a few extra loaves of day old bread for the kids. I looked out the plate glass window and saw a last few Christmas trees. That's when I realized there was no Christmas tree at my sister's house, no presents for the children either. The clerk told me to choose a tree, and take it. These last trees were poor specimens, lop-sided or with bald patches. I chose one and I threw it and the groceries into the back of the pickup and made I made some other quick stops in town for supplies and trinkets. I got back up to the ranch before dusk. The four kids were waiting for me, and when they saw the scraggly tree, their eyes lit. I told them it would be a fine Christmas, and we'd decorate the tree after we ate. We had a real meal that night, my specialty, Chili Pie. The kids ate like champions. My sister nibbled, then went into the bathroom to cry, then back to the couch. We could hear her rasping breath. My sister's eldest, Tommy and I shoveled manure and fed the sheep and horses. We cracked the ice on the water trough while the little ones shooed the animals inside the barn . . . I discovered strength I did not know I had.' Evaleen looked up, pleased, Jig nodded.

Katie played with McKenzie's curls while he binked.

'We got the lop sided tree standing up in the corner and the children decorated it. My sister did not move. She lay wrapped in a blanket, waiting by the phone, hoping that her worthless husband would call, waiting for his permission to breathe, even his permission to exist, though he is cruel and thankless. She should have got rid of him years ago. I said so. Why do you want him back, I asked her. If you can't breathe, why do you want him back?'

Evaleen blew on her fingers and rubbed her hands. She suffered from incipient arthritis. She glanced from Katie to Jig.

'My sister was too defeated to answer,' offered Jig. 'She could see no path in front of her, and the past was too painful.'

Evaleen typed that, adding, 'All that Christmas season, we, the four children and I, worked hard to keep the place running. We looked after each other. I cut out patterns from the materials I'd bought in town. I showed the older ones how to sew the sides up and the younger ones stuffed the little rag dolls. I showed them how to sew on buttons for eyes, all the while watching my silent sister. All that season, we were exhausted, but fulfilled and enjoyed a kind of happiness that comes from working hard and caring for others. Christmas Eve I cooked a turkey, stuffed with stale bread, rice and corn. I baked biscuits and a couple of cakes with all the eggs we had. I had apples for applesauce and I told my sister she must come in the kitchen and peel. She crawled off the couch and into the kitchen. She asked if I thought her husband would call on Christmas Day. I said no, but you're getting dressed for Christmas. You're not going to lie there any longer, and wait for his permission to live. And on Christmas Day, she did get up and get dressed, and the children all told her how pretty she looked. She came to the table. Her breathing was less labored when she was upright. Slowly, in that week between Christmas and New Year's, Sister Sarah emerged from her coil of grief and doubt.'

Jig and Evaleen regarded Katie McMichaels. They tried to imagine her as a woman who, on top of the ordinary obligations of life, could have nursed the sick, chopped wood, cleaned up after a marauding coyote, made certain that four children had gifts for Christmas, could have stuffed a Christmas turkey, made biscuits and a couple of cakes. Katie, with her slumped shoulders and tired mouth, did not inspire confidence.

Evaleen frowned, re-reading her letter. 'For Mr. Pierce, we'll keep it simple.' She set to editing, slashing words, phrases.

But Jig took off her glasses, cleaned them,

pictured Katie, axe in hand, chopping wood, bringing it in, feeding the fire as her thin Sister Sarah, asthmatic breath rasping, lay on the couch. Katie tucked a warm blanket around Sarah's knees and went outside with the four children. The cold, high desert wind whipped at their short hair as Katie directed the kids to collect the eggs and feed the chickens. The hens scattered before her, squawking as Katie shoveled the horse manure into a heap. Katie rolled a hay bale into the yard for the horses, and refreshed the trough, and made certain that the spigots were insulated against the freezing cold. She and the children secured the animals every night. The short winter dusk descended and the snow began to fall. In the hills the hungry coyotes called as Katie hurried the children into the warm house. Katie wore heavy man's boots and thick leather gloves, and her stride was not the defeated slouch of a woman who had married badly and too young, but someone with the confidence of the capable. By the time she got back inside, Katie's face was pink with exertion and her hands rough with cold and her eyes bright with hope. In doing this work, proving herself against unforeseen circumstances, trying circumstances, Katie McMichaels knew the peace of work well done and rewards well earned. Katie would herself be strong enough to go back to Mick and tell him to quit his bullying, his pushing and shoving and pummeling, his blaming her. To tell Mick she would not any longer absorb his anger against a world that failed to notice what a marvelous specimen of manhood he was. To tell Mick his choices were simple. Be a good husband and father, or live alone.

'What about the DVDs?' said Katie. 'Pierce'll want to know why I didn't return them.'

'We just told him why,' said Jig. 'Weren't you listening? Didn't you hear anything at all?'

Evaleen sighed, typed some more and then read aloud. 'I stayed at the ranch, helping my sister until spring. March. By which time she had recovered herself. This is why I did not return the DVDs in November. When, in March, I returned from my sister's ranch, I realized how derelict I had been, and I promptly brought them back.'

'You think it'll work? You think he'll believe me?' asked Katie.

Evaleen turned back to the computer, erased the last sentence and replaced it with 'By March I could hardly remember the woman I was when I rented them. That fearful, weak, immobile woman had vanished and I write now, taking full responsibility for my actions, or rather, for my lack of action. I ask, Mr. Pierce, that you recognize the extreme and unforeseen circumstances that I have labored under. The DVDs are returned. The $458 late fee presents a terrible hardship as my husband had not found work in Alaska. But neither has he come home.'

'I wish that was true, I wish he wouldn't come home,' murmured Katie. 'Mick treats the dog better than he treats me. Even if the dog gets kicked now and then, the dog gets a pat on the head sometimes. Mick only notices me if dinner isn't on the table, or if there isn't enough beer in the fridge, or if the kids are noisy, or if he's horny.' She slumped over the baby, her lank hair falling forward. The Katie they had imagined had vanished, and the woman before them seemed small and scant and paltry, unworthy of the eloquence waxed on her behalf. She asked Evaleen to add something to the letter about how she didn't have any money

'You've missed the point!' replied Evaleen. 'A woman with that kind of courage you have just demonstrated would not conclude in such a sniveling fashion. We will end with: Suffice it to say, Mr Pierce, I will reward your understanding and never again tax DVD Depot's goodwill.' Evaleen hit the print button. Camille coughed out the pages in halting little spasms.

When the letter was finished printing, Evaleen proofed it, squinting critically with her brown eye, glancing with her blue eye at the phantom Mr. Pierce. But he had dwindled, into the gray Formica chair, drooped, dripped, vanished into the beige linoleum. 'Pierce will cut the late fee in half even if he doesn't forgive it altogether,' declared Evaleen, 'You will get a part time job and pay him back.'

'Maybe he'll give you a part time job at DVD Depot,' offered Jig.

'But what'll I tell Mick?'

'Did you tell Mick that you owed this much money?'

'Of course not!'

'Then don't tell him this either. Find a part-time job,' counseled Evaleen, nodding toward Jig to find an envelope and a stamp. 'It will be good for you. Good to get out of the house, Katie. Good to get away from Mick for a while.'

'But what can I do?'

'You don't know until you look. Find some possibilities and come back and we'll write you a resume and some reference letters.'

'What about Mackenzie and my daughter?'

'If you ask your grandmother, if you tell your grandmother you want to earn your own money and get a little independence, get away from Mick, she'll look after your children. I think you can count on that.'

Jig marveled at Evaleen's methods: carefully constructing not what was, but what could be. People brought Evaleen their follies, their tawdry troubles, their wayward husbands and errant sons, their quarreling sisters, their insurance claims and forfeited deposits, their unpaid bills and ancient cars fixed by

204

unscrupulous mechanics, and Evaleen gave them the language and the courage and the confidence to right their wrongs and smooth their tempests.

'Do you think this will work?' asked Katie.

'The letter? Of course. I just told you what Pierce will do. The rest of it, well, that can work too. You're young. You have—'

'I don't feel young.'

'You don't feel anything at all. You're afraid to feel. It's living with Mick that's done this to you. But in fact, you are young, you are pretty. Don't squander all that. Take some steps. You have the strength. Look what you did for Sarah.'

'But that's a lie.'

On Evaleen's behalf, Jig stiffened, as she addressed the envelope to Mr. Pierce.

'I don't write lies,' said Evaleen. 'I write as much what could happen as what has. What actually does happen, well, Katie, that's up to you, isn't it?'

'I suppose so.' Katie McMichaels threw the original dunning letter in the trash. The baby woke when she stood. His back arched, he yawned, smacked his lips and snuffled; his binky fell to the floor. Jig picked it up and washed it off. Katie put the bawling baby on the chair, slid her arms into her jacket and took her stamped envelope from Jig, put it in her the pocket, and thanked Evaleen on her way out the door.

Evaleen lowered her bones into a chair, pulled Juno on her lap, closed her eyes, and put her feet up on the chair, lately graced by the phantom Mr. Pierce. Jig dawdled. She busied herself at the sink full of dirty dishes, letting the old water gurgle down the drain and adding fresh hot water, more soap. She was elbow deep in bubbles and enveloped in a cloud of steam that wafted over her glasses, obscuring her vision.

Presently Evaleen's roaming blue eye fastened on the kitchen clock. 'Get your jacket. We're off to Holy Names.' She rose and took the keys from the hook by the door.

' I don't want to go. Haven't I learned more here this morning than Ms. Richards could ever teach me in social studies?'

'That may be, but it doesn't count. What Ms. Richards teaches you, that counts.'

Jig did not believe this, but she did not protest. She put on her jacket and picked up her lunch, and put her social studies book in her backpack. Social studies were predictable, neat little chunks processed into chapters, and laid out in uninspired text, passing for facts. It might count, but it didn't finally matter. What mattered is that between Christmas and New Year's you might bridge that chasm between what is and what might be, that life's unforseen circumstances might yield unexpected rewards.

DAYTIME DRAMAS

The bench at the top of the stairs was much scarred, and pocked with oblique invitations to unnatural acts. They were oblique because this was a Catholic school, after all. The bench sat in the school secretary's direct line of vision, and just above it was a picture of the Virgin Mary, looking vexed and heavenward, as if she were asking God what could be done with the misbehaving students for whom this bench was reserved. Jig, slumped there alone, her heavy jacket over her arm. The hall was unnaturally quiet. School was over, and ordinarily Jig would be riding the city bus home. She liked riding the city bus. She felt fine and independent. But now she waited for her grandmother. The school secretary had called Evaleen and told her Jig was in trouble. Evaleen said she would be there directly.

But Jig knew that even if Evaleen hustled right out of the house, and if the orange Toyota started right up, and if she hit every green light all the way across town, (Jig's neighborhood was far from Holy Names) there would a wait. The principal's office was three flights up and there was no elevator. Evaleen Dermott would never show up breathless and at a disadvantage; she would take her time up the stairs, stopping at the landings. One of

Evaleen's precepts was that you must never look winded or weak, or you got shown the consideration that the fox showed the hare.

Even so, when Evaleen finally appeared at the top of the stairs, she was a bit flushed. She wore a red rain poncho over thick sweaters and Wellington boots instead of her usual wools sock and sandals. She lowered herself to the bench with some weariness, and regarded Jig with her brown eye.

The school secretary from her vantage point saw Evaleen and stepped into the hall declaring that the principal was ready to see her.

'Not so fast,' Evaleen replied. 'Give us a minute.' And the secretary did.

'There was a little trouble. Nothing really,' Jig volunteered.

In forty years as a court reporter Evaleen Dermott had seen the worst of humanity, some in iron shackles, some in business suits. Though she was retired, she had acquired from her line of work a certain judicious eloquence and the odd turn of phrase. 'Are you innocent?'

'Not exactly.'

'I guessed as much. The knuckles on your right hand are scraped and bloody.'

'They say I picked on a fifth grade boy, but I didn't. I got into a fight with him, but I didn't pick on him. He was bullying a little kid, a second grader, pushing him round the yard, and laughing at him, calling him names because his ears stick out and his English isn't very good.'

'The Duty didn't see this?'

'No. But I saw it. So I told him to lay off the little kid, and he dared me.'

'To?'

'He said I'd have to punch him first. So I did. I punched a good one in the nose, but he got up and hit me back. There was a scuffle. I wouldn't call it a fight.

'Blood?'

'His. Like I said, I got him good in the nose.'

'Looks to me like you're alone here. Didn't he get into trouble?'

'I'm a seventh grade girl. He's a fifth grade boy. The Duty sent me up here because he was so much younger. But he wasn't smaller, Evaleen. Just younger. He was my own size.'

Jig was small for twelve, nearly thirteen. She wore round spectacles over her blue eyes, and she still had braces.

'So why am I here? Why doesn't the principal just settle this with you?'

Jig sighed. 'They want me apologize to him, and I won't do it. They say if I don't apologize, well, that's why you're here.'

The secretary opened the door, her prim lips pursed over a wordless *Now*.

'Should Jig come too?'

'No. Jig should wait here. The principal would like to discuss the incident with you.'

'Very well.' From underneath her poncho Evaleen drew a postcard and handed it to Jig. 'This came for you today. It's from your mother. She's coming.'

'For Christmas?' Jig's pale face lit.

'For Christmas. Her first in four years. I already sent her present to LA. I didn't expect her home.'

Jig looked at the picture. Palm trees and blue skies and small boats bobbing in a safe harbor. A place distant and romantic as Alicia herself. The Coast. The Islands. The Continent. All post cards from Alicia were scenic backdrops for something dramatic and exciting that would happen soon, though out of Jig's vision or knowing. The post card had a Mexican stamp. *Dearest Jig, we are through shooting Kings Road for this season ! Dave and I are taking a little break here, but I am coming to have Christmas with you! Flying in Sunday afternoon the 21st. Will take cab. C U Soon!! XXOO! and love, Alicia St. Clair.*

The signature was gorgeous, but Jig did not remember a Dave. A Dan, yes. Then, she thought perhaps she had confused the names and Dan had been Dave all along.

That Jig attended Holy Names was the extent of her Alicia St. Clair's day-to-day involvement in her life. Alicia paid the tuition, for the uniform and supplies, these fees and a monthly check for Evaleen came from Alicia's accountant. Alicia's life had brightened considerably when she landed the role of Shawna Leigh, the capable hospital administrator, a regular on the long-running daytime drama, *King's Road*. Before *Kings Road* Alicia's contributions to Jig's welfare were sporadic. She was near thirty, and despite her good looks and ambitions, she'd had only bit TV parts where the sum total of her lines was: *May I take your order?* The phrase was well rehearsed; she also worked part time as a barista with fairly flexible hours so she could audition. But then came *Kings Road* and Shawna Leigh.

Kings Road, the daytime drama, was full of fascinating people, urbane, wealthy, gorgeous, glamourous, and given to dramatic accidents and illnesses, problems that were often solved in Shawna Leigh's hospital. Love affairs were often started there too. King's Road, the place, had no special geography, though it was clearly near some unnamed wine country and a ski resort. It had no weather to speak of, just enough that the characters' could wear summer or winter clothes; there were no heat waves, and only the one snowstorm when characters were stranded in a mountain cabin.

*   *   *

On Saturday the 20th of December, Jig and Evaleen finished cleaning the house, and put up the small Christmas tree in the same corner where a tree had stood every year since Evaleen had come as the bride of handsome, feckless Desmond Dermott.

On the morning of December 21st Jig put a few sprigs of prickly holly into a vase and took it into Alicia's room. In a house that was otherwise casual and comfortably cluttered, Alicia's room was spare, and in its shabby way, formal. They had forgotten to air it out, and the room was close with a slightly musty smell, the ghosts of dried flowers and ribbons that had gathered dust on the mirror for years. Alicia had left when she was eighteen, but this was still indelibly her room, though there was little beyond two dusty pom poms bedecking the mirror, to testify that she had once been Darla Alice Dermott. Alicia had returned home only once, briefly, for those few months before and after Jig was born. Jig swung the door back and forth many times to create a draft, mingling the air in Alicia's room with the rest of the house.

She smoothed the chenille bedspread and regarded the wallpaper with affection. The original wallpaper, perhaps once a cheery yellow and green and pink, had faded to a sort of gravy color, the green gone mustardy and the pink bleached sallow. Endlessly repeated— even behind the high dresser, the mirror and inside the musty closet—were some two or three idealized Western scenes, all of them set at the base of high, snowy

212

distant mountains. There was a small ranch with a windmill and a barn in the background, chickens in the barnyard, sheep just beyond, and sunflowers in the foreground. A woman hung laundry on a line while nearby a boy played with his dog, and two girls rode a small pony. The figures were indistinct. Smoke plumed from the chimney, and tumbleweeds rocked against the fence. In another scene against the same mountain backdrop, two figures on horseback tore over the hillsides, streaking across a meadow and toward a river, their horses sleek and stretched. Though you could not see the riders' faces, you knew their eyes were intent, looking ahead. In another, a coyote ogled some sheep from afar. Alicia herself had chosen the wallpaper when she was perhaps eight or nine and horse-crazy. For Jig the wallpaper scenes were like a much- loved movie or book, people she knew, a community of friends whose stories could change and grow as Jig changed and grew. She used to tell Evaleen their stories, some billowing from her own imagination, some compounded of Laura Ingalls Wilder novels and other books. In the last few years though, the wallpaper people and their stories had diminished, and Jig wasn't sure if she had outgrown them, or if they had outgrown her. She turned on the lamp by the bed, in case Alicia came home after dark, and left the door open.

Late that afternoon Jig, combed, clean,

wearing just-ironed jeans and a sweater, positioned herself at the livingroom window, the cat, Juno by her side. She parted the lace curtains, anticipating the cab, a gash of yellow in the sepia streets. Cabs were rare on Australia Avenue, and usually meant someone was mortally ill, and their relatives were coming to take charge.

In the Empire Projects, everyone was old, wan, without energy, as though houses and people alike, had quietly agreed to their own forthcoming oblivion. The houses on Australia Avenue were all narrow and set close together with pale tar-paper shingles, narrow windows, two up, two down; the rooms were cramped and poky. They had anemic gardens, small splotches of grass out front, and backyards with low chain-link fences. Some backyards still had the original incinerators, no longer legal, and many had fruit and shade trees. In Empire Projects, only the trees had prospered. Once skinny saplings now towered, their roots gnarled up under the clotheslines in the backyards. In the front yards, their roots rose like knuckles, clenched fists under the sidewalks. In summer their branches provided leafy summer refuge in the for sparrows and starlings; now, in winter they were merely black scratches against a gray sky. Today scabrous patches of snow blotched the landscape, much of it in dirty little piles in the gutters.

At last the cab arrived and Alicia emerged from the backseat, smart boots peeking out from the cuffs of trim wool pants. She wore a hat and a thick scarf, both at a jaunty angle. Alicia waved to Jig and Evaleen who had opened the front door. Jig tore down the short path to the street and into her mother's fragrant embrace, a noisy, public reunion, as much to satisfy the neighbors' curiosity as anything else. Jig knew the neighbors would be jealous. No one had relatives as glamourous as Alicia St. Clair.

'How you've grown!' Alicia cried, whirling Jig at arm's length. 'Such a young lady!' Laughing, she paid the driver who dragged her heavy wheeled bags behind him. He and the bags stopped at the step where Evaleen waited, leaning against the door frame.

Arms wide, Alicia embraced her mother. Evaleen held her close, but her expert sense of smell detected the odor of Alicia's infectious discontent, invisible as her cologne but every bit as heady and present.

'There,' said Alicia, stepping back, smiling as though some distracting bit of lint had been tidied and the effect was pleasing. 'You look fine, Evaleen. You haven't changed!' She looked up and down Australia Avenue, the cars up on blocks, the windows of other houses where unseen eyes flickered behind their yellowing curtains. Here and there Christmas lights were strung around doorframes and

215

plastic Santas stood in small yard. She turned to Jig. 'Nothing's changed, has it?'

'I dunno,' replied Jig kicking herself. Whenever Alicia visited, Jig said inconsequential, stupid things like *I dunno*. This visit would be different, she promised herself. After all, she was nearly thirteen. Pulling the wheeled but defiant suitcases, Jig followed them inside. Alicia never traveled light. *Shoes* was one of her mottos, *Shoes* and *silk lingerie*. Alicia always said these words in such a way as to envelope them in a tissue of significance.

Alicia's gaze took in the Seventies shag carpeting, the musical plaques and pictures still on the walls, the crocheted doilies under family photographs. The threadbare slipcovers over the old chairs, assorted afghans tossed here and there. The couch with its pillows from Expo '86. The stained coffee table with cracked glass. She took off her hat and fluffed her bright, blonde hair, curling and cut in fashionable layers. When she came back to Australia Avenue, Alicia was like a mateless shoe, a single stiletto in a closet full of comfy boots, scuffed slippers and frayed sneakers. She wondered how anyone endured the place. She wondered how she would endure it till December 26th. 'Nothing ever changes,' she said.

'Everything changes,' said Evaleen. 'Nothing is static. If you're not growing and

216

expanding, then you're dying. Nothing stays the same. I've always said that.'

'You always have!' Alicia's laughter sparkled like a roll of foil falling to the floor. 'That has stayed the same!'

Alicia made a fuss over the tree glowing in the corner, and the dozen present wrapped, be-ribboned. 'I already sent your present to Los Angeles,' said Evaleen. 'I didn't know you'd be coming home.'

'Oh, well, it was rather an spontaneous decision to come back, but I thought, it's been so long since I've had Christmas with you and Jig. I did my Christmas shopping in Mexico, most of it anyway. I still have some shopping to do here. Shall we go shopping, Jig? Won't that be fun?' Alicia made a fuss over Jig's school picture atop the big color TV, as though she had never seen it, though they had sent her a copy. She asked after the television as if it were a family friend; it had been her gift to her mother when she got the role of Shawna Leigh. 'Do you watch *King's Road,* Mom, now that you're retired.

'What else have I got to do?'

'You mean you aren't writing letters for any old body with a sad story and postage stamp?'

'When people need a little help putting their thoughts on paper, well, I can do that.'

'Summer vacations, we watch *Kings Road* together,' Jig chimed in. 'We pull down the blinds and crack pistachios, one o'clock

217

weekday afternoons. Rain or shine.'

Alicia touched Jig's cheek, and smoothed her short, unruly hair. 'When will your braces come off?'

'I dunno.'

'Two more years,' said Evaleen. 'Then she will have a smile for the ages.'

Two heavy suitcases bounced and growled behind Jig, up the narrow staircase to Alicia's old room. Alicia was peering into the mirror, adjusting her contacts: her eyes were as green as Astro-turf. Jig regarded the vase of holly with exaggerated affection. Alicia laughed, bounced on the chenille bedspread and said again that nothing had changed.

Certainly Evaleen's cooking had not changed or improved. Dinner was hash and greens. Or maybe the greens were hashed. Or the hash was just a little bit green. Alicia bravely made her way through it, exclaiming all the while how delicious it was! She cascaded on about the upcoming season, her credits and costuming, catering on the set, about makeup and properties, and Dave (Dave was new) about the producers being such tyrants. The corona of her glamour was the more dazzling here in the florescent light of the kitchen, the gray Formica table and beige linoleum floor. In the corner the computer brooded under faded flowered sheets, like a great idol that might suddenly come to life and demand sacrifices. Alicia sat on the chair that was officially Juno's. Juno tried continually to regain her throne, jumping into Alicia's lap. Juno was not playful. What goddess is? Finally Evaleen snatched her up and put her in the back porch with the boots and jackets on hooks and unceremoniously closed the door. Juno mewed piteously.

'Do you want to know a secret?' Alicia offered. ' Next season I'm going to have a much bigger role on *Kings Road*. Shawna Leigh falls in love with Dr. Pryce.'

'Which doctor is he?' asked Jig. 'They're all so beautiful, we can't tell them apart.'

'He's like the central character! His wife Cynthia dies, and Dr. Pryce is just absolutely grief-stricken. That's when Shawna confesses she's always loved him. Not right away. She waits for his grief to pass. Sort of. The producers love me. Last season they gave Shawna a lot more responsibility, and an ex-husband, and the audience loved me. This season I have a reunion with my younger sister, Chelsea, who married my ex-lover, Alex. Only, that was all before Shawna came to Kings Road. Now, Alex is sick with a brain tumor and Chelsea wants Shawna to forgive her, and let Alex have his operation at the Kings Road hospital. Shawna breaks down and confesses all this to Dr. Pryce. That's how they start.'

'Start what?' asked Jig.

'Start their . . .' Alicia twirled her fork in the

air, '. . . love affair.'

'Isn't Dr. Pryce married?' asked Evaleen.

'Yes, he married Cynthia about two season ago, but then Cynthia got amnesia and she got lost and when they found her, she had go to the psychiatric hospital. Well, next season, she's going to run out in front of a car and get killed. That's the worst thing that can happen to you. To have your character die. When they told Liana Clark that Cynthia was going to die—Liana's the actress—she fell apart. She started crying right on the set. She told them she'd do anything, get AIDS or get pregnant, or anything, just don't kill her off. But there's nothing Liana can do about it. Anyway, Cynthia's death is great for Shawna. A love affair with Dr. Pryce, well that's just about the best thing that can happen to me.'

'Until you get amnesia and walk out in front of a car and Dr. Pryce moves on to someone else,' said Evaleen.

Alicia bravely took another bite of hash and greens.

Jig and Evaleen had all but finished their dinners by the time Alicia had exhausted the excitement of her immediate professional life, and all the plots of the films up that would probably be nominated for Best Picture. 'Tell me about Holy Names,' she said at last.

'I dunno.' Jig and Evaleen had agreed that the fight with the fifth grade boy would not be mentioned. 'I guess Holy Names is fine.'

'Oh, I don't mean the school part. That's important of course, your grades and the like,' she added with a nod to Evaleen, 'But I meant, are you making friends? I wanted you to go to Holy Names so you'd meet better people and have more friends. Nice friends from nice families who live in better neighborhoods. I couldn't bear the thought that you'd go to Empire Elementary or Hoover Junior High like I did. People around here are just, well, they're hopeless. I mean, that really, literally! They have no hope and there's no hope for them. They're old for one thing!'

'That can happen to anyone,' said Evaleen.

'Well, the people who go to Holy Names are much nicer. You'll be glad you go to Holy Names once you start dating. You'll be dating soon.'

'Who would I be dating?' asked Jig, 'The Velveteen Rabbit?'

'Seventh grade is a big change for a girl! You're blooming! Growing! It's all so exciting!'

'Jig is very mature,' said Evaleen. 'And very responsible and very reliable and imaginative.'

'She's developing, physically, into a woman.'

'That happens to everyone. Mature and responsible and reliable, you have to work on.'

Silence followed this, broken only by Juno's protests from the back porch.

With her fork Alicia pushed a bit of hamburger past a crowd of jeering greens to the edge of the plate, daring it to jump. 'Well,

221

Jig should be having fun.'

Jig began to conjugate fun: to have fun, to make fun, to be fun. She wanted to jump up and do a little dance, live up to her odd name, just to prove herself fun. Funner. Funnest. But she grinned and shrugged and said, 'I'm having a lot of fun.'

'Tell me about your friends. You have friends, yes? Lots of them.'

'I dunno.' At Holy Names Jig was easily over-looked, a reader, but not an especially brilliant student, certainly not an athlete, and not aggressive enough to be part of the girl-gaggle cliques. Her old neighborhood friendships had dwindled in the five years she'd been at Holy Names; the local girls had their own rituals and Jig did not attend Hoover Jr. High. She had picked up many of Evaleen's odd mannerisms and turns of phrase, and seemed, even to herself, both older and younger than her years, caught outside the teenage enclosure, but having outgrown the assumptions of childhood. Still, she did not want to disappoint Alicia. 'I have lots of friends. Lucy, Isabelle, Zoe,' she threw out some names of classmates.

'And is there a boy?' Alicia winked. 'And don't try and tell me it's the Velveteen Rabbit!'

'There's no boy.'

'Well, there will be. A girl is never too young to look pretty. Let's go shopping tomorrow and get you some pretty clothes for school. Now, I know what you're going to say, Evaleen, ' Alicia glanced defiantly at her mother, exactly as Shawna Leigh had glanced at the malpractice lawyers besieging the Kings Road hospital, 'You're going to tell me it's Monday and a school day and the answer is no, Jig can't cut school to go shopping, but playing hooky for one day isn't going to turn her into a tatooed dropout. Jig and I need to have some fun. How often do we see each other?'

To this question there was no reply, or at least no one spoke. Sitting between them, Jig felt like a rickety footbridge connecting the two, as though she might collapse under the weight of the old resentments these women carried like stones bulging in their pockets. Jig said, 'I don't wear pretty clothes to school, Alicia. I have to wear a uniform at Holy Names. And I don't have to play hooky tomorrow. It's Christmas vacation.'

'Well that's settled! We'll go shopping and get you something really chic. I've always said,' she tossed her blond hair in a show of great spirit, 'with Italian shoes on your feet and silk lingerie next to your skin, you can be equal to anything!'

'You do always say that,' said Jig, and again Alicia's laughter rippled around the kitchen.

'They have such cute fashions now. We'll find you some clothes.'

'Jig is not a doll you dress up and play with

223

and put down,' said Evaleen. Her blue eye seemed fixed upon the nascent future or the kitchen clock, but her brown eye, squinting, rested on Alicia.

'Oh you take everything so seriously! I just want to do something nice for Jig, for my own daughter. Is that so very terrible? I want to see her look pretty.'

'She looks fine.' Evaleen, stacked her empty plate on top of Jig's empty plate.

'Well she looks fine for a boy! Or a kid! But really, she's growing up! It's time she wore something besides a t-shirt and sweater and sneakers and overalls. It's time she had some style.'

'You need to expand your notions of beauty,' said Evaleen who tended to extract bits of irritating wisdom from simple statements, as you might pluck a pearl out of a can of chili.

*   *   *

Charles of the Chez Charles salon at the mall was a young man, coiffed, polished, with hazel eyes and a trim goatee framing his perfect mouth. He had elegant hands. Walk-ins, Charles left to his assistants. But when he saw Alicia come through the door, his station was suddenly open. She explained that the haircut was for Jig. Charles pointed Jig to the chair, and to her everlasting humiliation, asked her if she wanted the booster seat. She declined with what she hoped was a withering sneer.

He whipped the cape over her and picked up his scissors and comb, holding them as a conductor holds the baton. He turned to Alicia, 'What kind of haircut would you like for your little sister?' When she did not immediately reply, he scowled, the furry frame of his goatee around a perfect 'O' of surprise. 'Surely you are sisters, not mother and daughter!'

Alicia flushed and brightened. Brightening was one of the things she did well. She said they were sisters like Shawna and Chelsea on *Kings Road*.

'I knew I recognized you from somewhere! You're Shawna Leigh!' He turned Jig with more respect. 'What kind of haircut do you want?'

'I dunno.'

'Something chic,' said Alicia, fluttering around him as he snipped, offering fashion tips. With her hair newly primped and shorn, Jig surveyed herself in the mirror. She was still slight, bespectacled and with braces, like an insignificant star pulled in Alicia's solar orbit, but now she had style. Her unruly brown hair was layered, and Charles had used the blow dryer, and the curling iron. She smiled at herself in the mirror while Alicia chatted with Charles. Alicia decided she would get a manicure. 'You too, Jig! We'll have manicures

225

together.'

They had tables side by side while Alicia kept both manicurists and Jig enthralled with insider wisdom from *Kings Road*. At one o'clock, as if on cue, the TV high in the corner began with the music for *Kings Road* and everyone in Chez Charles watched spellbound as Shawna and Chelsea had a tearful reunion. They had always been rivals, and had not spoken since Chelsea ran off and married Shawna's lover, Alex. Now, Chelsea tells her that Alex has been diagnosed with a brain tumor. Chelsea and Alex want Shawna's forgiveness. And the money for the operation. And to have the operation at the Kings Road hospital. Then there was a commercial. When they returned, Shawna Leigh told Chelsea, 'I will be there and you will find me. And I will always be there for you. I love you. You mustn't forget that.' The episode ended, and Alicia gratefully accepted the applause of everyone in Chez Charles.

Their nails gleaming, Jig and her mother wandered the crowded mall, while Alicia checked her cell phone messages and carried on brief, enviable conversations. The mall throbbed with shoppers, blinking lights and inescapable Christmas Muzak. People jostled and ignored one another, and seemed to move at the behest of inescapable tides or currents rather than their own volition. Jig's attention was caught by a stall at the end of this aisle,

226

and she gestured to Alicia she'd be right back. Alicia sat down on a nearby bench and continued her conversation.

The stall sold crystal figurines of different shapes and sizes, so beautiful and fragile and brightly colored, the details worked out in glass so finely spun it looked like thread. Across the top were a row of tiny crystal figures suspended on ribbons of different color.

'They catch the light,' said the vendor. 'You hang them in your window and they send rainbows all around the room. They're all made by hand. Hand-blown glass.'

Jig pondered between the crystal palm, the crystal dragonfly, settling finally on a crystal butterfly with blue and yellow-tips on the antennae, and many-faceted wings for maximum color. It was the perfect gift for Alicia: beautiful, its brightness splashing, spilling on anyone who walked across its path. She paid for it, tucked the little box in the pocket of her heavy jacket and raced back to Alicia who just then, snapped her phone shut, and said, 'Dave says hello.'

They loitered in front of stores with crisp, hard-consonant names. They looked in the windows at headless mannequins in impossible poses that suggested what you would look like in these clothes if you had no head and no butt. There were lots of party dresses, and Jig asked if Alicia went to holiday parties.

227

Tons of them! The two lingered in front of the make-up counter at the big department stores. Finally, Alicia looked at the time. She got down to business on Jig's behalf, and marched her into the Juniors department. She moved purposely through the racks, picked up different items, held them up to Jig, frowned and put them back, or piled them in her arms until a salesgirl came to help. 'Put them in a dressing room,' said Alicia. 'We're still looking.' To Jig she said, 'These can be your Christmas presents, can't they? You don't mind if they're not wrapped, do you?'

'I dunno. No. I don't mind.'

'Christmas is really just a shopping spree anyway. Put some lights up, get a tree and a shop till you drop. That's what it's all about.'

'Not at Holy Names it's not.'

'Of course not Holy Names! I'm talking about everyone else. You're bombarded with ads telling what and how and who to buy for, but finally, it's just like what the Kings Road producers did. They found a mindless present that suited everyone, bath towels with the Kings Road logo, and handed them out at the Christmas party. Everyone has a big grin on their face, and everyone agrees to ho ho ho, but really, you'd just rather be screaming somewhere.'

'Where?'

'What?'

'Where would you want to be screaming?'

228

'Really Jig,' said Alicia, steering her into a dressing room, where the clothes she'd chosen lay everywhere and hung off the hooks, 'you ask the stupidest questions. You sound like Evaleen.' When Jig's plain sweater and jeans came off, Alicia gave a little cry of horror. 'What's that?' She pointed squarely at Jig's chest.

'An undershirt.'

'You're nearly thirteen and you're wearing an undershirt!'

'I dunno.'

'Why don't you have bra?'

'Well there really isn't anything to hold up. Yet.'

'Don't you have to change for gym class at Holy Names? Aren't you humiliated to be the only girl still wearing an undershirt?'

'I'm not the only girl,' Jig replied, adding with some chagrin, 'there's one other.'

'Why didn't Evaleen get you a bra?'

'I never asked her for a bra.'

Alicia regarded her sadly. 'Of course you didn't, Jig. You have low expectations. Wait here. I'll be right back.'

Jig sat down among the unworn clothes, their stiff fabrics irritating her skin. She put her glasses back on and stared in the mirror, her reflection bleached in the fluorescent light. She stood and looked from the side. Maybe there was something to hold up. Both sides. Did she have breasts? Did she have low

229

expectations?

They were famished by the time they'd made their purchases. Alicia insisted that Jig wear the new bra and underpants. While the underwear wasn't silk, Jig began to understand something of Alicia's mandate for having silky fabrics against your skin. Underneath her old jeans and sweater, she had a new awareness of her body. She watched Alicia's walk and tried to emulate it. She wondered if Alicia's Italian shoes (which made crisp, emphatic sounds against the pavement) would fit her, and if Italian shoes might actually give you the wherewithal to face challenges. She knew that Evaleen would scoff at the notion that shoes could make a difference, but she began to suspect it was true.

They put their packages in the car. 'Get in,' said Alicia, 'and we'll to Delara's Deli for lunch.'

'What's that?'

'I used to go there all the time in high school. In fact, I had my very first kiss in one those booths.'

Delara's was dark and smokey, and the booth where Alicia had had her first kiss was taken. Delara's too, it seemed, had not changed, save for a few blinking lights draped over the menu, and a reminder that gifts certificates were always available for last minute shoppers. Alicia ordered pastrami sandwiches with two sides of potato salad and extra pickles. Their sandwiches were swiftly made, and they took them back to the booth. Each plate had potato salad in two neat mounds, a green olive on top.

'Exactly like little green nipples,' remarked Alicia, popping the olive between her lush lips. 'Dave and I found this Hungarian place we love. We eat there so often, Dave started calling me Paprika! Don't you think that's sweet?'

'I dunno.'

'Sometimes he just shortens it down to Rika.'

'Well, that's better than being called Pap.' The look on Alicia's face made Jig take a big bite of the pastrami. You couldn't talk with your mouth full. It wasn't polite. You had to listen.

Jig chomped contentedly and got used to her new bra while Alicia nibbled and told stories of Dave. They had met at the gym. He was a line producer on another show. Jig wondered what lines he produced, but did not ask. Dave had two kids, boys about eight and nine, Riley and Bailey and they were coming to LA for Christmas. Alicia had never met them. Jig nodded, sipped her chocolate milk shake, feeling happy, to be sisters, with the equality, camaraderie and shared secrets of sisters. Alicia talked about the *Kings Road* characters and cast members in a low confidential voice, bubbling here and there with laughter. Jig learned of their face lifts, foibles and feuds. Dr. Pryce and Cynthia, for example. Though their characters were madly in love, the two actors detested each other and played cruel tricks on one another that neither could acknowledge. 'Right before their love scene, Dr. Pryce ate a whole garlic salami, and when he took Cynthia in his arms to kiss her, she just about gagged, but she couldn't let anyone guess, and so she had to kiss him, and then when the cameras quit rolling, she stood right there on the set and barfed! Just chucked her cookies right on the set!'

Jig eyed the second half of Alicia's sandwich, left untouched.

'You want it?' Alicia asked. 'Sure. Go ahead. You're right, you better eat up now. There'll be something awful for dinner again tonight. Hard cooked fried eggs on toast. Beans and weenies. Tuna noodle casserole. Does Evaleen still make it with the ground up potato chips on top?' Alicia shuddered.

'Corn flakes.'

'I got her a waffle iron for Christmas. There's nothing you can do to ruin a waffle, and the mix comes in a box. It'll spare us the usual Christmas brunch, peanut butter and bacon sandwiches. And God! Christmas dinner! I hate to think of it.'

'I dunno, it's not so bad.'

'You say that because you don't know any better. Where else have you eaten besides the cafeteria at Holy Names?'

Jig evaded the question. 'We don't have Christmas dinner at home. Not for years. We go across the street, to Mrs. Riasanovsky's.'

'Oh God, do they still live across the street?'

'Not him. He died. But Mrs. Riasanovsky likes to cook, and so we go there. So do some of the other neighbors.'

'Well, anything's better than Evaleen's cooking, even that awful old Russian Jew.'

'They're not Jewish. It's Christmas dinner. She makes these little Russian pancakes.'

'Yes, they're so weird! Don't you just wish you could have turkey and mashed potatoes?'

Jig said I dunno, but she smiled conspiratorially, feeling uneasy, unused to pastrami and disloyal to Evaleen.

To make up for this Jig had a second helping of tuna noodle casserole at dinner while Alicia warbled on about the fun they'd had, and how Charles had thought she and Jig were sisters, and so all day long they were sisters, like Shawna and Chelsea (minus the part about Alex and the brain tumor). She repeated the story of Cynthia, Dr. Pryce and the garlic sausage and laughed, and in demonstrating, stuck her finger down her throat too far and had to bolt for the bathroom.

*   *   *

In the three days before Christmas, Alicia and Jig went to the late matinee three times. It was the only time Alicia turned her cell phone off. The mall multiplex had insufficient ventilation, the air was close and the floor was sticky. The acoustics were inadequate and screaming rockets and warfare from the film in the next theatre thundered through the love scenes on the screen before them. Throughout the pictures, Alicia leaned over and confided to Jig the Secrets of the Stars: who had a drug problem, who was a closet case, who cheated on their wives or husbands, who was on the Way Out. Jig nodded, but she got them all confused with *Kings Road* actors and characters. They all melded in her brain, like the crowds of Christmas shoppers all over the mall.

After the movie, the two of them sat at a food court table with ice cream cones in hand. This afternoon, December 24th, the mall was packed with gray-faced shoppers, restless, bleating children and bored teenagers. Voices echoed and tinny Christmas music blared, giving Jig a headache. She'd never spent so much time at the mall in all her life. Alicia's cell phone rang again, and she had a brief, bright chat with someone, not Dave. Alicia had a special voice for Dave, even a special vocabulary. For everyone else, her voice rippled and the conversation rattled with names that in the last few days had become vaguely familiar to Jig.

She clicked the phone shut and smiled radiantly. 'Bernie has an audition set up for me on January sixth. A feature film. Just think, Jig, you'll be seeing my face up there on the screen, just like the movie we saw today.'

'That'll be great.'

'You can take all your girlfriends, Lucy and . . .'

'Isabelle and Zoe.'

'And tell them Alicia St. Clair is your mother.'

'They always ask me what's it like to have a famous actress for a mother.'

'Well, what do you say?'

'I say it's fun having a mom who is a movie star.'

'Evaleen's always hated the movies. She was dead set against my being an actress. She hates anything that's not solid and sensible as her wool socks and sandals.'

'I don't think she hates the movies. She says if it's daytime drama you want, you only have to go and sit in Superior Court. It's free. Superior Court even sounds like a theatre, doesn't it? Come to the Superior!' Jig threw open her arms and got a laugh from Alicia.

'You think after forty years, she'd be sick of courtrooms.'

'Sometimes on really hot afternoons in summer we go to Superior Court and just watch the trials. Evaleen knows the judges and attorneys and who puts on a good show. It's free,' Jig repeated, 'and it's air-conditioned, and our house isn't.'

Alicia gave a rueful laugh. 'Yes, well I guess that's the courtroom's the place to look for a crime story. Personally, I like love stories.'

'There are some love stories there.'

'Like? How can there be any love stories in burglary, and shoplifting? Drunk driving? Grand theft auto and fraud and forgery? How can criminals and felons and crooks have love stories?'

'I dunno.' Then she remembered Agnes Frazier, the embezzler who lived in Empire Projects. 'You remember Agnes, don't you, Alicia?'

'I do not remember Agnes.'

'She lived over on Alberta Street. Evaleen didn't know Agnes till the trial, but they recognized each other during the trial. I mean, they recognized that they were neighbors. Everyone from Empire Projects who could come to the trial, did.'

'How do you know about Agnes Frazier? That happened when I was in high school.'

'So you do remember her.'

'How could I forget?' Alicia sighed.

'Evaleen told me the whole story. Evaleen said Agnes's public defender had kitty litter for brains. Evaleen took down every word Agnes said. Agnes wouldn't plea bargain. She said she was innocent over and over.'

236

'Is she out of the pen yet?'

'Sure. She comes over sometimes.'

'I might have guessed as much.'

'She only embezzled about a thousand dollars, I mean, it was wrong, of course, but it wasn't like millions.'

'It was pathetic.'

'She could have worked and paid it back, but the judge gave her three years, and a long talking-to before he imposed sentence, just ripping her up one side and down the other how she had betrayed the trust of her employer and all the people who worked there. Evaleen took it all down, but there was no way you could transcribe Agnes's sobs. Agnes would not say she was sorry. She said she had been betrayed too, that her son had betrayed her love, that he was a drug addict. The judge didn't care. He gave her three years. All the money that she embezzled went into her son's veins. Everyone knew it.'

'And no one cared. She was guilty as sin.'

'Yes, but Evaleen said it was a kind of love story, and you had to respect that, even if you condemned the embezzling.'

'Oh God, that's so Evaleen! Listen, Jig. It's not a love story. Agnes was a dupe, a dope, and she deserved what she got. A mother and son cannot be a love story.'

'What about a mother and daughter?'

'Don't be stupid. You need lovers for a love story.'

'You and Ted were lovers. Were you a love story?'

Alicia flinched. She'd been caught off guard. She finished her ice cream and tossed the cone into the trash can, picked up her purse as though she would leave, but Jig put a hand on her arm. Jig knew almost nothing of her father, though she pictured him as handsome, glamourous as Alicia. How could Alicia St. Clair's lover be anything else? Jig asked about Ted Thomas whenever the oblique opportunity presented itself, though Alicia's answers were never satisfying and often confusing. .

Alicia patted her hand, and smiled gently. 'Oh yes. If you like. We were a love story. We loved each other, but it was not to be.'

'Am I a love child?'

'What a silly, old fashioned expression. Who told you that?'

'I read it in a book. It doesn't sound all bad. Love Child,' she savored the expression along with her pistachio ice cream. 'Why don't I ever hear from Ted? Not even a birthday card.'

'I don't know. He isn't interested in anyone but himself. I knew I couldn't change him. I had to move on, to grow up and move on.'

'Do you ever see him?'

'Look, Jig, Ted Thomas is long long gone. He's not an actor. He was nothing to do with my career. You won't ever see him on TV. He doesn't even live in LA anymore.'

238

'Where does he live?'

'I don't know.'

'Last time you were home you said he lived in New York.'

'Well, that's probably right. New York.'

'Do you wish you'd married him?'

'No.' She drew a deep breath. 'Even if we got married, it wouldn't have been like that.'

'Like what?'

'Like what you imagine: Mommy and Daddy and the white picket fence, and all that.'

'I don't imagine that.'

Alicia scoffed. 'All kids imagine that. I imagined that after my father left, even though I knew we'd still be living on Australia Avenue if he had stayed.'

'What was Desmond like? Your father?'

'Who knows? He left home too. Just like I did. He had to get away from the tuna noodle casserole. Who can blame him?' Alicia drew a long breath, and seemed on the verge of saying something important, but instead she laughed, and reached across and tousled Jig's hair. 'Listen, Jig, here's the truth of it. I'm telling you the truth like you were my sister. When I met Ted, I was nineteen, just a kid, too young to be a mother. Ted was about twenty, too young to be a father.'

'Why didn't you name me Jig Thomas?'

'I didn't name you Jig anything! You're Angela. I named you Angela. And then, when

239

I came back to see you, everyone was calling you Jig.'

'I was always jumping up and down. Everyone said I was dancing a little jig. I like Jig.'

'I like Angela. Changing your name was Evaleen's doing.' Rancor laced her voice

'If you didn't like it, you should have come back for me earlier.'

'I'm here now! What has Evaleen been telling you? That just because I got knocked up, I should have stayed on Australia Avenue? Get a job *here?*' She strangled slightly over the very word. 'To spend my life spreading peanut butter on white bread? To join the Empire Mothers' Club?' Alicia gave a little shudder as if they were in the same league with tuna noodle casserole.

'Evaleen doesn't say any such thing. She doesn't criticize.'

'But she judges! Oh, she judges constantly.'

'She was in the courtroom for forty years.'

'Yes, yes yes . . .' Alicia massaged her temples thoughtfully. Then she continued, 'I had my career to think of, Jig. Ted and I were both too young to be parents. We agreed to part, that's all. I came here to have you. He left LA. I haven't seen him in . . .' Alicia did her math, 'thirteen years.'

For the first time Jig pictured Ted Thomas bespectacled, astute, small for his age, easily overlooked like Jig herself. In fact, so

240

insignificant was she, he had overlooked her for thirteen years. Easily replaced. Her ice cream melted, dripped down her wrist and hit the floor in little green teardrops.

'Look, Jig, I've made some mistakes. Who hasn't? But I did the right thing leaving you here. I couldn't look after a baby. I had to look out for myself. I couldn't bring you up. I had to get out of here. From the time I was a kid, I knew I had to get out of here! I loathed Empire Projects and Australia Avenue. It was a fitting name. A poor prison. It was like a prison for me! The people around here, the people who are always coming to Evaleen for something, they're hopeless. They're pathetic. People come to Evaleen, day or night, looking for her advice, always squabbling over disgusting little family quarrels, or overdue rent or some malicious mischief or petty theft or someone caught working without a green card and injured on the job, embezzling small change like Agnes. Sometimes there was a real murder, but it was never an interesting murder, like when Dr. Locket killed Nurse Haines—and then we found out she was pregnant and it wasn't his child, but he thought it was.'

'When did that happen!'

'On *Kings Road*. Oh, Jig, don't you ever get sick of this place?'

Jig, in her grave way, considered this as though they were a real questions and not a

241

plea for understanding, even absolution. She didn't want to sound spiritless, and so she said 'Everyone has to grow up somewhere. Australia Avenue is as good as any other place.

' Don't let her run your life, Jig. You will have to fight her, but don't let her do that to you. She'll make you fulfill her dreams, and not your own.'

'Did she have unfilled dreams?'

'Look at the way she lives! Does anyone *dream* about growing up and living in Empire Projects, a court reporter for forty years?'

Jig had to admit the answer was no.

'Evaleen wanted to be a lawyer,' said Alicia.

'No, really? She never told me that.'

'Well, it's true. Can you imagine anything worse?'

'I'm surprised because Evaleen thinks poorly of lawyers,' replied Jig happy to have stumbled on a subject on which Alicia and Evaleen agreed.

'Follow your own dreams and do what you want! I followed my own dreams and look at me!'

Alicia paused, winded, waiting for Jig to pick up her lines, a promise to Follow Her Dreams No Matter What. But Jig could not do this; neither could she grin or shrug or shuffle. She felt like Agnes Frazier maintaining her innocence in the face of overwhelming guilt

Alicia's cell phone rang and she talked for

ten minutes with Dave. She clicked the phone shut and grinned. 'That was Dave. He says hi.'

'Hi.'

' You want to see his picture?'

'Sure.'

She opened her cell phone and flipped through a dozen pictures, some from Mexico, some not, some where Dave was solid, shirtless and tanned, and some where he held a beer, and some where he stood beside a sleek, black automobile. One where he was naked. 'Oops,' Alicia cried, snapping the phone shut . . . 'Not that one!' She laughed, a warm, confidential laugh, and leaned across the small table. 'You want to know a secret? I might marry Dave. I love him. We're living together now and it's working out really, really well, Jig. Really well.' She beamed. 'I haven't met his kids, but I'm sure I'll like them. Riley and Bailey can be your brothers and Dave can be your dad.'

Riley and Bailey and Dave. They were like characters's names from a soap opera, like Shawna and Chelsea. Jig suddenly understood why Alicia was home for Christmas for the first time in four years. Neither Jig nor the season had brought her back. Riley and Bailey were with Dave, and Alicia had not been invited. A couple of brats Jig had never met, that's who she had to thank for Alicia's being home for Christmas. 'I don't want brothers,' Jig said without stammering or shuffling or grinning. 'I don't want the white picket fence. I don't want

Dave for a dad. Why would I need a dad when I've gone all these years without one? Why would I need anything more than what I have?'

'You are utterly ungrateful,' snapped Alicia, gathering up her purse. 'I don't know why I bother to come back when you don't even care about me one bit.'

Jig followed her silently, chastised, but not repentant. It was like the fracas with the fifth grade boy. She would not say she was sorry.

*   *   *

Snow fell that night. Christmas morning saw Australia Avenue cleanly limned in black and white, the geography of the lives within each house more clearly, crisply demarcated. Jig looked out the kitchen window while she waited for the kettle to boil. The clothesline, the long-unused incinerator stood solemn, erect, more interesting than they really were. The snowfall somehow dignified everything it touched. Even the garbage cans, and the swingset. The low, chain link fence looked delicate, ephemeral. The windows across the way, the curtains framing them like small stages lit up against the gray morning light.

Alicia and Jig had hardly spoken beyond 'pass the peas,' at dinner the night before. Alicia went up to her room on Christmas Eve, and stayed there. Door closed. Jig and Evaleen could hear her upstairs, pacing while she talked on the phone, railing now and then. Jig felt terrible, as though now she too were part of everything wrong with Australia Avenue, in the same category as tuna noodle casserole and Agnes Frazier. Evaleen asked if something had happened at the mall today. Something had, but Jig wasn't certain what. So she just shrugged and mumbled.

The kettle whistled and Jig made the tea. While it steeped, she washed her glasses, and put them back on. She wondered if this Christmas was the coming attractions for being an adult, this awful feeling of being torn, and wrong, no matter what you do. Jig put the pot and three mugs on a tray and carried it into the livingroom where the tree sparkled brightly. Alicia was just coming downstairs. She wore an ecru peignoir, lovely but inadequate to the winter morning. She wrapped herself quickly in a purple and yellow afghan and sank into the one of the chairs. She still looked wounded. Jig poured her tea, and took it to her like an offering, fighting the urge to fling herself on Alicia's lap and say that yes, yes she would follow her dreams no matter what, that all Alicia's choices were wonderful, that she couldn't wait to meet Riley and Bailey and Dave, to have a stepdad and little brothers. But that moment had passed.

'Well, Jig,' said Evaleen, pulling Juno on to her lap, 'why don't you hand out the presents?'

'Give Alicia mine first, will you? She looks

like she needs it.'

Evaleen had bought Alicia wooly slippers like the ones that she and Jig wore. Alicia put them on her feet and said how warm they were. But she sat silently while Jig opened her presents from Evaleen. Everyone, even Juno seemed to radiate static electricity. In addition to the waffle iron, Alicia gave Evaleen a bath towel with the *Kings Road* logo on it, and a sunny ceramic dish from Mexico. Jig opened a Mexican serape in bright colors and a pair of hoop earrings which Jig said she would wear, first thing, when she got her ears pierced.

'And don't forget you have a whole closet full of new clothes, thanks to me.'

'Thank you, Alicia. I love my new clothes. You're right about nice underwear. It really does make you feel good. Here. I hope you like my present.'

'Thanks,' said Alicia, peeling the paper away, revealing a small box. Inside the box was a crystal butterfly suspended on a red ribbon. 'Is this a necklace?'

'No, I mean, it could be, I guess, but you're supposed to hang it up, in a window, see?' Jig took it to the livingroom window, and twirled it around. Rainbows ricocheted around the room. 'You see? It sends the sunshine everywhere. It reminded me of you. You just sort of light things up wherever you go.' There, Jig thought, that was the truth. 'It's made by hand.'

246

They all three watched the light dazzle about the room, Juno suddenly alert, as if the spinning reflections were some new prey for her.

Finally, Evaleen sighed. 'Will one of you tell me why you're you both sulking on Christmas morning?'

'Ask Jig.'

No good stammering and saying I dunno. Jig was almost thirteen now. She had breasts and higher expectations than she'd had a week ago. She spoke in an even, unruffled voice. 'Alicia's going to marry Dave and she wants him to be my stepdad and I don't want one.'

'Oh, you know that's not it, Jig!' Still clutching the afghan, Alicia stood bolt upright. 'I am upset because you are so ungrateful. Because after everything I've done for you, you don't even care. You don't want me to be happy. You won't even give Dave a chance. You've ruined my whole vacation.'

'Jig isn't Mexico,' said Evaleen, a look of surprise draped oddly over her features. 'We're not a destination or a pleasure cruise. We're a family. Why can't you just enjoy being with us?'

'Being here? Enjoy this house? Hah!'

'Not forever,' Evaleen clarified, 'just for Christmas.'

'You've turned my own daughter against me.'

'I have not.'

247

'You've made her absolutely content to live here with you and the cat. She's perfectly happy living this dull life in this poky house in Empire Projects'

'What's wrong with being happy?' cried Jig. 'What's wrong with—'

'Because, Miss I-Never-Even-Asked-For-A-Bra, you don't even know when you're deprived. You'll never accomplish anything if you don't want more than this!' She gestured roughly around the living room with its threadbare furniture and fading pictures, and doilies 'If you're content to live in a place where people like Agnes Frazier bring you their squalid little troubles, you'll never do anything.'

'Everyone has troubles, Alicia. Squalid or not.' Evaleen paused. 'Everyone has follies and regrets. If they didn't, there wouldn't be any *Kings Road*. What is that but made up squalid follies and troubles and regrets? Agnes Frazier's are no worse than Shawna Leigh's.'

'Shawna Leigh is beloved by everyone,' Alicia pulled the purple and yellow afghan around her as though it were ermine. 'People love me! People recognize me on the street, and they tell me how much they love Shawna Leigh! You want me to give all that up?'

'I never said that!' cried Jig.

'You thought it.'

'I didn't,' Jig protested. 'I'm glad you're Shawna Leigh. I never wanted you to come

248

here and live. But I'm glad you're home for Christmas, Alicia.'

'I'm not home! I'm back. This will never be home to me. I got out of here, and you never will, Jig. You'll never see anything better than this, or want anything more. Don't you have a single dream? What do you want, Jig?'

'I dunno.' And this was the truth.

'Oh, you are so like Evaleen! You're like the Before and After of the same woman, but that woman isn't me! How can we all be in the same family?'

They regarded each other oddly, as if the answer to the question might suddenly materialize there in front of the Christmas tree.

Evaleen's blue eye seemed to cloud over. 'Are you suggesting that Jig shouldn't be happy here? That being happy means you think of no one but yourself. Act only in your own best interest?'

'I did not do that! I had dreams and I followed them!'

'Alicia, you have never thought of anyone but yourself,' said Evaleen.

Alicia's lovely features pinched together 'I think you're getting tired, Evaleen. I think you're getting old and tired and you shouldn't be raising a teenager. Jig needs a change. She needs a chance to experience something outside of Empire Projects. She should come back to LA with me. She can be Angela for

249

once. Like she was always supposed to be. I'm her mother. She should be with me and Dave. You better pack up your new clothes, Jig, Angela, I mean. We can leave today.'

Jig made a move as though to dash toward Evaleen, but stopped immediately when her grandmother raised up one hand in gesture at once swift and certain. Evaleen dumped Juno from her lap, and rose. The planes of her face were stark as if they had been powdered with snow. 'Jig is not doll to be dressed up and carried around. She is not a toy you can play with while she amuses you, and then cast aside when you tire of her. A mother has obligations.'

'You don't think I can be a good mother? Fine! I'll take her to LA with me and prove it.'

'You're too young to be my mother,' cried Jig, the words tumbling over one another. 'We're more like sisters. I'd rather be your sister. Like Shawna and Chelsea. It's funner that way. Funnest. Besides,' she cast about, ' I don't want to leave my friends at Holy Names. Zoe and Isabelle. And it's Christmas Day, Alicia. You can't disappoint Mrs. Riasanovsky. She watches *King's Road* every day. She's always talking about Shawna Leigh. She'll be so happy when you tell her that Cynthia's going to die and Shawna will get Dr. Bryce.'

'Pryce,' said Alicia. 'As long as you know, you don't have to stay here, Jig. Anytime you want to come live with me and Dave.

Anytime—'

'I know who to call. I do!' Jig put the little box with the butterfly in Alicia's hand, and folded her fingers around it. 'Here. Take your present. Merry Christmas.' She wrapped her arms around Alicia, a genuine, a spontaneous hug.

Alicia thawed, and smiled. 'Merry Christmas, Jig.' She planted a quick kiss on Jig's forehead and started up the stairwell. Resting her hand on the bannister, she turned back to the livingroom, as though she were about to declare some deathless line or another, as though the situation cried out for daytime drama, but apparently the theatre was too poor a venue for what she had in mind. 'Merry Christmas, Evaleen. I hope you like the bath towel. They're one of a kind.' And with that, she went upstairs.

'We better make waffles for breakfast,' said Evaleen. ' I think if we made peanut butter and bacon sandwiches, Alicia will fly right out that door.'

'She doesn't even know that Agnes Frazier will be at Mrs. Riasanovksy's this afternoon.'

Evaleen stifled a chuckle. 'Where's the waffle iron?'

Jig searched around amid the wrapping paper and ribbon. ' Did you ever want to be a lawyer, Evaleen?'

'I did, actually.' She picked up the teapot and the three mugs, and put them on the tray.

'I thought you have a low opinion of lawyers.'

'I do. But I didn't know that then. There's the waffle iron. In the chair beside Juno. So it's just as well that I didn't become a lawyer, isn't it?' She took the tray into the kitchen. 'Just as well I became a court reporter.'

Jig picked up Juno and moved her to the floor. Resenting the upset, she mewed loudly. 'Get used to it,' Jig said to the cat. 'Nothing stays the same. Nothing is static. Not even for you, you old goddess, you.'

The Delinquent Virgin

The Reverend Hamilton Reedy often wrestled with uncharitable thoughts. For instance, he wondered—uncharitably—if seventeen-year-old Lisa Kellogg ought to have the role of the Virgin in the church's Christmas pageant. Then he dismissed the question as needlessly legalistic. Of his superior, Bishop Throckmorton, Hamilton Reedy believed (uncharitably, but correctly) that the Bishop used sincerity to mask his colossal ineptitude and gross opportunism. However, as Hamilton sat in the church study penning one of his usual defensive letters to the Bishop, he took a rather different tone, explaining his unorthodox attitudes (as the unorthodox always do) in lofty terms. He had crumpled this draft and trashed it just before the church secretary, Mrs. Leila Doggett, tapped at his door and announced that the police were here.

The Reverend rose to greet the two officers who identified themselves as Washington and Green, the former a black man, about forty with a lined face and graying hair. Green, a much younger white man, suffered from a pronounced overbite and a weak chin. 'Thank you for coming so quickly,' the Reverend extended a hand to each man. 'Would you like some coffee?'

'I don't think we have time,' said Officer Washington, whipping out an official set of forms in triplicate and poising his pen over them.

'You've seen the empty Nativity scene in front of the church, I take it,' the Reverend said gravely. 'It's a sad testament to the tenor of our times, gentlemen, that someone would actually steal the Holy Family from in front of the church itself.' At that moment he considered dispensing with the Christmas Eve meditation he'd already written and substituting something along these lines—but then again, no. Too grim. Christmas was about uplift, not theft. *Hark! The Herald Angels Sing.* Christmas was about glory. Leave the thieves for Easter, Good Friday, darkness at noon, that sort of

Officer Washington cleared his throat, calling the Reverend's attention back to the topic at hand. 'You'll be happy to know, Reverend, that we've found your Holy Family.'

'You have? Well, this is good news.' Hamilton rubbed his hands together and smiled.

Green and Washington glanced nervously at one another. Green continued. 'The Holy Family was on the steps of the city jail, the downtown police station this morning when our shift came on. We didn't know, until we got your call, where they'd come from.'

'On the steps of the police station?'

inquired Hamilton. 'That's a very odd place for thieves to leave them.'

'We suspect kids. Malicious mischief.'

'Rather nervy kids to leave them on the police station steps, don't you think? This sounds graver than mere mischief.'

Rather than reply, Officer Washington began asking a series of predictable questions. Naturally the Reverend's answers were unsatisfactory: he had driven past the front of the church this morning, noticed, to his alarm, that the Holy Family was missing from the Nativity scene and called the police. Simple.

Completing his form, Washington stuck his pen back in his pocket, gave a copy to Reedy and assured the Reverend that no harm was done. 'I'm afraid, though, you'll have to come down to the station to collect them. You'll have to sign. Stolen property, you know.'

Green offered: 'The duty officers took them off the station steps and brought them in the waiting room. They look mighty strange there among the derelicts and hookers and drunks.'

The Reverend said he would pick the Holy Family up in the church van late that afternoon.

'The sooner the better,' said Washington as they took their booted, uniformed selves from the Reverend's study.

'Nasty brats did this,' announced Mrs. Doggett, refreshing the Reverend's coffee cup. She was a prim woman, fond of cardigans and polyester pants, over-fond of chocolate toffees; the scent of chocolate toffee clung to everything she touched. Mrs. Doggett heaped calumny not only on the perpetrators of this crime, but on their parents and grandparents as well. 'Is your letter to the Bishop ready for me to type?' she concluded.

'Not just yet, Leila. It must be perfect, you know—or as close to perfect as we can come in this imperfect world.'

Leila Doggett gave him the look that had annoyed him for the whole twelve years of his tenure at the St. Elmo Episcopal Church: as if pearls had suddenly shot from his lips and she might scuttle to catch them.

'Well, since you're not finished, would you mind the phone for an hour or so while I do some last-minute Christmas shopping?'

'Of course, Leila.'

After she left, Hamilton Reedy went back to struggling with his letter to the Bishop. His thoughts, however, wandered along more pleasant paths, toward the annual Winter Solstice cocktail party this evening at the holly-decked home of Dr. and Mrs. Gorman. Rachel Gorman was one of those tireless committee women and hostesses (like the Reverend's own wife, Catherine), but unlike Catherine, Rachel had the gift of making all her undertakings appear graceful, easy, effortless, fluid. Her parties were earthly pleasures. Hamilton Reedy enjoyed his earthly pleasures, perhaps too much so. He knew this. Indeed, he knew it so well that he had always cherished visions of himself leading a very different sort of life, a life physically and spiritually strenuous: Hamilton Reedy, the inner-city pastor, a sort of *Going My Way* cleric, ministering to street toughs, bringing drug addicts to God. He often longed, nostalgically, for the old Civil Rights days, the glorious days when religion had marched on the side of Right. He saw himself there too: Hamilton Reedy in shirtsleeves, leading the integration of buses and lunch counters. In fact, however, during those glorious days Hamilton Reedy had been assistant pastor in a Seattle suburb and the only thing he had done in his shirtsleeves was raking the leaves in his front yard.

He swivelled in his chair, watching the palm and pepper trees sway outside his window and wished that St. Elmo might offer him some grander theater of religious endeavor. Perhaps a few Central American refugees to whom he might give sanctuary, the huddled masses crouched in the shelter of his church. Imagine Bishop Throckmorton's response to that! He laughed out loud. He chewed on the end of his pen.

Hamilton Reedy was a stout man, with a fringe of gray, fraying hair, serious eyes and a whimsical mouth. He had a trove of anecdotes (religious and otherwise), a gift for conviviality, a sonorous voice that extolled what he liked to think were inspirational sermons, though he knew they were not. A fundamentally honest man, Hamilton Reedy was aware that his sermons were well crafted, but seldom moving, and never disturbing or demanding. In a word, tidy. However, he exonerated himself from complacency: after all, his tidy sermons suited the tidy lives of his well-heeled congregation. St. Elmo Episcopal was in a fine old section of the city, with big trees and wide parkways and irrigated lawns emulating the nearby country club where Hamilton often played golf with Dr. Gorman and a few other parishioners. At St. Elmo Episcopal, the congregation was largely professional, lawyers, judges, bankers, administrators, city officials, teachers, everyone well-dressed on Sunday, and the rest of the week as well. St. Elmo Episcopal parishioners had swimming pools, three- car garages and investment portfolios; they had good retirement plans, good jobs, good credit and good marriages, or at least, durable unions. Their children played soccer and piano, violin and varsity football, honor roll students. Occasionally someone's daughter got pregnant, and there might be a boy flunk out at the university, or find himself on social probation. Occasionally people got miffed, or indignant, but never outright nasty (though choir politics were known to be intense). But mostly these were the sort of people who taxed only the Reverend's power of eulogy when they died. They would not demand that Reverend Reedy wrestle with those chronic demons of American life: drugs, divorce, alcohol, adultery, broken homes, broken hearts, broken vows. His own life was equally and mercifully tidy: married to Catherine for thirty years, three children, all of them happily married, two grandchildren. The only true cross that Hamilton Reedy had to bear was Bishop Throckmorton. As long as the Bishop so disliked him, advancement would not come to Hamilton Reedy. Oh, well. He'd advanced quite far enough to suit himself. He was a contented man. But he was hungry.

He put the draft of his letter in the drawer, took up the schedule Leila had left him and decided to begin early on the round of seasonal calls that he and his curate, Tim Voight, traditionally made each Christmas season, dividing the congregation between them. No doubt his parishioners would offer him something good to eat.

He took the list, his coat and hat (to protect the bald spot on his head), put on the voice mail, locked up the office and crossed the church courtyard, pleased to feel the wind coming down from the east, ruffling the lacy branches of the pepper trees, rattling the palm fronds. Hamilton Reedy never missed the gray and gloom of his Northwest boyhood; he loved Christmas in California. It was so, well, so cheerful and undemanding.

His first call was a Mrs. Robin Vance, a newcomer to the church, he remembered. Her address (he was surprised to note) was an apartment; not many of his parishioners lived in apartments, save for a few old ladies. He found Shadetree Gardens Apartments, parked in the lot and wandered the huge unkempt complex, looking for 23B. He might never have found it at all, but he recognized the two Vance children, a boy and a girl, playing outside their apartment in the dirt, building roads for toy trucks. The girl ignored him, but the boy, Patrick, about five, recognized the Reverend Reedy. Patrick jumped up, opened the door and ushered the Reverend into a room furnished with cast offs.

Led by Patrick to the kitchen, Hamilton was dismayed to find Mrs. Vance kneeling on the kitchen floor, crying, and another woman sitting at the table with the phone in her hand, looking at it as if it had just sprouted a goiter.

'Forgive me—' he began ineffectively, '—if I've—'

Mrs. Vance raised her eyes. She was young, thin, nervous; had it not been for her swollen eyes and tear-stained face, she might have been pretty. She was still wearing a blue bathrobe and her feet were bare. She pushed her hair away from her face and gazed at Reedy who could only mumble that he called on all his parishioners at Christmas.

She mopped her face with a wadded

Kleenex and rose unsteadily to her feet. 'Well, you've just stumbled on a broken commandment, Reverend. Caught my sister and me in the middle of bearing false witness. A gross, sordid lie. A useless lie.'

'Oh, Robin,' the other woman pleaded, 'please, don't—'

'What does it matter, Renee? What can it possibly matter now?'

'Can I be of some help, Mrs. Vance?' the Reverend inquired reflexively.

'Not unless you're God. Or Santa.' She blew her nose. 'All I want for Christmas is my husband. All I want is the gift that money can't buy. You know, one of those gifts? The happy family reunited around the Christmas tree.' She scoffed, and wept some more as she walked to the window, stared past the dead geranium in the pot. 'He was my husband and I loved him.'

This was an untidy life, that much was clear. Hamilton could not think quite what to say, but he composed his features soberly.

She swallowed her tears and stared at her Kleenex. 'Six months ago I left him. Jon was cheating on me. It was intolerable. But now all I want for Christmas is the chance to forgive him. It is the season of forgiveness, isn't it, Reverend, isn't it? But you can't say something like that on the phone.' She turned to Hamilton and her sister beseechingly. 'You have to be face to face. Jon could get a ticket,

261

fly here in time for Christmas, there's time. If he'd only come, if he'd only see Heather as an angel and Patrick as a shepherd, he couldn't help but...'

'Oh, Robin,' Renee sighed.

'But of course, I couldn't ask him myself, could I? So I had Renee call him, just now, like she was at her own house, like I knew nothing about the call. I had Renee tell him she was just sure, if only he'd fly out for Christmas, if only we could all be together, I'd forgive him and . . .' Robin Vance began to cry again.

'What did he say?' asked Hamilton, his curiosity not wholly professional.

Pain contorted Robin Vance's features. 'He said he'd think about it.'

'Well, that's something,' Hamilton offered optimistically. 'That means—'

'It means he won't be coming. He doesn't care if I forgive him. It means the season of forgiveness will pass and there won't be another chance. It means this is an irrevocable tragedy and not just a temporary separation. That's what it means.'

Renee hugged her sister's quivering shoulders. 'He might come yet and surprise you, honey. There's still three days. He might.'

'He might,' the Reverend offered hopefully. 'It is Christmas.'

*　　　*　　　*

262

The picture of Robin Vance in her robe, on her knees, crying on the kitchen floor troubled Hamilton Reedy for the rest of the day, troubled him as he drove the church's van (donated by Dewey Schultz of Dewey Schultz Chevrolet) to the police station where he filled out triplicate forms for the release of the Holy Family. As he stood at the desk, Hamilton glanced over, surprised, somehow, to see the figure of the Madonna (baby Jesus in her lap) on the waiting room bench. Beside her, standing, Joseph dispassionately regarded a young thug with rings gleaming in his nose, his lower lip, his eyebrow. He had a swastika carved into his haircut, handcuffs on his wrists, and a chain tattooed around his neck. Mucous bubbled at his nose and his pupils swam like black fish in his blue eyes.

A drunk, brought in as Hamilton was filling out his forms, fell on his knees before Mary and began to scream, to rage and wail and weep. All this exertion caused his ripe personal bouquet to fill the room. He peed himself. He had to be dragged to his feet.

'Sorry, Reverend,' the duty officer offered. 'Human litter, you know?' The articles were described as *1 Madonna, 1 Jesus, 1 Joseph* and Hamilton signed on the dotted line.

Two young officers hoisted the plaster figures of Mary and Joseph into the back of the van. Hamilton himself laid the Christ child on the passenger's seat. Mary had to be laid on her side so that she appeared to be curled into a fetal position and Joseph was laid on his back beside her. It crossed the Reverend's mind that they might have been lying in bed beside one another, but he chased the thought away.

With the help of Curtis Frett, the church's groundskeeper, Hamilton once again established the Holy Family at the Nativity scene there before the church. Enclosed on three sides by a plywood shed, the plaster, life-size Mary sat on an orange crate beside the manger (complete with straw) that held the baby Jesus with his little outstretched arms. Joseph looked on reverently. Plastic baby lambs and calves regarded the Holy Family with smiling bovine indifference. The silver star, stuck on a long pole behind the little shed, trembled in the breeze.

Satisfied, the Reverend Reedy paid the rest of his seasonal calls for the day. He dawdled pleasurably so that they occupied the entire afternoon (thus freeing him from finishing his letter to Bishop Throckmorton). He chatted amiably, drank tea or coffee, nibbled cookies, gingerbread or pound cake, at each home, all of these parishioners tidy, cheerful, downright fa la la la la. *We Wish You A Merry Christmas*. Tidy lives. None of them on the kitchen floor, barefoot, crying their eyes out, caught in a lie told to no avail.

From the last house on his list, he went

directly to the Gormans' cocktail party where the specter of Robin Vance was all but dispelled in the flow of spirits (of all kinds), good cheer, the grace Rachel Gorman trailed in her wake. Her tree sparkled, her canapés artfully arranged, the glitter of her crystal punchbowl, all filled him with seasonal pleasure as did the whispered invitation that he and Catherine should stay for dinner. Rachel Gorman had ham and rice, candied yams with pineapple for those select half dozen she always invited to stay after her cocktail parties.

Amongst the other guests so honored were Eleanor Kellogg and her husband (parents of the virginal Lisa). Lisa was there too since she was the girlfriend of the Gormans' oldest son, Michael. Watching the two young people, Hamilton felt fairly certain that acting the virgin was a role Lisa played in life as well.

After dinner they reassembled in the living room for coffee, and as Eleanor was director of the children's choir and producer of the entire Christmas pageant, Hamilton took the opportunity to ask after Robin Vance's children, Patrick and Heather. Eleanor Kellogg could not place them. 'The family is new to the church,' he added, 'they only started coming this fall.'

'What does the husband do?' asked Eleanor, stirring her coffee.

Hamilton hesitated. 'I don't think there is a

husband. I mean, there was, there still is, but he lives far away, he doesn't—of course he might—'

'A broken home,' Eleanor stated soberly.

It occurred to the Reverend Hamilton Reedy only then and for the first time that the term broken home was absolutely odious, pernicious and wrong-headed, that as long as children were loved, a home could not be broken. Hearts got broken, but homes did not need to be. In Robin Vance's defense, he corrected Eleanor Kellogg. 'A fractured family, not a broken home.'

The distinction was lost on Eleanor. She said she thought that yes, the Vance children were in the pageant and in fact Mrs. Vance had donated several afternoons in the church hall sewing angel and shepherd costumes. She added, beaming, that her daughter, Lisa, was sewing her own costume for her starring role as the Virgin Mary. 'This will be the best pageant ever.'

As Hamilton left the Gormans' and drove back to the church to park the van and pick up his own car, he noted that the electrical system was shorting again and that one of the spotlights on the Nativity scene was blinking on and off. He resolved to have it fixed tomorrow, parked the van, checked all the church doors and was about to go to his own car when he felt impelled, oddly, to check on the Holy Family again. He was pleased

266

to note they glowed serenely in the short-circuiting spotlight, their plaster faces rapt with adoration.

* * *

They were not there, serene or otherwise, the next morning. Again Reverend Reedy asked Mrs. Doggett to call the police. Again, officers Washington and Green arrived, took down the information in triplicate. The officers vowed to find the culprits, and stated moreover that the joke was no longer funny. The St. Elmo police would double their night patrols, that is, as soon as the Holy Family was recovered. With these assurances, they left the Reverend Reedy who continued work on his letter to the Bishop. Hamilton struggled for a full hour over a single paragraph in which he defended himself against the Bishop's unpleasant innuendos: that Hamilton Reedy was a *laissez-faire* pastor, that he was not sufficiently vigilant in routing out sin. The Bishop had further chastised Hamilton that commitment to Christ meant obedience to the church (i.e., the Bishop). Hamilton declared his fealty to Christ and to the church, at the same time reminding Throckmorton that historically it was the right of Protestants to approach God without benefit of an intermediary. That was as far as he got. Lunchtime.

Late that afternoon, surfeited with coffee,

267

tea, spirits, Christmas cheer from his seasonal calls, Reverend Reedy drove home, picked up the St. Elmo *Herald* off the lawn and greeted Catherine with a kiss. She was wearing an apron, picking up after a committee meeting in their living room. Hamilton loosened his collar, sat down, about to open the *Herald*, but just then the phone rang. It was Officer Washington. 'You've seen the afternoon paper, I guess,' the officer said.

Hamilton unraveled it in his hand and beheld the church's Virgin and child sitting on the St. Elmo County courthouse steps. That is, the Virgin was sitting. The child lay on the cold, hard flagstone. The caption read: *No Crib For A Bed.*

'She isn't at the courthouse anymore,' Washington added. 'I picked her up and took her in.'

'For questioning?' the Reverend replied automatically.

There was a brief silence, as if the officer were uncertain of the joke. 'For safekeeping.'

'And Joseph?' Hamilton inquired, 'do you have him too?'

'No, just Mary and the baby. We're still looking for Joseph.'

The short December day had contracted into darkness by the time Hamilton arrived again at the downtown police station, the cop shop, he liked to call it. So much cheerier. He entered and found the Virgin in her same

268

place on the bench, her blue robe soiled here, paint flecked off her outstretched hands; the Child's swaddling had grayed and His little nose chipped.

The downtown police station was crowded this evening and Hamilton was told to take a number while the duty officers processed those before him. He tried to remember the last time he had been called by a number. Perhaps Cake Box Bakery on the day before Thanksgiving—last year. Here, he watched as police processed half a dozen kids arrested for shoplifting. They wore pants so huge they each looked like full sail clipperships and from the cargo holds of these ships there issued forth an astonishing array of stolen goods, including four videos from the boxer shorts of a boy who had refused to sit down. He had also refused to shut up. With his compatriots he spat and smirked and swore. All four gang members addressed one another and the cops—indeed everyone present, male or female—as *puta*, whore, bitch, inviting them to suck various substances and informing them they all sucked in general. Their oaths counterpointed the yelps of a dreadlocked, gray-bearded veteran (wearing a VFW denim jacket) who alternately protested and wept about a chain of human ears. At least that's what Reedy thought he said. The veteran was being charged with disturbing the peace, assault and public nuisance. He didn't seem to care; he begged Reedy to look at the chain of human ears he wore around his neck. There was no such chain. There was nothing.

All this clattered against the ring of phones, the blip and natter of computers, the clank of handcuffs. Suddenly the waiting room split with the screech of a battered woman in a short dress and running shoes, dragged in by two armed officers while she clutched at, refused to relinquish the handle of a baby carriage. She screamed that she wasn't going to steal the baby, just talk to it. To Hamilton's horror, as she wrestled with the cops, the baby carriage overturned and garbage bags with her belongings tumbled out, as did a doll, a baby doll warmly clad in soiled jammies who bleated out a weak, *Maaa-Maaa, Maaa-Maaa.*

'Next! Number 56!' cried out the duty officer. 'Number 56! Where are you?' Hamilton rose and went to the desk. 'There she is, Reverend, your Virgin. Sign here and a couple of the guys will carry her out for you.'

Hamilton signed for *1 Virgin* and *1 Child* and they were carried outside and slid in the back of the church van, the Madonna on her side. Basically the Virgin seemed none the worse for wear, still tranquil, even benign, Hamilton thought. Though, as he placed the Christ child on the passenger seat, he reminded himself these were only plaster statues (*no graven images)* and their expressions, painted on, were not likely to change, whatever their circumstances.

Officer Washington came to the window of the van. 'My advice, Reverend, is to go the Home Center and pick up a couple of locks and chains. Chain the baby to the manger and the Virgin to her seat, lock them up and you won't be having this problem again. When you been a cop long as I have, you learn that you can't stop anyone from stealing. All you can do is make it hard for them. Lock 'em up, Reverend, make it hard for them. But I don't think it will happen again anyway. The patrol car is going by the church every hour tonight. If they try again, they'll get caught.'

'Then I won't be needing the chains, will I?' Hamilton asked pleasantly.

The thought of a shackled Christ, a manacled Madonna was repugnant to Hamilton, intolerable, anathema. You couldn't chain up the light of the world or the woman who had given that light flesh. He bade Officer Washington a Merry Christmas and drove to the Gormans where he engaged the good doctor and his two sons (Michael, varsity tennis, Paul, varsity baseball) to help him return the Virgin and Child to the Nativity scene in front of the church.

'What about Joseph?' Paul Gorman asked, after they had put them in place.

'It looks awfully weird without Joseph,' Michael chuckled, 'like maybe Mary is an unwed mother.'

'That child's father is in Heaven,' the

271

Reverend replied. Though he had not meant it as a pompous remark, it came out sounding that way. Hamilton flushed, thanked the Gormans and then drove home, wondering not about Joseph, but about Jon Vance, not about the fractured Holy Family, but about the fractured family at 23B Shadetree Gardens. While, certainly, it was the historical right of all Protestants to approach God without an intermediary, he prayed for Robin Vance to get her Christmas wish, not as he might pray for world peace or an end to strife and starvation in the great theaters of the globe, but for the Christmas spirit to enact itself in the tiny darkened theater of the human heart. He prayed that the season of forgiveness would not pass in vain.

*   *   *

This—and every other thought—was blasted from the Reverend's mind the following morning when he opened the *Los Angeles Times* and gaped at the picture from the St. Elmo paper, plastered on the front page, complete with its caption: *No Crib For A Bed.* Indeed, the Associated Press had picked up the picture. It was running all over the country.

Driving to work, Hamilton saw a bevy of unfamiliar cars clustered near the church and so he turned, avoiding the front and drove round to the back, parked. Unfamiliar figures milled in the church courtyard; he walked past them without comment and dodged into the large church office, but even here, reporters swarmed out of the wood-paneled walls. They assaulted him with questions and Leila Doggett could not protect him. To the clamoring hordes, Hamilton muttered something cheerfully inspecific and ducked into his study where the lights on the phone flashed and flurried. There was a sheaf of phone messages, some from as far away as New York, Cleveland, Miami and Blytheville, Arkansas. Unwisely he picked up line 1. It was a stringer representing *People Magazine* who wanted to know how to get to St. Elmo. Gesticulating wildly from the door, Mrs. Doggett indicated that Bishop Throckmorton was on line 2.

The Bishop sputtered questions, accusations and innuendos without a single pleasantry.

'The police have assured me,' Hamilton began, hoping to put the onus on their secular shoulders, 'that they will patrol the church every hour. They did so last night.'

'Is that so?' snarled the Bishop. 'Did they perchance then see who stole these things?'

The dreadful thought accosted Hamilton. He had not driven by the front this morning, had not seen the Nativity scene. Could it be . . . ? He lay the sqwuaking phone down very gently on his desk and dashed to the outer office, *sotto voce* inquired of Mrs. Doggett if the Holy Family were missing again this morning.

'Why do you think all these people are here?' she wailed, pointing to the reporters, camera crews, photographers and other assorted hangers-on who were swilling the church's coffee and munching the church's goodies. In a great mass they lunged toward Hamilton, but he escaped behind his study door, and picked up the phone just as the Bishop was demanding, *Well? Well?*

'What can I say,' Hamilton replied prudently. 'What would you have me do? Chain Jesus to the manger? Chain Mary to Joseph?'

'You'll have to find Joseph first, won't you?' the Bishop retorted. 'Never mind. I'll call a firm here in L.A. and have one delivered this afternoon. And you better hang onto him, too. You can't have a Holy Family without Joseph.'

Less prudently Hamilton added, 'I don't know why not. There are lots of families without fathers these days. That doesn't make them any less families, does it?'

'Very funny, Reedy. You really are too much. You had better see that this doesn't happen again. This—' Hamilton heard the rattle of a newspaper in the phone '—is not what we like by way of publicity.' The Bishop hung up.

From these inauspicious beginnings, Hamilton Reedy's morning deteriorated.

The church—venerable institution that it was—degenerated into another venerable institution, the madhouse. Traffic snarled for blocks as reporters congealed and collected, mini-vans double-parked and mini-cams taped the serious reflections of pretty men and well-coiffed women. Sound men adjusted the volume for these representatives of the four networks, CNN and two independent L.A. stations. Cell phones buzzed and pinged, and people sought the privacy of the church's flower beds for inconsequential conversations. Standing sturdily before the insta-cam, on-the-spot reporters gravely told their anchor persons on the morning news what anyone with a brain to play with could clearly see. The newspeople's power needs plugged up all the church's outlets and thick cords snaked across the courtyard, over the lawn. Finally the uncertain electrical circuits blew altogether. The place shut down: computers died, lights went dark, nothing worked. A cameraman called the electrician on his cell phone. Mrs. Doggett's stash of chocolate covered toffees had been raided and she chose this moment to bring the theft to Hamilton's attention. Just then one of the women reporters popped her head into Hamilton's study and told them the women's toilet was backed up.

Officers Washington and Green rescued Hamilton from Mrs. Doggett, from the plumbing and electrical problems. He regarded them hopefully and they did not disappoint him.

'Marconi and Tuttle found your Holy Family about 5 a.m.'

'Where?' asked Hamilton weakly.

'County Hospital. Emergency ward. Marconi and Tuttle were bringing in some suspects—'

'You couldn't call them suspects,' Green argued. 'Marconi and Tuttle saw it. Damn near got it themselves.'

'It was a domestic violence call,' Washington explained, 'and when Marconi and Tuttle got there, they could hear the man beating on the wife, threatening her with a gun and so they called out and kicked open the door, but the guy fired once at the door, turned back and fired again at the woman. Hit her.'

'And?' Hamilton asked urgently. 'And?'

'She was OK.'

'She's not OK,' Green corrected Washington. 'She's not dead. She's not seriously wounded, but she's not OK. Could have been a lot worse.'

Washington gave a mirthless laugh. 'No kidding. By the time they called the ambulance for the victim, and they've read the guy his rights, got him handcuffed, Tuttle looks up and there's the woman, up off the floor, bleeding and all, raging towards her husband with a butcher knife in her hand. She stabs him before anyone could stop her. Well, they couldn't put them in the same ambulance after that, could they? Not in that kind of murderous rage.' Washington shrugged. 'So they get to County Hospital, the ambulance with the wife, the squad car with the husband, and everyone's just struck dumb to find your Holy Family in the waiting room beside the potted palm, just like they're there, waiting for word on their nearest and dearest.'

'They're not my Holy Family,' Hamilton protested without any particular verve. 'Did anyone see them, well . . . arrive?'

'There was another guy there, a patient checked in just before the domestic violence, but they haven't asked him yet.'

'Why not?'

'He was still having his stomach pumped, last I heard. Suicide.'

'Attempted suicide,' Green clarified. 'Poison.'

Hamilton paled, felt rather queasy himself, but he asked nonetheless if Joseph was with them, if Joseph had been found.

'No. Just the Mother and Child. We're still looking for the man.'

'I guess I need to come down to the station and sign for them.' Hamilton rose wearily, put his coat over his arm.

'Well, no, Reverend—'

'Listen!' Hamilton cried, surprise, delight wreathing his face. 'It's quiet in the front office! Thank God, the reporters have gone!'

Washington and Green exchanged uncomfortable glances. 'They're not gone, your Reverence,' Green said at last. 'I think they're all out front of the church. You see, we have Christ and the Virgin in the squad car.'

As Hamilton Reedy walked between the two cops (as though he were the one in custody), he positively kicked himself that he had ever wished for some grander, more dramatic theater of ministry. Gone was the picture of the shirtsleeved Hamilton integrating lunch counters and converting young toughs. He longed only for the tidiness of his placid congregation, Sunday School recitations, choir politics and homebound ministries. Washington and Green protected Hamilton as microphones were thrust in his face, and cords and cameras barred his progress. Men and women shouted at him. Hamilton reminded himself of the sufferings of the Holy Martyrs. Torture.

Worse yet: there she was, locked in the squad car. Behind the thick grill in the squad car sat the delinquent Virgin, the blue in her robe chipped, but her expression unblemished, her eyes untarnished by anything she might have beheld—suicide, violence, vomit, poison, blood, bullet holes, stab wounds—in the Emergency Ward of County Hospital. The Reverend Reedy prayed to God to take this affliction from him, to protect the Holy Family

from theft, to protect him from the
wrath. 'All is calm,' he murmured t
though clearly this was not true. 'All is

Officer Green unlocked the squad car
out wafted the stench of cigarette butts, spilled
coffee, stale hamburgers and apple cores as
the two cops hoisted the Madonna from her
sitting position and carried her to the Nativity
scene, the humble plywood shack, where
plaster animals gazed at straw in the empty
manger. A reporter thrust the baby Jesus into
Hamilton's arms and took his picture. Lots
of pictures. The crews and cameras tumbled
over one another to follow Hamilton back
to the Nativity scene where he lay the Christ
child gently in the manger, there beneath his
mother's benevolent gaze.

*   *   *

The Bishop was as good as his word and a
Joseph was delivered to the church by the last
light of afternoon and placed with the holy
group. Joseph looked new to the job. Mary
and Jesus showed signs of wear. Manicured
newspersons and their cam-crews, their sound
men still milled through the huge crowd that
had gathered round yon Virgin, mother and
child. Everyone in St. Elmo, and some from
afar, had thoughts on the matter, including
Lisa Kellogg who told KNBC that all this
stuff really made her like think a lot about her

le as the Virgin in the Christmas pageant tomorrow night. The reporter then asked Lisa if she would join an all-night candlelight vigil which people planned to hold here at the church to protect the Holy Family from further mischief. Lisa said she had a date. But later, sure. Cool.

However, it rained that night, a torrential downpour that quashed all thought of a candlelight vigil, and cut off power to two-thirds of St. Elmo from 12:27 to 4:54 a.m. At six a.m., the Reverend Mr. Reedy was awakened by a phone call. A young voice, allying itself with the St. Elmo *Herald*, wanted to be the first to ask him if he had any idea where the Virgin might have got to this time, since she was not in front of the church when the power came back on.

'What about Jesus and Joseph?' Hamilton asked.

'They're there. It's just the Virgin who's gone off this time.'

The Reverend rang off and slowly rose from his bed, rumpling what was left of his hair. For some reason a smile tugged at his lips, at least he thought he was smiling. The suspicion was confirmed by the bathroom mirror. As he shaved, Hamilton found himself wondering if he could find a Biblical citation to support the notion of Joseph babysitting Christ.

Despite Catherine's furrowed brow and anxious questions, Hamilton's feeling of well-being, perhaps downright euphoria, persisted through breakfast. Driving past the front of the church he felt no twinge of yesterday's tortures and apprehensions, yesterday's dismay. He was merely curious, and clucked inwardly over the damage done the church's narcissus beds where the people were taking snapshots (this early!) Of the Virgin-less Joseph and Jesus. He parked his car at the back, whistling *God Rest Ye Merry Gentlemen,* and stepped lively toward the office, eager, full of good cheer and good will, as if last night's downpour had washed an accretion of invisible tarnish from his very soul. He felt somehow expanded. Ignoring the ringing phones and stuttering fax machine, he greeted Mrs. Doggett jovially. And when she asked if they'd found the Blessed Mother yet, Hamilton patted her hand and replied that she would certainly turn up. He did not doubt it for a moment. He smiled. Mrs. Doggett thought him unhinged.

*　　*　　*

She did turn up. By mid-morning of Christmas Eve Day, every newspaper in California and beyond had been apprised that St. Elmo's Vanishing Virgin had been found on the steps of the State Hospital for the Criminally Insane, some twenty-five miles from St. Elmo proper, near a town called (of all things) Vassar.

Mrs. Doggett heard it on the radio and

told the Reverend who was calmly working on his letter to the Bishop. He thanked her and returned to the task. He finished the letter. He thought it one of his best, a model of defensive dignity. Then he tore it up and decided not to be defensive at all. His next draft was dignified, succinct, and completed in a matter of minutes. He handed it to Mrs. Doggett to be typed. He went outside and stood in front of his church, waiting, along with Joseph and Jesus, for the return of the Virgin Mary, as though Mary worked the graveyard shift at an all-night diner and would be home soon.

And soon she was. Brought by the police (sirens blaring), trailing a caravan of mini-vans, bearing mini-cams and sound men shepherding mannikin-reporters, followed by dozens of other cars, all horns honking, the whole procession of pilgrims (as Hamilton thought of them) returned the errant Virgin from Vassar to the Episcopal church. Hamilton watched.

As the cameras rolled and newspeople nattered into hand-held mikes, police placed Mary back with her husband and God's son. And then, for the especial benefit of Channel 7, Mr. Will Dance of the St. Elmo Home Center volunteered free locks, free chains to keep her there. The cameras then panned to the Reverend Reedy who, despite the chill, was in his shirtsleeves, leaning against the church door. The reporter asked if St. Elmo

Episcopal would take the Home Center up on their offer. The Reverend declined. He added, for all the world (to say nothing of Bishop Throckmorton) that you could not chain up the light of the world, or the woman who gave that light flesh. 'If the Virgin wants to stray, to deviate from the paths mere mortals have assigned her, who are we to insist she stay put?'

'Reverend Reedy,' the reporter inquired gravely, 'they're saying that maybe the Virgin Mary was never really stolen, sir. What do you think? Has there been a miracle here?'

Hamilton's eyebrows shot up. He regarded the reporter ruefully. 'A miracle?' he said, 'in St. Elmo?'

*   *   *

Some hours later for Christmas Eve services, Reverend Reedy, clad in his vestments, stopped off in the church hall to see all the little shepherds and angels getting ready for their procession. They were subdued for a band of angels, and the shepherds clutched their fluffy sheep as much for comfort as for effect. Eleanor Kellogg was beside herself, issuing cues and instructions. Hamilton then took his customary place, and on the opening notes of *O Come All Ye Faithful,* he entered the church following the acolytes, the brightly-robed choir and curate, Tim Voight. From the

283

altar, overlooking the congregation, Hamilton inwardly grinned; never had he seen so many faces in these pews. Standing room only. He blinked into the floodlights which had been set up at the back of the church to illuminate the pageant and when his eyes accustomed to their glare, he searched for Robin Vance, finding her finally in the sixth row, sitting beside her sister. She kept turning toward the doors at the back, looking for her husband to appear, visibly disappointed when the church doors closed. She stared at her twisted hands.

Following the benediction, the pageant began, the littlest children leading the way into the church: shepherds and angels hand in hand, their little voices piping *Angels We Have Heard On High.* The choir took up the bright refrain and eased into *O Holy Night* and at that swelling chorus, *Fall! On your knees*! Michael Gorman as Joseph escorted Lisa (the Blessed Virgin) Kellogg down the aisle. Clad in a simple blue robe, her feet bare, her perky cheerleader's gait subdued, a satisfied smile played at Lisa's lips, but her gaze was straight ahead. Inexpertly she cradled a blanketed babydoll in her arms. Hamilton thought he heard the bleat of the babydoll in the cop shop where the sight of that homeless, childless, manless, jobless madwoman shocked Hamilton, indeed, revolted him. But here in the context of the church, he was moved. Why was that, he asked himself. Why? The

Three Wise Men followed behind Mary and Joseph, walking more like cadets than sages; these were boys Hamilton had known since their Sunday School years, watched them grow through Cub Scouts, the Science Olympiad, Junior Varsity, all that. But in these youths he so well knew, he saw too the clippership shoplifters spewing defamation, the kid with the mucous bubbling from his nose ring, his empty eyes, his neck bearing a tattooed chain. In Michael Gorman who played Joseph (his hair all floured make him look mature), Hamilton, quite against his will, saw the grizzled veteran, dreadlocked, mad, endlessly atoning for his chain of human ears. All this rang in Hamilton's head, in his heart, above the congregation's *It Came Upon a Midnight Clear.* Hamilton forgot to stand. He sat rooted, looking out upon the crowded church as the carol ended, as the angels and shepherds ringed themselves round Mary and Joseph, and the narrator began the familiar tale. Suddenly, there was a crash at the back, and a tier of lamps smashed down and the church's eccentric electrical system crumbled under the strain. The whole congregation was momentarily thrust into absolute blackness. The angels and shepherds began to cry.

Instantly Hamilton was on his feet, his sonorous voice booming out, 'Do not be afraid!' Quickly, sharply, indelibly, understanding flooded over him, 'This is the

285

dark the world lived in for thousands of years!'
he called out. 'There will be light. Tonight, of
all nights, there *will* be light and that light can
never be shackled or chained or dimmed.'

After considerable scuffling, the tier
uprighted and the lights came back on. A man
at the back shouted, 'Nothing to worry about.
A guy just came in late and tripped over the
cord.'

And with those words Hamilton Reedy saw
Robin Vance bolt from her seat, start up the
aisle toward the church door, and Hamilton's
eyes, too, scanned the back of the church,
looking for a man he pictured bearded as
Joseph, searching, with Robin, for sight of Jon
Vance, willing, as Robin must have willed, for
that man to appear out of the darkness and
step into the light.

So strong was the willing, the wish, the
prayer that Hamilton almost thought he saw
Jon Vance, but the only man who came to
meet Robin was Dr. Gorman who gently took
her arm, murmuring that everything was all
right.

Robin stared at the doctor for a moment.
Then she allowed him to return her to her seat
beside her sister. She picked up the hymn book
she had dropped, opened it. Her eyes met
Hamilton's. His heart broke to see sorrow and
disappointment drape her face. *It is the season
for forgiveness and it will pass in vain.*

No, Hamilton thought. It cannot. It must

not.

The sermon the Reverend Reedy delivered that night was not the one he had so tidily written days before. It was not tidy at all, but rather inchoate and incoherent, rambling, unconventional, alternately pompous and poetic, certainly impassioned. His dawning understanding, his attempt to frame that understanding into words, to offer it in speech (judging from the puzzled faces of the congregation) only confused them.

Hamilton looked right at Robin when he began, saying the reason Christmas was celebrated year after year, was so that we should remember that the season of forgiveness never passes away entirely. 'Like all seasons, it returns. Like all seasons it brings the promise of renewal, shrouded in nostalgia.' He said we should resist nostalgia and look 'forward, to the promise of renewal, of forgiveness, to the goodwill we might yet spread in this sorry world.' He opened up his arms; his gaze swept over the crowded church. 'But first we must see that sorrow. For that we must look into the institutions. Go into the institutions. Reach into the courthouse and the jail, the hospital for the criminally insane, the hospital for the terminally ill, for the suicide, for the wounded. We must wring that sorrow with our hands. Feel it. Free it. Recognize it as our own sorrow. Who says we are immune? We might one day be amongst

287

those shepherded into one institution or another. To the jail where they are booked, to the courthouse where they are tried, to the hospital where their bodies break down, and the madhouses where minds crack up. Do you think Jesus was unacquainted with these places? With these institutions? Do you think the Holy Family was immune from strife? From struggle? From anger? From anxiety? From heartbreak? The true beauty of the Holy Family, my friends, is not so much that they are holy, but they were a human family. As difficult as your own family. They were a fractured family, but not a broken home. Jesus was the original stepchild.'

A quiver of outrage riddled the congregation and then Hamilton pointed out Jesus was in good company, Moses too was a foster child. Though this hardly mollified the faithful, Hamilton continued, unabashed.

'Jesus well knew the courthouse, the jail, the madhouse and hospital. Jesus suffered through all these institutions. You need only to read the New Testament to know He suffered. You need only to consult your heart to know his mother suffered with and for him. At Christmas we acknowledge that He was born amongst the homeless. At Easter we acknowledge that he died amongst the thieves.'

Hamilton then denied the rumor that there had been a grand miracle in St. Elmo these past few days. 'There are no more grand miracles,' he told the faithful and the curious alike, 'only tiny miracles enacted daily in the individual heart.' He further confounded them, asserting that although there had been no miracle, neither had there been a theft. 'There was no theft. The St. Elmo police will not find who fractured the Holy Family because families—even the Holy Family—exist in order to *be* fractured. By time if nothing else,' he reasoned, 'by death, finally and for certain. After all, children grow up, leave home, parents grow old, die. We might, any of us, you—or you—or you—' He pointed randomly into the crowded pews, 'You might one day find yourself cast far from home, shackled in an uncongenial institution, in a jail or courtroom, or hospital having your guts pumped out, your wounds sewed up, your heart still broken. None of that renders the family—any family—invalid. Flesh, blood, bone, life—these are finite! Love is not. Love, unlike life, is infinite and exists beyond time. My dear friends, time will make fools of us all, of our sufferings, indeed, even of our pleasures. Life is finite. Love is not. Love can bend like light!' Hamilton paused, expecting applause. The thought was so spectacular, so appropriate, so obvious he marveled that he'd not understood before. He hazed out to the confused faces and concluded with a few random thoughts. He sat down. He was a little

289

confused himself. The delinquent Virgin had shed her light, restored his vision.

The curate, Tim Voight, visibly checked Father Reedy's's breath for alcohol when he whispered to him after the service that the police were waiting for him in his study. Hamilton crossed the church courtyard alone, up the flagstone paths, his cassock and surplice blowing in the cold winds that came off the desert, the vestments billowing until he closed the door of the office and then they seemingly died around his ankles.

Officers Washington and Green greeted him. With them they had four teenaged boys slouching on folding chairs. Hamilton judged them to be about fourteen, surly, tattooed and earringed; voluminous pants hung from their skinny hips and their enormous feet were planted defiantly apart. Permanent sneers twisted their features and one picked his nose with his third finger. Officer Washington made them stand up. 'We caught them hanging around out front,' said Washington. 'We think they're the ones who have been stealing your Holy Family.'

Hamilton considered telling Officer Washington once again that they were not his Holy Family, but he resisted. He turned to the biggest boy. 'Have you been stealing the figures from in front of the church?'

'Hell no,' said the boy. The others guffawed.

'Well, if you're lying—and I assume you

are,' Hamilton scrutinized their beardless faces, 'allow me to congratulate you on your good work. Allow me to be the first to thank you for a job well done, men. Excellent! And please, I beg of you, in the name of the church, of Christians everywhere, on behalf of the Spirit of God and the message of Christ, go on stealing the Holy Family! Go on leaving them in places where people will notice them. I commend you! No one notices the Virgin and child in front of the church, do they? Of course not. It's expectable, isn't it? Conventional. Ordinary. But! The Virgin and Child in the mess and muck of the Emergency Room where people who have despaired of life are having their guts pumped out—now, no one could overlook the Virgin there! No one could miss the Virgin even if they were bleeding from knife wounds, riddled with bullets, beaten in anger, could they?'

The boys rustled uncomfortably among themselves.

'And the Holy Family on the courthouse steps where families are dissolved every day, amidst all the wretchedness, the squalor of divorce—oh, boys, I tell you that was perfection! The courthouse where crime and degradation, desperation are everyday judged. Oh, brilliantly thought out. I have to hand it to you. I am dazzled by your vision. And the madhouse? The *criminally insane?* What a coup! What imagination! Which of you men thought of taking her out there?'

The boys' sneers melted into disbelief. 'Are you fucking dicking with my head?' one blurted out.

'Shut up,' commanded Washington. They shut up.

'The Virgin in the madhouse. That's where she belongs, isn't it? That's where she's needed,' Hamilton continued. 'Her tenderness and mercy among the criminally afflicted, the truly wretched of the earth. And I shall always be impressed with your conspicuous bravery in the first place, men, your certain fore-knowledge in leading us, in taking the entire Holy Family, all three of them, and placing them on the steps of the downtown St. Elmo police station. You put her there. The pure, chaste Virgin there in the police waiting room where the nightsoil of humanity is collected. You are the kind of men our country needs. Men with bravery. Vision. Forgive me, men. I ask your forgiveness, truly. How could I have contradicted your wisdom? How could I have brought the Holy Family back to the church? Men—I beg of you—continue always in this great and glorious work! Merry Christmas. Go with God.'

'What the hell, your Reverence!' cried Green, 'You can't mean you don't want to press charges.'

'You can't mean you don't want us to take these guys in?' asked Washington.

'And have them spend Christmas Eve in Juvenile Hall? Yet another sordid institution? Never. Can it have escaped your notice, Officer Washington? It is the season of forgiveness.' He gave them all a maddeningly benign smile.

The boys shuffled silently out. The cops stalked out, muttering. The Reverend took off his tippet and academic hood, his surplice and cassock and hung them in the closet. As he put on his coat and turned out the lights, made ready to depart by the back door, Hamilton Reedy thought—at least he entertained the notion—that he heard a tiny round of applause in that darkest theater of all, that untidy chamber of hope and remorse, the human heart.

293